LONGING IS VIOLET DUSK

THE HAZEL DEAN MYSTERIES
BOOK 2

JOSALYN MCALLISTER

EBURNEAN
BOOKS

EBURNEAN
BOOKS

LONGING IS VIOLET DUSK

To Carrie: Hazel's real life BFF.

ONE

Nina shouldered her backpack and slammed the trunk of her Impala shut. She took a deep breath. The air smelled like damp dirt, like spring. It was her favorite time of year for hiking — warm enough to be pleasant but early enough that the hiking trails weren't congested with hiking tourists, outsiders. The bare arms of pine and oak trees opened wide, welcoming her home. For the first time in months, maybe years, a spontaneous smile took over her face. The air was cold and nipped at the tips of her ears and nose, showing her breath in thick clouds ahead of her as she made her way from the parking lot to the trail head.

It didn't take long for her to get winded. She hadn't done any legitimate hiking in years. Four kids under nine and an allergy-overwhelmed husband put a stop to her habitual jaunts. But being out in the woods, with how quiet it was, how beautiful, it reminded her how much she missed it. It made her feel like herself again, even if her body wasn't as limber or resilient as she remembered.

It wasn't far up a steep incline that she had to stop and

catch her breath. She sat down on a wide fallen tree and took a sip of water.

She swallowed the water, relishing the sensation of cold traveling down her throat. She felt supported and protected by the trees around her, the low-growing bushes, the occasional bird chirps, even the overcast sky. A feeling of comfort enveloped her, and she felt herself relax. But the tension that had been living in her shoulders and neck was her only shield against her feelings. When that shield disappeared, a deep sadness welled up inside her, so intense it felt like a physical ache. She clutched at her elbows and hugged her arms to her stomach, like she had been punched in the gut.

Her throat constricted, and she began to cry. Tears streamed down her cheeks. Occasionally a sob hiccupped through her labored breathing, but she didn't try to quiet herself. There was no one else in the woods. The idea cheered her a little and a half sob, half laugh escaped from her.

She couldn't remember the last time she had been alone. She realized that she hadn't let herself cry with this kind of abandon since she had been married almost twelve years before. This last-minute solo hiking trip wasn't something she had ever done before.

That morning she had packed up her trunk and told her husband that she would be back Sunday evening, two days later.

"But what am I supposed to do with the kids?" he whined.

Nina looked down at her one-year-old with his dirty cherub face. Objectively, she knew her kids were adorable, but looking at them didn't stir anything in her heart. "I'm sure you'll think of something," she said. She knew he would just call his mom and complain about her. Then grandma would come and rescue 'her sweet babies,' which is what 'Mimi' called her four grandchildren because she couldn't seem to keep their names straight.

And that's exactly what had happened. Mike's mom, Karen, had been perfectly anxious to send Nina off. She had appeared before Nina had even left, with a bag of homemade energy bites for her. It would have been sweet, if Nina didn't know that all Karen wanted was to get rid of her.

A few months before, Nina had realized something wasn't right with her brain. Maybe it had been wrong for years and she had been too busy and overwhelmed to notice. The joy and pride she read on other moms' faces didn't feel familiar. She avoided her children and only tolerated her husband. She had stopped responding when her friends reached out to her, stopped leaving the house.

The only exception was the bookstore, Books and Chocolate, where she had attended Hazel's book club with her friend Nora for several years now. She still went to that, unable to deal with the combined scolding of Nora and Hazel if she didn't, but she had stopped contributing to the discussion. She even stopped drinking Hazel's famous escapist hot chocolate she used to look forward to.

She thought she might need some help, but getting it was too daunting. She figured if her kids were fed and clothed, she was surviving. She'd be okay. But when Dansby messaged her a few weeks previously, it had turned her slightly-tortured mind into an unbearable furnace of discontent. His intense, focused personality was visible in every photo he posted on social media. After traveling around the world on daring adventures, he was back home visiting his parents, and he wanted to see her.

Nina began reminiscing about when she was Dansby's girlfriend—before. Back when she was young and full of energy and spunk. It threw how much she had changed over the years into sharp relief. Like a before and after picture of her personality. She missed that girl she used to be.

She couldn't resist messaging Dansby back. Since then

every second of her life was holding its breath, waiting for communication from him.

Even now, she wondered what he was thinking. She hadn't responded to his last several messages. She couldn't. She needed time to think. Nothing had happened between them yet, but she knew where things would lead if she continued to communicate with him.

She had begun to realize it when she was at Hazel's book club just a few days before. She didn't remember which book they had been discussing. She didn't read it or have anything to say about it. She sat in one of the overstuffed chairs by the fireplace in the cafe staring at all the people talking. The words they said didn't register in her brain. She watched their mouths move and thought about how ugly mouths really were. Disgusting, really.

She tore her gaze away from the hideous sight and looked at her hands instead, but they were ugly too. They were too dry; she had hangnails and jagged, bitten fingernails. She stared at her wedding ring, trying to remember the feelings that had motivated her to put it on her finger. She shook her head and rolled her eyes at her naive young self. She had thought that marriage would fix everything. So pathetic and stupid.

She became lost in thought and self-loathing, and when she looked up again, she saw that everyone was standing up, milling around and chatting and eating the treats that Hazel had set out.

Nina had tried to summon the energy necessary to get up, but her core muscles wouldn't tighten, and her legs wouldn't move. She gripped the arms of the chair hard and grimaced down at her lap as the tears came hot, scalding her cheeks as they ran down her face.

"Nina?" Hazel usually had a bright theatric voice that carried, even in a crowded room. She wasn't exactly soft-spoken, but in that moment, her voice was soothing and quiet.

Nina plastered a smile onto her face and surreptitiously wiped the tears from her cheeks, hoping Hazel wouldn't say anything about them. She looked up at Hazel.

"Thanks for hosting, Hazel. I'm just so comfortable I could sit here all night."

Hazel smiled, but it was tinged with concern. "Sometimes it's hard to go back to a house full of noisy kids after you've had a chance to sit down and relax for a minute. My two were enough for me; I don't know how you handle four!"

I don't. Nina thought. *I don't handle anything.* All she could manage was a pained smile.

"Oh, my dear," Hazel seemed to know that Nina was just barely keeping it together. "It's hard sometimes when they're little. But it gets better. You'll get through it, and it will all be worth it."

Nina felt like snorting. *What did Hazel know about it?* She had the perfect marriage and the perfect teenage children and a beautiful bookshop and more friends than anyone had a right to. She choked back her bitterness, nodding instead.

"I want you to have this," Hazel handed her *Anna Karenina*. "It's my gift to you. It's a heavy one, but so good. It's not my favorite translation, but *Anna Karenina* is pretty accessible as Russian literature goes."

Nina took the gigantic paperback into her hands. There was a painting of a woman dressed all in black on the cover, looking haughtily down from a carriage. She wore an old-fashioned hat with a gigantic white feather attached to it. Nina couldn't decide if the woman looked happy or sad. She placed her palm on the cover, almost reverently. "Thank you so much," she whispered.

"It's my distinct pleasure. You can sit here for as long as you like," Hazel said before she swept away to interact with another guest. Nina so wished that she were her.

Everybody at book club knew that if Hazel gifted you a

book, you read it. She had a knack for knowing exactly what you should read. Jacob swore that she handed him *The Last Lecture* before he had told anyone about his cancer diagnosis. "It's one of the reasons I was able to beat it," he whispered to a few of them one day when Hazel was getting treats out of the cafe. Brittney said that she was struggling to navigate an adult relationship with her mom when Hazel gave her *The Great Alone*. "My mom and I are best friends now," she said.

Nina could barely wait until she got home to start reading it, but she didn't want to start it at Hazel's shop. She needed privacy. This book was the answer. It would solve all her problems and show her what to do.

Nina never thought of classics as page turners, but she stayed up almost all night reading *Anna Karenina* and spent the next three days doing little else. She started out just skimming the portions about Levin but found that she was just as fascinated by his story as Anna and Vronsky's.

However, as much as the novel gripped her, the lessons she gleaned from it were convoluted and contradictory.

Anna Karenina was happy enough with her boring marriage until she met Vronsky. But his intense personality and flattering attention made her realize how much she was missing in her life.

The situation was uncomfortably similar to her own life. Except that she had been completely miserable even before Dansby turned up. Could Hazel Dean have possibly known about Dansby? Is that why she had given Nina *Anna Karenina* to read? The thought made her burn with shame. No, she couldn't have known.

Nina was embarrassed by how irritated she was with Anna for resisting the affair. She was relieved and excited when she finally gave in and agreed to have a relationship with Vronsky.

Meanwhile, the Levin character extolled the virtues of monogamy and family values. All he wanted was to get married to a sweet girl and settle down but he couldn't seem to manage to achieve that.

When Levin fled to his country house after his love rejected his proposal, Nina had a stroke of inspiration. She could flee to the country in her own way by going backpacking. The influence of nature and the solitude would surely help her sort out her thoughts and feelings.

It had only been a few days earlier. She had put her plan into motion almost immediately. Now that she was here, it seemed foolish. What good would it do to sit all alone and let herself give in to the dark feelings inside her? It was just one more thing to add to the list of stupid things she'd done in her life.

Nina cried for a long time, sitting on a log by herself in the woods. Finally, she wiped away the snot and tears from her face, finding she had no tears left. She picked up her backpack again and shouldered it. She took decisive steps up the trail, determined that the woods would yield an answer to the question that her whole body pulsed with: should she leave her family for her high school boyfriend?

* * *

The rain pounded onto the glass roof, but Hazel didn't mind. Relentless raindrops had melted the stubborn shaded snow tenaciously bordering the glass wall around her cafe. The crocuses weren't bothered, and their cheerful yellow, purple, and white blooms brightened the gloomy day. Green daffodil shoots poked out of the ground; their golden petals outstretched. Hazel noticed grape hyacinths budding, as if waiting until the crocuses were done before they enjoyed their time in the spotlight.

It was a Monday morning in the shop, slow by definition. Lazy, rainy spring mornings called for romance, so Hazel chose

Outlander from the romance section of the shop. Hazel shelved her inventory by color. Not the color of the book's spine, but by the colorful emotions Hazel could see glowing from them.

The romance shelves were filled with the rosy pinks of happy endings, the dark rose reds of the steamier ones, the moody purples from unrequited love and tragic endings.

Hazel settled into her favorite overstuffed chair by the fire and allowed herself to become lost in the book. The picturesque scene outside added to the swell of longing that filled her whenever she read about people in love. Hazel lived for atmosphere, and this morning oozed with it.

She had completely relaxed into the chair and gotten lost in the book when a chill ran down her spine and the hairs on her arms stood on end. The nourishing, cozy feel of the rain morphed into an ominous and cold feel. It felt a bit like when her kids were younger and had been quiet a little too long. She would find them trying to fix something they broke or rigging up an elaborate tower of chairs and books to get into the cookies.

Hazel slowly closed the book and sat at attention, listening. Her brow furrowed. She got up slowly and made her way through the tall bookshelves towards the front of the empty shop. She looked out the front window onto the street, expecting to see a car accident or some other catastrophe.

Outside, the rain fell in sheets. The wind blew in gusts, driving the rain down the street in a pattern that resembled ocean currents. It was stormier than she had realized. A shiver ran through her. The mountain must have protected the back of the store from the frigid wind. The weather had predicted some rain but not such a severe storm.

Something was wrong. Hazel could feel it deep in her heart. She just couldn't put her finger on what it was. Her two sons should both have been in school, so it wasn't likely they were hurt. Maybe something happened to her husband, Jason. She got her phone out and was about to call him when the bell attached to the front door jangled. She held her breath, her fists clenched. She steeled herself, as if waiting to be hit. A large figure in a dark coat rushed into the store. Hazel flinched, but then relaxed when she recognized the form as her uncle.

"John!" she exclaimed. Her surprise was overtaken by increased worry. John wasn't exactly a regular in the bookshop. Especially not on weekday mornings. He radiated concern with a carrot orange glow.

Since she was a child, Hazel had been able to see other people's emotions as colors that surrounded them. Hazel had been watching John's colors long enough through the years to know that carrot orange was not a good sign. "What's wrong?" she said.

John hung his coat on the rack and turned towards her. "Hazel," he began. His terse tone wasn't unusual; years as a police captain had made it a habit. Her childhood was one long interrogation. "I understand you sell all kinds of caffeinated beverages here. It's going to be a long day and a late night. What do you have to keep us awake?"

Hazel recognized John's signature stall tactics. Whenever there was something he didn't want to tell her, he would always talk about something culinary instead. As a child she had been easily distracted by food. "Did something happen to Jeremiah or Elias?" Hazel asked, ignoring his request and clutching at his arm.

"No, no, nothing like that." John said, patting her hand. "I'll tell you over drinks."

Hazel crossed her arms over her chest without moving an inch. "That's not going to work this time, John. I have a great espresso. But I'm not going anywhere until you tell me what's wrong."

John sighed, shifting his weight. "I believe there's a woman in your book club named Nina?" he almost whispered.

The blood in Hazel's veins turned to ice. Her breath caught in her throat, but she managed to get out a nod.

"She's missing."

Hazel could feel the color drain from her face. John put out a hand to support her arm and tugged her gently toward the back of the store.

"It's not as bad as it sounds, Hazel," he assured her as he made his way through the bookshelves toward the café. "She hasn't been gone that long. Once we get a search party going, I'm sure we'll find her in a matter of hours. Her husband said she left Friday night for a spontaneous backpacking trip and was supposed to come back last night. The moron didn't call us until this morning."

Hazel shook her head. "No, no, no," she murmured to herself.

"She's going to be just fine," Uncle John repeated. "I'd be willing to bet that she turned an ankle or something and is having a hard time getting back to the car. She'll be hungry, but fine. Probably turn up in the next couple hours." He glanced at Hazel and hesitated before continuing. "The only thing that worries me a little is the storm. That's why I came to see you. We'd like to get a big enough search party together that we find her sooner rather than later. I knew that you'd be able to galvanize the community to participate better than I could." John reached the bakery counter but didn't sit down. He stood by the display case looking at all the treats inside.

Hazel nodded again and went around the counter to make him an espresso macchiato. But she couldn't. The ingredients and machinery on the counter seemed foreign to her. The steps necessary to make the drink didn't come readily to her mind, even though she had made it countless times before. Her hands froze in midair. She knew that John was right. They would probably find Nina in no time, and everything would turn out okay. But she couldn't shake the feeling that something was seriously wrong.

She looked at John with wide eyes. He gave her a little nod. "Are those the same blondies you used to make when you were a kid?" He asked, pointing.

"Yes, with the brown butter." The question grounded her, like John probably knew it would. Apparently, she wasn't all that different than she was when she was a kid and he had to say no to the latest toy she wanted. She tried to focus. It might not be what she thought. It might not be too late. Nina needed her. She had to pull herself together. The steps to make the macchiato returned to her.

She got a blondie for John, then began to beat milk with the frothing wand. Her motions were automatic, almost robotic; her mind was racing.

"Did she leave a hiking plan with Mike before she left?" Hazel had a professional dislike of Nina's husband who was on the city council with her. Hazel had disliked him ever since he had taken credit for the recycling initiative she and another council member had been working on for two years before Mike was elected. He enthusiastically offered to help them with the implementation and then made public statements that the change had been propelled by his "young blood" revitalizing the council. Plus, he was constantly cracking his knuckles. It drove Hazel up the wall.

"Sounds like the trip was a spur-of-the-moment thing. Mike wasn't sure she knew where she was going herself; he has no idea where she is."

Hazel frowned. She tried to imagine the quiet, reserved woman she knew taking off on a sudden backpacking trip. It seemed out of character. Why wouldn't Mike have been more concerned? Or at least curious?

She poured John the macchiato. Hazel had consumed less caffeine as she got older, but she would need it today. John was right, it would be a late night. She poured herself a mug too. John drank without sitting down.

"Wow," he said, holding the mug up to his eye level to raise an eyebrow at it. "That's good."

Hazel nodded absently, sipping with unfocused eyes.

"I wondered if you might do what you do and get some people together?" John asked. "I know you'll know who to call. We're meeting down at the Twin Pines trail head. Brandon is at our base of operations. He'll be there all day and tell people where to go and what to do. We just need people to show up." John pointed out the window. "Particularly because of the weather. It's getting cold at night still, and there will still be snow in some spots. If she's injured, she could potentially get hypothermia."

"I'll get as many people as I can," she assured him. She set down her coffee mug so he wouldn't see her trembling hands. She couldn't believe how strong her voice sounded.

"Alright." He took another sip of his coffee before grabbing a to-go cup to pour it into. "I'm headed out there." He took the blondie and put it in his front shirt pocket.

She blinked at him. "Do you want a bag or something for that?"

"No, it's fine," he said.

"Thanks for letting me know in person, Uncle John," she said. She walked around the counter and gave him a hug, careful to avoid smashing the blondie in his pocket.

He hugged her back and headed back up the aisle towards the exit. "Well, I know how sensitive you can be about your friends. Ever since that business with the McCleary boy..." He shook his head. "Just be careful, okay? I know you'll be out looking for her, but take care of yourself. Don't do anything rash."

Hazel nodded but didn't say anything. She followed John back through the bookshelves to the front of the store, lost in thought. Sometimes the situation called for rash action, but not now. Now they needed as many people as possible searching for Nina.

"I'll probably be out in the woods by the time you get down there," he said. He pulled on his heavy coat again and glared out the window. He turned back to Hazel and put a hand on her arm. "Don't worry, we'll find her."

"I know," Hazel said, avoiding eye contact she knew might make her cry. "I'll get on the phone. You'll have tons of people out there in no time."

John gave her a grim smile and turned to the door. The wind had gotten worse. When he opened the door, the first two feet of carpet became soaked with rainwater. The gutters were overflowing. John ducked his head and ran out through the rain. The door slammed behind him with a bang and the clatter of bells.

Hazel turned in a circle after he left, unsure of what to do next. She spotted the chair behind the counter and collapsed into it. She took several deep breaths then said a quick prayer and called her husband.

"Oh, Jason, have you heard? It's all my fault," she moaned, "What am I gonna do?"

"What's happened?" Jason asked, panic causing his voice to rise. "Is it Jeremiah?"

"No, no," she said impatiently. "It's not the boys. It's Nina. Oh, why did I give her that book?"

There was a long pause on the other end.

"Jason?"

"I'm sorry," he replied. "Who's Nina?"

"Nina, you know, from book club."

"Hazel, you have like four book clubs, and they each have at least ten people in them."

"Yes, but I told you about Nina, remember?" Hazel's voice

was clipped with impatience. "She's seemed down lately... She's Nora's friend from high school... She's Mike's wife..."

"Mike Mitchell?"

Hazel groaned. "Of course, you recognize her from her husband."

"Hey, that's not fair." Jason protested. "I know Mike because of all the city council stuff you've dragged me to. I've never met his wife before. 'Nora's high school friend who's depressed' didn't ring any bells."

"Yes, yes, yes," Hazel said impatiently. "But I gave her *Anna Karenina* last week and now she's *missing*."

There was another long pause on the phone. Hazel brought it away from her ear and looked at it. The call was still connected. "Jason?!"

"What? I'm waiting for the rest of the story."

"That *is* the story!" Hazel spluttered. "She's missing! After reading *Anna Karenina*. A book that *I* told her to read."

Another unending pause. If only her husband was a verbal processor. Hazel felt desperation rising in her throat. It came out as a sharp whisper. "Jason!"

"Maybe if you could remind me the plot of *Anna Karenina*?"

Hazel was speechless for a moment. Even if he had never read the book, which she realized he probably hadn't, they had gone to see the movie with Keira Knightly when it came out. "Jason, she kills herself at the end of the book! She is involved in a passionate affair that doesn't end well, and she kills herself. You know, just to sum up an eight-hundred-page book."

"Oh," Jason said, sudden realization in his voice. "You're worried that Nina took a page out of Anna's book and..."

"Yes!" Hazel shrieked.

"But Hazel," Jason soothed. "You're getting way ahead of yourself. How long has she been missing?"

Hazel looked at her watch. "Since last night."

"Okay," Jason went on in a maddeningly calm voice. "That's

less than twenty-four hours, which doesn't even formally classify as missing. Do you know how often moms of young kids disappear for a day or two and then come back? There's no evidence to suggest that she's dead, let alone that she killed herself."

"Except that I gave her *Anna Karenina* to read."

"That's not evidence," Jason said. Hazel interrupted him with an impatient noise in her throat, but Jason went on. "Hazel, seriously, that's not evidence. And if she does turn up dead and it turns out that she had killed herself, that doesn't make you responsible."

"It does! I am!" Hazel wailed; tears stung her eyes. "I've always just matched people with their books based on color. I decided a long time ago not to second guess things. It's always worked out before, but I knew deep down that something like this was bound to happen, and I kept on just handing out books. Like candy." A horrible realization dawned on her. "I gave Cash a book right before he died too! I'm basically a serial killer!"

"Hazel, try to calm down." Jason spoke in a stern voice that Hazel hadn't expected. "What has gotten into you? You are not a serial killer. Don't be ridiculous. Just breathe for a second, Hazel."

Jason began to take deep breaths on the other end of the line. Hazel tried to match her breathing to his. After a couple minutes her mind cleared a little bit.

Jason had been helping her breathe through her anxiety since they met. It was the closest she ever got to seeing her own emotional colors. Her outgoing breath came out in clouds of brown that crumbled and fell like chocolate that had taken on moisture and seized up. She continued to breathe until she couldn't see her breath anymore. "John did ask me to spread the word and get some people out to look for her."

"Then that's exactly what you need to do. Where are they organizing the search?"

"At the Twin Pines trail head."

"Okay, I'll spread the word around here. Hazel, let's just focus on finding Nina before we jump to conclusions about what happened."

Hazel nodded even though Jason couldn't see her. "Okay."

"I'll meet you down there in one hour."

She bit her lip. She changed the audio to speaker phone and began scrolling through her contacts, mentally planning the best order in which to call people. "Sounds good."

"Hazel?"

She stopped scrolling, her thumb hovering above the phone. "Yeah?"

His voice softened. "Everything is going to be okay."

She sighed. "Thanks."

Hazel ended the call and let her hand drop. She knew she couldn't allow herself to stop and think about Nina anymore.

The first things she did were call the fire department and the ranger's station at the National Forest, in case John forgot to notify them. It was a good thing she did. He had remembered the fire department but forgot the ranger's station.

"Can you get a helicopter out looking for her or something?" Hazel asked them.

"Not in this weather, ma'am," the ranger said apologetically. "I'll look over my trail maps though and try to figure out the likely places she could be. You say she left Friday evening?"

"That's what I was told, yes."

"Well, if she stuck to a trail, we should be able to narrow things down a bit."

"Thank you," Hazel said. "Please call the police station with any updates; they'll be able to communicate with search parties. I'll let them know."

"Happy to help. We'll be in touch."

Hazel knew she needed to call Nora next before she started calling around town. It would never do to have her hear it from someone else who heard it from Hazel.

When Nora's feelings were hurt, she turned a very sad ocean blue. Sometimes, for no reason at all, Nora would grow quiet, and the ocean blue would settle on her. Hazel assumed that in those moments, she was thinking about a past hurt and reliving those old feelings.

Turning towards the bookshelves, Hazel ran her hand along the spines of her books as she made her way back to the cafe. She drew strength from the stories. She headed to the counter and took a long sip of the now-cooling macchiato. Focusing on Nina, lost and alone in the woods, wasn't helping her maintain her composure. Instead, she focused on Nora. The next step. She hit Nora's name on her contact list.

"Hi, Hazel," Nora answered on the fourth ring. "I just got my little one settled in front of the TV for a minute so I could work on a few more bags for your shop. Tourist season will start up before we know it!"

Hazel's throat closed up. Nora's voice was bright and cheerful. Hazel cringed at the thought of ruining her day. "Nora, I have some bad news."

"Oh, no," Nora said, without a distinguishing change in tone. She thought it was something trivial. The sound of a sewing machine suddenly created a dull roar in Hazel's ear. "What is it?" Nora asked loudly.

"Nora, it's Nina...she's missing."

"What was that?" Nora yelled over the sound of the machine.

"Nina's missing!" Hazel shouted into the phone.

The sewing machine stopped, punctuating Nora's intake of breath. "Missing? What do you mean missing?" she gasped.

"She went hiking several days ago and never came back."

"No," Nora choked on the single syllable.

"I wanted you to hear it from me," Hazel said. "I'm organizing people to go look for her, so I'll be calling all over town."

"What happened?" Nora choked. Her audible tears were
almost too much for Hazel. She bit her lip.

"She went out hiking by herself," Hazel said. She was
repeating herself, but she knew that a lot of times people
needed to be told traumatizing information several times
before it actually sunk in. She remembered when she was a
little girl, how many times she made her grandmother explain
about her parents and the accident. "She was supposed to
return yesterday afternoon, but she didn't."

"Hiking?" Nora said, confused. "I don't think Nina's been
out hiking since she got married."

The puzzle-solver in Hazel came to life. "Is that something
she did a lot before her marriage?"

"Oh yes, she would hike all the time. Alone, sometimes. She
used to go with her dad a lot, and then he left, and so she went
with her boyfriend. But then he left town, and so she'd go by
herself. I went a couple times, but I'm a little picky about my
weather. Then she met Mike. Mike isn't really an outdoorsy
kind of guy."

"I see," Hazel said. "I wonder why she decided to start again
now?"

Nora sighed. "Well, you know I was telling you at book club,
Nina hasn't been herself for the past while. It's like the life
slowly went out of her over the years. It got really bad when her
last baby was born."

"Do you think she may be suffering from post-partum
depression?"

"It would make a lot of sense, but can it really last this long?
Her baby is almost one. But about when her oldest was born
was when it started, I think. I'm not sure; we weren't as close
back then. I wasn't even married yet. It kind of freaked me out
that she was having babies."

"I'm afraid I don't know too much about post-partum," Hazel mused, making a mental note to research the condition. "I'll ask about it more. I'd better go. I've got a lot of calls to make."

"You should try talking to Nina's mom. Maybe Nina told her what she was up to before she left. I think she's living in Florida now. I could be wrong though. She's a little bohemian. She can't seem to stay in one place for too long."

"That's a good idea," Hazel said.

"When are they meeting? I'd like to go if I can get my mom to watch Harley and Jamie."

"You can go anytime," Hazel told her. "John said that Brandon Teeter is going to be at the Twin Pines trail head giving directions. You can come whenever for as long as you can."

"Alright, I'll see you later then," Nora said, hurrying to hang up the phone.

Hazel spent the next forty minutes on the phone. She started with her book clubs and the city council members, people with a strong connection to Nina, asking them to spread the word as well. Then she moved on to local church leaders. A couple of them promised to activate their prayer trees, an organization specifically designed for this kind of emergency. Their promises energized Hazel. Next, she called all the high school sports coaches and the diner where all the retired men hung out on Monday mornings.

Finally, she put her phone in her pocket and prepared to close the shop and head out into the woods herself.

TWO

Rain pelted the windshield as Hazel inched her way down Main Street. The wipers were on their fastest setting, and still Hazel could barely see the street signs fifty yards ahead of her. She squinted into the sky, wondering if hail was in their future. The storm had been in the forecast for several days. An experienced hiker like Nina would have known about it and planned to end her hiking trip before it started on Sunday night. Hazel shook her head. She couldn't imagine what Mike had been thinking. If it were her, she would have called the police as soon as the rain started.

Tim McGraw's *Live Like You Were Dying* began to play on her car speakers. Hazel pawed at her phone blindly until the music stopped. The rain was enough of an audio track for Hazel's current mood. She shuddered when she thought of Nina out in the weather, hurt or lost, and already in a shaky place mentally. Would she feel like no one cared about her? That no one would mind if she gave in to hypothermia?

Hazel gritted her teeth. She would make sure that this was the biggest search party Red Gap had ever assembled. When they found Nina, she would be overwhelmed with love and care.

Hazel imagined the scene to cheer herself up but found that driving in the weather took her full attention. When she turned off the highway onto the dirt road it got even worse. Any speed over ten miles an hour had her slipping and sliding on the wet roads. Hazel was surprised they were still open and worried that there would be a fatal car accident in addition to a missing person with all the people that would be driving up that afternoon. It took almost an hour, instead of the usual twenty minutes, to drive out of town and to the Twin Pines trail head.

About fifteen minutes into the drive on the dirt road, the rain let up slightly. Since the visibility was better, Hazel risked speeding up a little bit. Vague motion sickness set in as she bounced down the bumpy road. It seemed to take forever, but finally she saw a police car with its lights on. Additional bright lights shone further down the parking lot.

She pulled in next to the police car, pleased at how many trucks and SUVs were already there. She got out of her car, pulling on her heavy rain slicker, and pulling the hood over her head. She grabbed her backpack, umbrella, and a brown paper bag, and she found where Brandon had set up a headquarters for the search.

A generator emitted a dull roar underneath a pop-up canopy tent. Two construction grade task lights shone through the murky wet. A folding table stood nearby laden with insulated cups, waxy donuts, and a coffee dispenser. Hazel frowned at the table while she waited for Brandon to finish talking to an older couple. They were wearing galoshes and hooded waterproof ponchos with flashlights in their hands.

"Hello there, Hazel!" called the woman.

"Bob and Suzie!" she exclaimed, recognizing her neighbors. Suzie walked over to give her a hug and Bob extended a hand.

"It's so good to see you!" Hazel said, putting her hand in his. "Are you going to be okay in this slippery, wet weather?"

Bob chuckled at her concern, and Suzie waved a hand dismissively. "We didn't have anything on the calendar until later this afternoon, and I couldn't bear to think of that poor young mother out in this. We just had to do something."

Bob nodded in agreement. "I've been wandering these woods for years now," he said, "I have a few ideas of where someone might go in weather like this."

"Do you know Nina?" Hazel wondered.

Suzie shook her head. "No, but we've helped with a few search parties in the past. The value of experience can't be overstated." She winked.

Hazel felt tears stinging the corners of her eyes. She was touched by this couple's willingness to help.

"Thank you so much for coming," she cried, clasping Suzie's hand impulsively.

"We'll get going," Bob said. "Don't worry, we'll find her. Red Gap hasn't lost anyone to these woods yet."

Hazel smiled and watched them head into the trees on sure feet. "I love this town," she declared, turning towards Brandon.

He grinned. "It's been nice to see how many people are willing to drop everything to come out and help."

"There will be more on the way," she said. "Especially once school gets out." She held out a brown paper bag. "Here, I brought you some real food."

Brandon snatched the bag from her hand and opened it. He put his face partway into the bag and inhaled. "Bless you, Miss Hazel! I'm starving."

Hazel smiled. Brandon reminded her of her teenage sons. Jeremiah would be a lot like him in another ten-ish years. Hazel felt a pang of longing for the baby Jeremiah with his pudgy hands and sticky kisses, but she swallowed it. She couldn't stand the thought of him being another ten years older.

Since her misadventures the previous fall, Hazel and Jason had invited Brandon and his wife, Isabel, to dinner several times and even got to babysit for them once for an overnight trip. Hazel had loved watching her two teenaged sons interact with the toddlers.

"There's a club sandwich, some chips, cinnamon apples, and a brown butter blondie from the shop."

Brandon sat down in a damp camp chair and started to unpack the food onto his lap. "This is so much better than those terrible donuts. The coffee isn't any good either."

Hazel nodded. "Where do you want me?" she asked.

"Bringing up more food for hungry searchers."

Hazel laughed. "Maybe later. Where do we need to search?"

Brandon shook his head. "Sorry, Miss Hazel, but policy is you can't go out to search unless there's at least one other person with you. We don't want to have to start looking for the rescuers or anything."

"Well, I wish you would have told me that before Bob and Suzie left," Hazel said, crossing her arms in front of her. "I could have gone with them."

"Just hold your horses," Brandon said, eying the sandwich he had freed from its wax paper wrapping. "Someone else will be along in just a minute."

Hazel couldn't sit still and paced underneath the canopy tent while Brandon ate his lunch. Hazel's impatience asserted itself in her muscles. Electricity shot through her fingers and calves, a mixture of anxiety about Nina and the coffee she drank earlier. She sat in a camp chair for only a second or two, then jumped up again to pace. She glanced at Brandon occasionally, realizing that she had forgotten to include a napkin in the lunch bag.

"How's the wife and kids?" she asked when he had polished off most of the lunch.

Brandon didn't need a lot of encouragement to talk about his family. His monologue soothed Hazel's nerves a little.

Finally, headlights bounced into the far side of the parking lot.

"Oh, good, another person," Hazel said. She checked her watch. It was a little before Jason thought he would make it, but she hoped it was him. Either way, she would head out to search with whoever it was. She couldn't sit around waiting anymore.

She walked several paces out into the rain to meet the person getting out of their car but froze when she recognized who it was.

Mike Mitchell slammed the door of his car and looked up at the rain pouring down on his face. Hazel expected him to shake his fist at the heavens, but he just shook his head and ran through muddy puddles towards her.

Hazel ducked back under the canopy, trying to think of the best thing to say to him. 'I'm so sorry' felt so cliche but was so accurate. She wondered if she should mention *Anna Karenina* to him and then was horrified by her own thought.

"Who's that?" Brandon called through the rain.

Mike had a hood pulled over his head and was looking down at the ground, so his face wasn't visible.

"It's Mike Mitchell," Hazel said, turning towards Brandon.

Brandon flashed a few different colors, and Hazel thought the look that sprang to his face was one of exasperation. "He's here *now*?"

Hazel nodded.

Mike made it under the canopy and took off his hood, shaking the water from his hair. "Oh," he said when he saw her. "Hi, Hazel." He tinged pink. "I'm sorry you got dragged into this."

Hazel blinked. "I wouldn't be anywhere else," she answered. "I just hope we are able to find her quickly."

"I'm sure she'll turn up," he said, taking a seat in one of the camp chairs.

Hazel looked at Brandon, who shrugged. "Did you want to head out to search with Mrs. Dean?" he asked, "We can't let people go out by themselves, but..."

"No, I'll wait for Captain Tate."

"I don't know if he'll be here anytime soon," Brandon said. "He's in a meeting about the search and rescue with the rangers."

The pink surrounding Mike darkened. "Search and rescue? Aren't we overreacting here? She's just a little late coming home. I'm sure she's fine. I wouldn't have called anyone, but my mom thought I should, as a precaution." He pulled another chair over and put his feet up on it.

Hazel and Brandon looked at each other again. Neither seemed to know what to say.

Behind Mike, rain dripped down from the edge of the canopy in big drops. The dull roar of pouring rain numbed Hazel's hearing and created a surreal atmosphere. The man with the missing wife relaxed under a tent while a storm raged around him.

Hazel was grateful to recognize Jason's car pulling into a parking spot next to Mike's.

"I think a lot more people will begin to show up now," Brandon said. "I just hope we won't have to close the roads. If it keeps coming down like this, I don't know if we'll have a choice."

Hazel looked up at the sky. The rain was still steady, but it had let up and the sky looked lighter, but the wind was still gusting in cold bursts. "I think it will clear up," she said.

Jason got out of the car and pulled out an umbrella. He held it above his head as he ran across the parking lot towards them. Hazel could see the wind catch it and try to pull it away from him a couple times.

Hazel smiled to herself.

"I got here as soon as I could," he huffed when he made it under the tent. "They're shutting down the county offices and the courthouse early today so everyone can look for Nina." He folded up the umbrella and leaned in to give her a quick kiss.

"Thank you," Hazel said.

"You doing okay?"

"I'll be fine. It helps to be doing something. Brandon wouldn't let me go searching by myself, so I'm glad you're here."

Jason gave Brandon a salute. "Good man, Brandon."

Brandon grinned.

Jason startled a little when he saw Mike, who was staring at the forest through the rain. Jason glanced at Hazel and Brandon. She gave him a grimace, and Brandon shrugged again.

Jason approached Mike. "Hey, Mike," he said, crouching down next to the chair Mike was sitting in. "How are you holding up?"

"I'm doing just fine," Mike replied, "I just..." he hesitated and looked at Hazel and Brandon. Hazel looked away from the two men. "So, Brandon," she said. "What do you think the forest rangers are going to be able to do to support the search?"

Brandon's eyes darted back and forth between her and the two men. "Oh, uh, well, they have a lot of resources available that we don't have and a lot more experience with this kind of thing, so I think they'll be able to help us out quite a bit."

"That's so good to hear," Hazel said, trying to think of something else to say so Jason and Mike could finish their conversation in relative privacy.

"Are you ready to go, Hazel?" Jason called.

"Yes, I'm definitely ready," she blurted.

"Alright," Brandon jumped in. "I'm sending each group out about five degrees away from the previous group. Do you have a compass?"

"Of course," Hazel said. Since she and Jason got tied up in

the woods for longer than they expected the past fall, she made sure that she had all the tools necessary for an overnight camping trip before she came out to look for Nina. She noticed that Jason had forgone his fancy hiking boots and opted for some nice, worn-in tennis shoes instead.

"Hazel?" Brandon was saying. "Hazel, did you hear me? That's north twenty west."

"Oh, yes, got it," she said, pulling her compass out of her backpack.

"GPS watch?" Brandon asked the two, and they both replied with an affirmative. "Go ahead and start a walk, then stop it when you turn around, so we know how far out you went. That will help us know how to plan out our future search. Call her name." Brandon stopped short and looked over at Mike. He took another step away from him and lowered his voice before he went on. "But remember that she might not be able to speak. Make sure that you look underneath logs and inside of caves because she probably went somewhere to seek shelter when the weather got bad."

Hazel glanced over at Mike too before nodding.

"That about sums it up," Brandon said. "We'll be sending people out for a while, but we'd like people to meet back here around five-thirty, so we can do a shoulder-to-shoulder style search." He looked out from underneath the canopy at the sky. "Well, as much as we can do something like that with this kind of geography and weather."

"Maybe that makes it easier," Jason pointed out. "Because there are some areas that she couldn't possibly be."

"Maybe," Brandon sighed, rubbing his face with his hand. He tinted a burnt orange. "Sending people out like this, a couple degrees apart, it feels so hopeless. It would be so much better if they are able to calculate her most likely route or something."

"We'll find her," Jason said. "Don't worry. There's a lot of people coming to look for her."

Brandon grimaced. "Sorry, I shouldn't have been so negative." He gave a short firm nod of his head, but Hazel noticed the burnt orange didn't fade. "We'll find her," he repeated.

Hazel had Jason leave the umbrella there 'in case someone needs it.' Then they left Brandon and Mike behind and headed out, following their bearing. The light was murky, and Hazel tried her flashlight, but it wasn't quite dark enough yet, so she put it away again. The rain had let up even more, and once they got under the cover of the forest, it was more quiet and less windy. Hazel took off her hood so she could see her surroundings more clearly.

"I've never been a part of a search and rescue before," Jason said. "It's always so hectic and hurried in the movies."

"We have to find her," Hazel declared.

"It's most likely she's hurt and pulled herself somewhere out of the rain," Jason said. "We'll find her. She might be a little banged up, but she'll be fine."

"What did Mike say to you?" Hazel asked.

"Just that he's embarrassed that so many people are putting themselves out trying to help find Nina. He doesn't seem to think that she's in any danger. Just that she lost track of time or something."

"I would be a wreck if I were him," Hazel said.

Jason nodded. "I think I would too, but you never know how people are going to react in times of crisis. I think he's just in denial. It happens."

Hazel nodded, trying not to judge Mike too harshly. "I love you, babe," she said to Jason, swallowing a lump in her throat.

"I love you, too, sweetheart," he said, squeezing her hand. "Let's find your friend."

THREE

I n Hazel's imagination, she would be the one to find Nina. She would duck her head under a ledge, and Nina would be huddled up at the back of a shallow cave, her ankle wrapped up in a makeshift bandage, her eyes filling with relief. She would stay there with her, while Jason went back to get help. Nina would spill everything about the depression she had been feeling recently. Hazel would listen sagely and offer support and advice. After that, they would be the best of friends, and Hazel would babysit when Nina went to therapy appointments and provide her with the support system she needed in order to find herself again.

After several hours searching, Hazel realized that her imagination was overly optimistic. The rain and wind had stopped but the clouds hadn't broken up and blown away. They still hung overhead, a threatening dark gray. She looked out over the mountains, bursting with new green, and felt vaguely sick. How would they ever find Nina in all of this?

There were too many cliffs and caves and dense sections of foliage. She could be anywhere. There had been no shortage of alcoves, fallen trees, or other small places a person might look for shelter. The search felt overwhelming. Hazel had read enough books to know that one shouldn't lose hope in a situation like this, but it was harder than she thought it would be.

Now, as they turned around to head back to the base of operations, Hazel was hoping that Nina would be wrapped up underneath the canopy sipping hot coffee. Or maybe Brandon would tell them that they had found her but needed help extracting her off the mountain, or that an ambulance had already come and gone, taking her to the safety of the hospital. Hazel could imagine plenty of positive outcomes and willed herself to focus on those instead of the even more numerous and diverse negative possibilities.

Once they were in view of the parking lot, she could tell that Nina had not been found, but she got a little choked up when she took in the number of people that had gathered to look for her. Hazel's heart filled to overflowing with love for her community. She reached out and grabbed Jason's hand. He gave her a grim smile.

"Don't worry," he whispered. "We'll find her."

A cloud had rolled in right on top of them, as it sometimes did in the mountains. A vague mist hung over everyone's heads and clung to their waterproof jackets. Hazel ran a hand over her sleeve, and water came pouring off it. They approached the canopy from the back end and ducked underneath. Uncle John stood amongst a small crowd of people, talking in a loud voice, his colors changing with each new person that approached him with a question.

"We're going to start a concentrated search in forty-five minutes so we're not sending individual groups out at this time," he boomed. "And no, this is not a catered event."

"I'll get you a cup of coffee," Jason said in her ear.

Hazel nodded and wandered out of the canopy and around the periphery of the large group of people milling around, waiting for the search to really get underway. The crowd emitted a veritable sea of emotional color that swirled together, resulting in a muddy, foggy brownish-gray muck. Hazel did not like to be in large crowds of people for this very reason. So many different people, with so many different and complex feelings overwhelmed her. She couldn't make sense of the input, and it threw her intuition off balance. It would have been easier if the people were spread out a little more, but the group tonight was hunched together to keep warm. Hazel could see cars lining the dirt road as far back as it turned into the trees. There was even a school bus, parked as much to the side of the road as could be expected but blocking a worrisome amount of the way out.

People who hadn't seen each other for a while conversed warmly with each other, but they were almost whispering. It felt like a funeral. Hazel shivered. She noticed a man standing a pace or two away from everyone else that she didn't recognize. She waved to catch his eye and gave him a welcoming smile, but when his eyes met hers, she froze.

For a minute she was sure her mind was playing tricks on her. It was all the caffeine and the stress.

"It can't be," she muttered under her breath. Suddenly she was sixteen again, wearing her Patty Loveless concert t-shirt and her hair was gigantic.

The man walking towards her through the mist raised a hand in greeting. She just stood there staring. It started to rain harder then, the cold drops felt like they were attacking her head and shoulders in a relentless onslaught. The man was squinting at her now. She didn't have time for reunions, not right now. Not when her friend needed her. She took a step backwards, wanting to avoid the inevitable interaction.

"Is that Hazel Randolph?" he said, surprise in his voice.

Hazel took another step back. She looked behind and around her, but she didn't see any easy way to escape.

"Lance Fuller," she reluctantly responded. "You would show

up at a time like this." Her attempt to sound natural, like he did, fell flat.

"Wow, Hazel," he said, coming closer. The space around him turned a rosy violet that stretched out between them and engulfed her. The heady haze of memory hung in the air. "It's so good to see you," Lance smiled.

"You too?" she said, without an ounce of believability. The awkward jawline in her memory was now covered with dark stubble that made it less noticeable, and she could tell that his head was clean-shaven underneath his baseball cap. Hazel's hand went to her hair. But then she shook her head. She didn't have time for vanity.

"What are you doing here?" Now that the initial surprise from seeing him again faded, she was feeling irritated by his intrusion. How could he think that he could just waltz back into town after so long and start searching for missing townsfolk?

"I just wanted to help," he said, looking towards the tent where John was barking orders. The purple around him changed abruptly to a muddy, mustard yellow. Hazel's eyebrows went up. He was lying, or at least not telling the whole truth. Seeing that color on him took her right back to when they were teenagers sneaking out after curfew. What motive could possibly bring someone into the wooded mountains on a stormy day *other* than wanting to help?

"Well, that's awfully community-minded of you," she said, following him through the parking lot. "Especially considering you don't live here anymore."

"Well," that violet color flickered back into focus. "I've actually been here for a few weeks now."

"Weeks?" Hazel was shocked that Lance could have been in town for so long without her hearing about it.

"Yeah, my mom and dad aren't doing too well." His color deepened again, this time to a cerulean blue.

Hazel's irritation melted. "Oh, no, Lance I'm so sorry. I didn't know." Hazel had not kept in touch with Lance's parents after he left town—in fact she avoided driving by their house. But she had fond memories of them from high school and had always wished them well in her heart.

"Yeah, dad's losing his mind, and mom's losing her body." He paused and turned towards Hazel and looked into her eyes. "I guess it's better that way, you know? Instead of the other way around? Dad never really used his brain that much, and mom didn't use her body. At least they can keep the most important pieces of themselves."

"That's terrible," Hazel whispered. In her mind, they were still in their forties, supremely capable and full of authority.

He reached out and patted her on the shoulder. "It's okay. We're coming to terms with it, Dansby and I. Remember my little brother? He's back too. We're going to stay with mom and dad for a while until we can figure out what to do about everything. It's like I'm eighteen again." He smiled at her. "I'm sleeping in my old bed and everything."

"How strange," Hazel smirked. "Me too."

Lance laughed. "Surely your bed is bigger now than it was back then."

Hazel felt herself blush. Lance seemed to suddenly realize that he put his foot in his mouth, and although his face didn't change color, his aura turned crimson.

He looked away from her. Hazel followed his gaze to Uncle John. "You should say hi to him," Hazel said. "He'd love to see you again."

Lance ducked his head and gave her a rueful smile. "It doesn't seem like a good time," he replied.

LaShay Trudgeon suddenly appeared by Hazel's side. "Hazel! Hi!"

Hazel's voice grew more cheerful when she addressed her friend. They had met the previous year when LaShay's son,

Wallis, had been arrested for a murder he didn't commit. Hazel had made it her mission to prove his innocence. Wallis didn't exactly appreciate Hazel's interference in his life, but she and LaShay had remained good friends. "LaShay! I'm so glad to see you. I didn't think you'd be able to make it."

"Oh, well, when I heard about poor Nina, I called up Mrs. Williams and told her that her haircut would have to wait for another day. She was fine with it; she's here now too, I think. I used to cut Nina's hair every eight weeks or so, but I haven't seen her since two babies ago. She was always such a sweetheart. It breaks my heart to think of her lost and alone."

"Me too," Hazel said, but then she caught Lance's eye and realized he was watching her have this conversation with her friend. "I suppose that it breaks your heart too?" she said sarcastically. "That's why you came down to help?"

"And who, may I ask, are you, handsome?" LaShay gave Hazel a hard nudge in her side while she looked Lance up and down with slow, lingering eyes.

Lance was at his most charming when he was in the spotlight. "Lance Fuller," he stuck out his hand, but when LaShay put her hand in his, he turned it, bowing in low to brush it with a kiss.

LaShay giggled. Hazel smirked and rolled her eyes.

"Hazel and I used to date, you know, back in high school. And who might you be?" he asked.

"LaShay Trudgeon," she said, blazing with magenta. "Hazel reconciled me with my son last fall."

Lance smiled again, his dimple just barely showing through his beard. "That sounds like Hazel."

"How would you know?" Hazel asked. "You haven't seen me for twenty-five years."

"I know there's some things never change and your essential meddlesome do-gooderness is one of them. It's one of the things I liked most about you when we were kids." Hazel felt her cheeks grow hot.

"She was always like that, huh?" LaShay asked.

Lance smiled, nodding. "She was always so sure of herself and her place in the world."

"Gimme a break," Hazel started but LaShay shushed her.

"I know what you mean," she chuckled at Lance.

"But not in a condescending way," he went on, seeming to think that LaShay had misunderstood him. "In more of an enabling way. Like because she was good, so were you. I gotta tell you, it was a little bit addictive." He took a sip from his coffee cup and looked over the rim at Hazel. She rolled her eyes.

"What happened to you two then?" LaShay asked.

"LaShay!" Hazel said, scandalized. It was the most inappropriate conversation to be having in the middle of a search and rescue operation.

"I enlisted," Lance said. "She Dear John-ed me."

"What?!" Hazel was shocked out of her righteous indignation by his interpretation of events. "I don't think that's exactly accurate."

Lance's eyebrows came together. "How would you describe it then?"

"You had no interest in getting married," Hazel said. "You wanted to... what was it? Keep your options open? Not be tied down? Be free to live in the moment? I can't remember what you said, exactly. Why would I put myself on the shelf for that?"

"Well, I didn't think that you were going to get engaged so fast."

"Well, it's not my fault I met the best guy on Earth while you were out trying to find yourself."

They glared at each other, their breaths turning to steam in the cold air. LaShay looked back and forth between them, her giggles had given way to a pained expression and a puce color.

"So..." LaShay said. "It was so nice to meet you, Lance. If you'll excuse us, I'd like Hazel to say hello to my daughter-in-law."

Lance found his easy smile again. "Of course," he said. "I hope to run into you again."

LaShay put an arm through Hazel's and pulled her away from Lance through the crowd. "Still have some hard feelings there, huh?" she said.

"Not at all," Hazel told her. "I'm happy with how things turned out."

"That doesn't mean that you don't have some hard feelings about how he treated you. It sounds to me like both of you do. Never got any closure, huh?"

Hazel didn't say anything. LaShay was too intuitive. It was a hairdresser superpower.

"Well, I don't blame you too much; he is a very, very good-looking man."

"Is he?" Hazel said, although she knew perfectly well how handsome Lance was. "Is Trudy really here?"

LaShay looked at her sideways. "No, I just wanted to give you an excuse to leave."

"Thank you," Hazel breathed.

"Wallis is here though," she said. "Would you like to say hi?"

When Wallis was accused of murder, Hazel had been the only one to insist that he was innocent. In any other case, it might have endeared her to him, but he was looking at a lot of money for taking the fall for it, so he didn't take kindly to her meddling.

"No, thanks. I'll steer clear of Wallis for the next ten years or so," Hazel said.

LaShay laughed. "I don't think he's mad at you anymore, but okay. How is that poor sweet boy doing? Eugene?"

Eugene was a teenager who had accidentally killed his brother, the one that Wallis had been accused of murdering.

"He's doing okay. About as well as can be expected I suppose. He's had a lot of contact with his grandparents and aunt. They're going to take him in when he gets out of the facility next year."

"I pray for him every night," LaShay said.

"Me too," Hazel nodded.

"You're an angel," LaShay leaned in and gave Hazel a one-armed hug. "I'll see you later. I sure hope we find Nina tonight. I don't like the idea of her out there in this weather."

"Who did you say is here now?" John's voice rose above the dull roar of the crowd. He turned toward his deputy, looming over him. The man took an involuntary step back.

Hazel's brow furrowed. John's tone had changed from his regular bluster to real irritation. He flashed with chevron orange. Hazel was certain that when her surrogate father eventually had a heart attack, it would be when he was flashing chevron orange.

"Excuse me," she said to LaShay. "I'm going to go see if I can help."

LaShay grinned at her. "I wouldn't expect you to do anything else." Hazel gave her one last smile and turned to make her way through the crowd towards John.

FOUR

"For the love of the Good Lord Almighty..." John muttered.

"What's wrong?" Hazel asked, putting a hand on his forearm.

"Oh, Hazel, good," John said, the orange immediately stopped flashing and melded into less of a zig-zag pattern. "You can take care of this mess."

"What mess?" Hazel chewed on her lower lip.

"The press is here."

Hazel choked on a laugh. "The press?"

"Yes, remember that idealistic youth that set up shop a couple months ago to run a paper in Red Gap?"

Hazel smiled. "Oh yes, I remember," she said. "She came into our city council meeting to make sure she had our blessing. She seemed like a nice girl. Why are you so agitated about her?"

John blinked at her like she had asked the right way to hold her gun. "My dear, reporters communicate with each other. You let one of them in here, and before long, there'll be press here from all over Georgia, Tennessee, and North

Carolina. The last thing we need is a bunch of reporters and cameras running around when we're looking for this...this lost woman."

"Nina," Hazel interjected. "Her name is Nina."

"Right," John said. "Can you please go talk to the kid? I don't have time right now. I'm trying to orchestrate a mass search party."

"Sure. Where's Brandon?"

"He went to get some dinner," John said. "He'll be back before we start."

At the mention of dinner, Hazel's stomach rumbled. She wished she had thought to bring herself a bag lunch. A steady diet of granola bars just wasn't going to cut it. They had a long night ahead of them still. Hazel stepped out from under the tent's canopy into the mist. She looked around for the reporter but didn't see anyone obvious, just a crowd full of people wearing various shades of gray.

For the second time that day, all the colorful emotions of such a large crowd overwhelmed her. She felt herself start to tighten up inside with anxiety. She closed her eyes and took some deep breaths, counting to ten. Then she opened her eyes again.

She began to scan the crowd again, this time trying to tune out the waves of color and focus on individual faces. She found the "reporter" hanging out towards the back of the tent. The title seemed too grand for what she seemed to be, which was an eavesdropping kid.

Hazel knew that this girl had recently graduated from Kennesaw State with an undergraduate degree, but she looked like she could pass for a high school senior. Her round, freckled face and rosy cheeks made her look quite young.

"Hello there," Hazel said.

The young woman jumped and turned towards Hazel. In her shock, her phone flew up out of her hands for a second, and she recovered it with some awkward fumbling. She instantly turned a bubble gum pink.

Hazel glanced at the phone, recognizing a voice recording app on the screen. Had this girl been trying to record Captain Tate's conversations? Why on earth would she want to do that?

"Hi," the girl replied, locking the phone and putting it into her pocket. Then she looked up and focused on her face, and the bubble gum pink that surrounded her intensified. "Oh! Councilwoman Dean. I didn't see you there."

"Hello," Hazel smiled. "I think at our meeting, you said your name was Ermengarde."

The girl turned crimson, and the bubble gum pink turned to more of a neon. "Yes, family name, but everyone just calls me by my last name McGee."

Hazel tried to remember the city council meeting McGee had attended to introduce herself. "Your grandparents lived here?" she asked.

"Yes, that's right. I spent every summer here until they moved away. I loved it."

"And you think that some reporting on a small town is somehow going to heal the political animosity in the country?" Hazel was trying to paraphrase her stated motive.

"Yes, that's right. I think that politics aren't really divided into left and right wing so much as rural and urban. If urban areas could read good journalism about rural areas, I think it could go a long way to bridge the gap."

Hazel smiled again. "That's very sweet."

The girl flushed deeper. "Oh... um, thanks."

Hazel realized that McGee probably wasn't interested in being sweet. She was a hard-boiled journalist after all. "Well, it's nice to meet you personally," she said.

"You too," McGee smiled.

"Captain Tate sent me over to give you a statement, although I'm afraid there's not much I can tell you. A woman in her late twenties went for a short backpacking trip alone in the woods, and she was supposed to return last night. Her family has not yet heard from her. Because of the weather, authorities are taking her disappearance very seriously. The search is ongoing, but we have an excellent turn out here," Hazel motioned towards the crowd. "And we hope to find her tonight."

McGee had grabbed her phone again and was typing furiously. Hazel marveled at her two-handed technique. Hazel was still a one-finger texter. "Can you release the name of the missing woman?"

"No," Hazel said flatly. "Her family has not given permission for us to do that; however, I'm sure you could ask anyone here, and they would tell you as unofficial sources."

McGee reddened (and pinkened) again but asked another question without changing her tone. "Did the hiker leave a plan or a route with anyone before she left on her hike?"

"No comment," Hazel said.

"Why did she go out alone?"

Why *did* she go out alone? Hazel frowned. Her stomach dropped. She imagined that it had something to do with *Anna Karenina*, but she didn't know how. "I don't know," Hazel answered.

"Is it possible she was meeting someone?"

Hazel stared at McGee. "What?"

"Do we know if she might have been meeting someone on her hike?"

Hazel narrowed one eye. "No." The kid didn't seem to fully realize what she was implying. If Nina went out to meet someone and then went missing... Hazel shook her head quickly.

"Oh, hello there..."

Hazel whirled around. Jeremiah was standing right behind her. "Jeremiah!" Hazel said. "What are you doing?"

"I just wanted to come and say hello. I don't know you; my name is Jeremiah Randolph Dean."

Hazel narrowed her eyes. Jeremiah was glowing with a dusky pink violet that she didn't remember seeing on him before. Also, Randolph wasn't even his real middle name. It was Hazel's maiden name. She came from one of the founding families of the area and her name carried a lot of weight with it. Hazel had seen him pull it out before when he wanted to be impressive. It was embarrassing. He was flushed and appeared to be sweating. "Are you okay?" she asked him.

He pushed past her and stuck out a hand towards the reporter.

"Um," she stammered. "I'm McGee."

"McGee...interesting name for such a beautiful woman."

Hazel's eyes bulged. "Jeremiah!" she exclaimed, but McGee's laugh covered up her reprimand.

"McGee is my last name," she explained. "But everyone calls me that. My first name is Ermengarde."

"Oh, wow," Jeremiah said, "I can see why everyone calls you McGee. But I like it, it's so meta."

"Meta?" Hazel asked.

Ermengarde McGee smiled.

"So, umm, I don't remember seeing you around town before." Jeremiah ran his fingers through his hair, tossing his head back.

"I'm relatively new," McGee said. "I'm a reporter. I'm here to report on small town life to the big city." The girl couldn't help herself; she was so excited about her idea on how to solve politics. "The problems in the country right now are directly related to the animosity between the people living in big cities and those who are in more rural areas. As the population of the cities increases, it becomes more and more important for the two different groups to stay connected in some way. That's where journalism comes in."

"Oh, that's very..." Jeremiah tossed his hair again. "Perceptive of you."

Hazel pressed her lips together so she wouldn't laugh.

"Um, thanks... Listen, Councilwoman Dean, here's my card," she handed Hazel a business card in the shape of a typewriter. "Please call me if you think of any other information you can give me."

"Oh, that card is so cool," Jeremiah said. "Can I have one?"

"Sure, I guess," McGee handed one to Jeremiah too. "Thanks, Councilwoman Dean," she said before she skulked off to try to pump out information out of another unsuspecting victim.

"What was that all about?" Hazel asked Jeremiah.

"Mom, that is the most beautiful woman I have ever seen," Jeremiah declared.

"Jeremiah, she has almost ten years on you."

"Age is just a number, Mom," he quipped.

"Not when you're fifteen, it's not," she said. "Please don't harass Miss McGee anymore, okay?"

The hot pink around him faded. "Don't worry, Mom," he said. "I'm not going to harass her."

For some reason, Hazel wasn't convinced.

"Come on," Jeremiah said, "Dad's been looking for you." He led Hazel back through the tent to where Jason and Elias were standing.

"Oh, good, you found her," Jason said to Jeremiah, handing Hazel a cup of coffee and a donut.

"I did find her," Jeremiah said, gazing goofily to where McGee was trying to maneuver closer to John.

"What's going on?" Jason asked, giving Hazel a quizzical look and raising his eyebrows in the direction of Jeremiah.

A smile played around Hazel's mouth when she thought about how tickled Jason would be by the story when she relayed it later. "I'll tell you at home," she assured him. "Um, there's something else I should tell you too. I ran into an old friend..."

"Attention!" Uncle John's voice boomed from a megaphone. "Can I please have your attention!"

Hazel turned towards him, taking a bite of the waxy donut. In her shop, she only made donuts in the fall, and she only made apple or pumpkin cake donuts. She grabbed the coffee out of Jason's hand and swallowed some to force the gluey mess down her throat.

Brandon had reappeared with a man wearing a forest ranger's uniform with him. Hazel felt a little of the weight lift off her shoulders at the sight of him. The forest ranger would know what to do. He should have way more experience with finding missing people in the forest than John and their town's little police force.

"This is a good turn out," John continued. "I know you all realize the importance of the first couple days after a person is missing. I've asked Reverend Combs to pray for us." The reverend stepped out of the crowd to stand next to John.

Hazel bowed her head for the prayer. She opened her heart towards heaven, willing God to aid them in finding Nina for better or worse.

Murmured 'amens' echoed through the parking lot.

In his uniquely gruff but efficient way, John gave the whole group instructions for the evening in about ten sentences. The search had officially begun.

Jeremiah and Elias instantly disappeared in the direction of their friends. Hazel sighed. Even a search and rescue operation could be a social event if you were a teenager, she supposed.

She turned towards Jason and was startled to see Lance on the other side of him. She jumped in surprise, letting out a surprised "oh!"

Jason raised an eyebrow at her and turned towards Lance.

"I'm Jason Dean, I'm sorry, I don't recognize you."

Lance looked up at Jason, who had about four inches on him, and then put a hand in his. Hazel half-smiled.

"Lance," Lance said. "Lance Fuller."

Jason froze and dropped Lance's hand. Jason had emitted varying shades of green and tan all day. Hazel knew that tan was a color that took over when he was thinking about something, analyzing, and putting pieces together. It was the color he wore every day when he came home from work. Green was his worry color. She saw that a fair amount too.

When Jason met Lance Fuller, he turned a reddish orange that felt distantly familiar to her. But it wasn't one that she could instantly match an emotion to. It was different than his normal surprise color, which was cotton candy pink. It wasn't panic exactly—that was a more saturated red without any orange in it. Hazel didn't know what to make of her husband in that moment and she was surprised by how uneasy that made her feel. "Lance Fuller?" he said, "As in, Hazel's high school boyfriend?"

Lance smiled and winked. "That would be me. I'm so flattered you've heard of me."

Hazel glared at him. Jason stood up straighter and glanced at her; she could see orange sparking off his body. "Well, I suppose I could say I'm glad to finally put a face to the name," he said finally.

Lance laughed. "Likewise," he grinned. "You look about the same as you did in the wedding invitation my parents got. Haven't aged a day. I don't know how you pulled that off, living with Hazel."

Hazel watched a smile tease her husband's mouth. The red and orange around him softened. Hazel felt a momentary flash of panic herself. The last thing she wanted was for Jason to develop a friendship with Lance, although she couldn't explain to herself why it would be so horrible.

"Let's go," she said, pulling on Jason's arm. "We need to find Nina. We're going to be left behind."

"Mind if I join you?" Lance asked.

"Not at all," Jason said.

Hazel cringed. It was truly the worst timing.

They had been instructed to stay within arms length of the people next to them, so they were plenty close enough to carry on a conversation. Hazel maneuvered so that Jason was in between her and Lance.

"So, Jason," Lance said.

"What's it like being married to Hazel Randolph?"

Jason chuckled. "The Hazel or the Randolph?" he asked. Lance laughed.

"I'm right here," Hazel called. "I can hear this conversation."

"Both," Lance responded, ignoring her.

Jason turned around and winked at her. "Being married to Hazel is great. Being married to a Randolph... well, it has its pros and cons. Being married to John Tate's pseudo-daughter? That's the hardest part."

"Oh, come on," Hazel groaned. Jason, as the district attorney, had a tumultuous working relationship with Hazel's surrogate father, the police captain. They clashed politically, philosophically, and generationally, but they always managed to be polite during family dinners.

"You have trouble with Uncle John?" Lance said, surprise in his voice. "I always got along great with him."

"Well, that tells me a lot about you, now, doesn't it?" Jason retorted, his voice going flat.

Hazel grimaced. Uncle John had loved Lance. He was exactly the kind of guy that John envisioned Hazel marrying. When she and Lance broke up, John still insisted that they would eventually end up together. Jason wasn't way off base if he was thinking that Lance was the guy John wished she had married. But Hazel didn't wish that, and isn't that what really counted?

"Hey, Hazel, does Jason know about your, uh... you know?"

Hazel's mouth fell open slightly. "My what?" What could Lance possibly be referring to? Suddenly every weird and embarrassing thing she ever did in high school came flooding to her mind. She had told Jason a lot of things, but there was probably something she had left out.

"You know, your superpower."

Hazel glared at Lance. "Of course he does." And if Lance thought there was a chance that he didn't, why would he ask about it?

She looked at Jason with a shrug and was surprised to see his face gray and contorted with pain, like he had been hit. "Are you okay?" she asked. "Did you trip? Are you getting a blister?"

"Lance knows?" he asked, in a voice too quiet for Lance to hear.

"Didn't I tell you that before?" she asked.

Jason shook his head. "No, you implied that you had never told anyone else. That no one knew except your dead grandmother."

Hazel winced. "Jason, I'm sorry. I thought I would have mentioned it, back when I first told you."

"I know that knowing what other people are feeling all the time is usually more trouble than it's worth," Lance went on, oblivious to their whispered conversation. "But I gotta tell you, it got us out of a bit of trouble a time or two when we were kids. Probably comes in handy in a marriage."

Jason looked sharply at Hazel.

"I don't want to talk about it," Hazel said in her best Grandmama Randolph voice. "Shouldn't we be calling Nina's name?"

She began to shout Nina's name loudly, and the two men joined in, effectively ending all conversation. The mood had turned from friendly to tense. It was going to be an awkward couple hours, and she would have some explaining to do later, but at least Lance and Jason weren't going to end up being best friends.

Any second, Hazel expected to hear jubilant shouts. They continued to call her name. A few hundred voices, all reaching out into the night to find their friend, an essential part of their little corner of the world. *Oh, Nina,* Hazel thought. *I hope you'll be able to see how important you are.*

The gloom intensified as time went on. The sun, though invisible behind cloud cover, made its withdrawal known. People began to take out their flashlights. Hazel saw spots of light in the distance, dancing on each side of her. Hazel's heart ached with pride in her community and worry for her friend. "We'll find her," she murmured to herself. "Together we can do anything. We'll find her."

Tears stung at her eyes. She blinked rapidly, chewing on her bottom lip to keep the tears from spilling over. It wasn't the right time to cry. She refocused her attention on the woods ahead of her, panning her flashlight in an arc, looking for anywhere someone might have gone to get out of the rain. "Nina!" she called. "Nina, we're here for you!" Her voice cracked.

"Hazel, maybe you need a break," Jason spoke softly to her. "We've been at this for eight hours now."

Hazel shook her head without speaking. She didn't trust her voice.

Jason sighed. "Just a little while longer. But it won't do Nina any good if you collapse in the woods."

"I'm not going to collapse," Hazel protested, but her voice didn't have its usual feisty note.

Lance looked over at her, but she couldn't see his facial expression or his emotional color in the dark. He didn't say anything.

Jason handed her a water bottle. "At least stay hydrated."

Hazel drank without pausing in her steps.

As they continued, the lights surrounding them became fewer and more spread out as some people had to go home. Elias and Jeremiah headed home with the rest of the high schoolers. It became so dark it was impossible to see without the flashlight. The leaves on the ground were so wet they reflected a blinding glare from its beam.

An ATV engine roared nearby. Minutes later, John's voice sounded over a loudspeaker. "Please, if you were searching during the day today, go home. Get some rest. Come back in the morning. If you started at six you can keep going."

"Come on, Hazel," Jason said, grabbing her arm. "He's right. It's time to call it."

"He wasn't talking to us," Hazel protested. "He's talking to old, frail people."

"Hazel Dean, if you can hear me, I *am* talking to you," John's voice crackled. "I will call you if we find anything."

Hazel twisted her mouth, and her eyebrows furrowed.

"I'm staying out for a while, Hazel," Lance said in an attempt to be reassuring. "Don't worry, there are lots of people still looking for her."

"Hazel..." Jason said, his voice full of warning.

Hazel let the air rush out of her. "Yeah, yeah, yeah. Fine, I'll go to sleep and come back in the morning."

Jason smiled. He gently turned her towards the parking lot. Hazel reluctantly turned her back on the woods where Nina could be just another few steps away and followed her husband back down the mountain to their safe, warm home.

FIVE

"I wish I could come with you," Jason said as she left early the next morning. "But there are some time-sensitive things at work that I put off last night, and I can't push them back another day."

"Don't be silly, Jason," Hazel said, pulling on her coat. "I don't expect you to come with me. I just can't not go."

Jason nodded, pulling her into a hug. "I know."

She kissed him and turned away to head towards the car.

"By the way..." he said in a tone that made her turn back around. He glowed the strangest green apple color. She had never seen anything quite like it on him before.

"What is it?" she asked, raising one eyebrow.

"You don't think that Lance will be searching again today, do you? He doesn't have some connection to Nina?"

Hazel laughed. "You're jealous! I'm seeing all kinds of new colors on you lately!"

"I'm not jealous," Jason said, his eyes dropping. His embarrassment color, sherbet orange, overtook the apple green.

"I've never seen you jealous before," she said, walking over to him. She hugged him around the middle.

"We never finished that conversation yesterday, you know about how I thought I was the only one on earth who knew about your gift, but it turns out I'm not?"

"I'm so sorry, Jason," Hazel reached out and put her hand on his shoulder. "I don't know why I didn't tell you. I guess I just never expected to see Lance again. Or maybe I thought he would have forgotten."

"Forgotten that he had a girlfriend once who could see his feelings?" Jason smirked.

"I don't know; I just..." Hazel threw up her hands and sighed. "He just wasn't real anymore."

Jason looked at her, his eyebrows furrowing. "I don't know what you mean."

"When he left... when I met you... It was like, I don't know. Like he was a character in a book I had read once."

Jason shook his head. "I don't understand."

"I know, I'm sorry. I wish I could explain it better. Anyways, you have nothing to worry about. You are the love of my life and about a thousand million times better than Lance in every way."

"I know," Jason chuckled, but then asked, "For example?"

"Well, you're taller, and you still have all your hair, for starters."

"I do still have my hair..." Jason mused, letting go of her to run a proud hand through it.

"See? You win. Besides, Lance probably isn't going to be out this early looking for Nina anyways. Neither of us will ever see him again." Hazel remembered that Lance had been lying about why he was out searching for Nina and wondered again what his true motives might have been. Maybe he was trying to bump into her. She shook her head to dislodge the thought. "Now, I'm going to go look for my missing friend."

"Did you pack a lunch?"

"An actual ham sandwich with an apple and carrot sticks. Like I'm in elementary school again."

"Good," Jason nodded. "I love you."

She patted his face before turning away. "I love you, too."

Driving to the Twin Pines trail head, Hazel was happy to see that the weather had improved. Overnight, the rain had stopped, and the clouds dissipated. Hazel thought the conditions would be better for Nina until she got out of her car and an extra cold morning greeted her. The cloud cover had trapped some warm air close to the ground, but now that it was gone, the temperature had dropped. The foliage that kept the forest cool in the summer wasn't around to keep it warm in the spring.

Hazel's breath was visible in thick puffs of condensation. The canopy was deserted except for Mike, who sat in a camp chair with his head buried in his hands. He emitted a silvery gray haze that Hazel thought might be sadness. Finally, the man was displaying the kind of emotions that a husband should have when his wife goes missing in dangerous circumstances.

"Hi, Mike," she said, her voice gentle. "How are you feeling today?"

Mike startled, his head snapping up to look at her. His eyes were bloodshot and red.

"Have you been out all night?" she asked.

He nodded. "I can't believe she did this," he grumbled. "What a nightmare. What am I going to do?"

"Did what?" A shard of ice pierced Hazel's heart. Was it suicide? Had they found Nina's body? Hazel knew it was all her fault.

"Took off like this," Mike said. "I don't understand why she went to begin with." He cracked his knuckles, one by one. The popping made Hazel cringe. "I don't know if she's going to come back."

"Mike..." she said, using a soothing voice. "Have you talked to Nina's parents at all?"

He barked a short laugh. "No point," he said. "She always talked to her mom too much. She's probably in on it."

"In on what?" Hazel asked. Her eyebrows furrowed.

"In on her plan." Mike waved a hand. "You know... to take off."

Hazel blinked. "You think she left on purpose? You don't think she's lost?"

Mike glanced at Hazel then looked back down at his hands. The silver in the haze surrounding him flickered, like it had been shaken up and was slowly floating down to settle. "She's been acting weird lately. She was really distant, and then she got all jittery a couple weeks ago." He shook his head. "No, not jittery. More like giddy. And distracted."

Hazel stared at him, but he didn't continue. "What are you saying?" she finally blurted. Hazel couldn't wrap her mind around the idea of a mother leaving her children on purpose. Women who abandoned their children had extraneous circumstances that made it impossible for them to stay, like extreme poverty. In the book, *Anna Karenina,* the title character spends most of it trying to maintain ties with her child. Women who walked away from their children for no reason did not fit into Hazel's world view.

"I think she ran off with someone." Mike blurted out. He buried his face in his hands again.

Hazel drew a sharp intake of breath. The question came out of her mouth before she could stop it. "Who?"

Mike looked at her sideways. "I don't know," he shook his head. "I don't know how she would even have met anyone. She never leaves the house, never talks to anybody." He rubbed his face. "She was... unhappy...with our life."

Hazel nodded. She had gotten that same vibe from Nina.

She remembered her conversation with Nora the previous day. It seemed like much longer than that.

"Mike..." Hazel struggled to find words that wouldn't make him defensive. "Nina's unhappiness—when did you start to notice it?"

Mike still didn't meet her eyes. The silver haze darkened and intensified around him. He buried his head back in his hands.

"Mike?" Hazel said.

Mike exploded out of the chair, balling his hands into fists. The silver around him raced as though it had been shaken up again. "I don't know, okay? I don't remember. I wasn't paying attention. I was so busy with the election, and everything seemed fine. I just didn't have the time to spend much time on Nina's *feelings*."

His voice became sarcastic with the word feelings, and Hazel had a sudden desire to knock the man upside his head. Instead, her voice became flat and full of contempt. "You didn't have *time*?"

For the entirety of their conversation Mike had avoided eye contact, but now his head snapped up, and he gave her a hard glare, his jaw clenched. His hands balled into tight fists, and he took a step towards her. Hazel wondered if he might hit her. She tilted her jaw upwards slightly, narrowing her eyes.

He didn't come any closer, but his voice came out more dangerous than a shout. "Don't judge me—"

"Time to go home now, Mike," Uncle John's voice boomed from the other side of the canopy. He walked towards them, completely relaxed except that Hazel could see a dangerous green and brown swirled cloud around his feet. She knew that color from hunting with him. He was preparing himself for a strike.

Mike's eyes widened when he noticed John. He took a step away.

"I'll give you a call if we find anything," John said quietly, taking slow steps in Mike's direction. "It's been a long night. Go get some rest."

Mike took one more cowering step backwards and then shook his head back and forth. He stood up a little straighter and looked at John, ignoring Hazel completely.

"You're right," he said. "I do need some rest." He gave Hazel one more hard glare and then turned to stalk towards his car.

Hazel watched him walk away. John came to stand next to her. "I'm not sure I should let him drive himself home," John shook his head. "Sleep deprivation and grief are about as mind-altering as alcohol."

Hazel snorted. "Yeah, grief."

John gave her a look. "Don't go making trouble," he chastised.

Mike's car reversed out of the parking space and then stopped a little too abruptly to change directions. He accelerated far too quickly out of the parking lot, his tires skidding a bit when he bounced onto the gravel road.

John frowned after him.

"Did anybody find anything while I was asleep?" Hazel asked, changing the subject.

"I'm afraid not," John said. "The ranger is thinking that maybe she didn't get as far as he originally thought. We're sending people back in the other direction. We searched a day's hike in that direction already, so it's a long shot. But if she only hiked the first day she was gone, it would make sense."

Hazel furrowed her brow. "So, she hiked for a day and then sat around at a campsite for the next two?"

"Maybe," John said, "or maybe she got hurt that first day and has been immobilized since."

Hazel's throat closed at the thought.

John patted her arm. "We'll find her," he reassured. "Don't worry."

Hazel bit her lip. If John was right and they did find her and bring her back home, then what would happen? Hazel began to wonder what more she could do to help her friend through the difficult time she'd been having.

"Have you notified her parents?" asked Hazel.

John balked. "Didn't Mike?"

Hazel shook her head, "It didn't sound like it," she said. She added 'get in touch with Nina's parents' to the to do list she was keeping in her head. Right behind 'learn more about postpartum depression' and 'find out if Nina was meeting someone in the woods.'

Mike seemed to think she was. The basic plot of *Anna Karenina* might support that as well. Maybe that's why the book wanted to be with Nina, because she was thinking about running away from her family.

"Mike thinks that Nina ran off with an old boyfriend," she told John.

He nodded. "Yes, he told me the search was a waste of time because she was probably out of the state by now." John scratched his head. "It doesn't sound right to me. She didn't take anything else with her aside from her backpacking gear. Didn't leave a note or any mementos for her kids... it just doesn't feel like that's what's going on here."

"Have you been to the house?"

"I was down there yesterday afternoon, just to take a quick look around. Her make-up bag was sitting on her bathroom counter still. A girl doesn't take a make-up bag to go backpacking, but she does to run off with a lover."

"That makes sense." Hazel didn't know whether to feel relieved or not. Everything John said rang true, but for some reason, Hazel couldn't dismiss the idea completely. Something was nagging at the back of her mind, like she was trying to remember something she used to know and forgot.

"So, you're a glutton for punishment, eh?" John grinned at her. "I can't let you go out searching alone, you know."

"No one else is around?" Hazel asked.

"Not right now. I think most people are still asleep."

Hazel ignored the hint. "What are *you* doing right now?" she asked.

"The forest ranger is supposed to meet me here with some maps, and we're going to strategize."

Hazel sat down in a camp chair. "Seems like maybe I should wait until after you do that so that I know the best place to go. It could be miles from here, right?"

"I suppose so," John said, taking a seat as well. "Ranger Rick should have been here by now; I wonder what's keeping him."

Hazel snorted. "It's kind of hilarious that his name is Rick," she said.

John smiled. "Maybe his family owns that kid magazine," he said.

"Actually, we do," Ranger Rick had approached the canopy from the other direction, and they hadn't noticed him standing there. "I'm the fourth generation of Ranger Rick in my family." He didn't crack a smile, but Hazel thought he might be joking because of the dancing yellow beams she saw around him.

John's mouth fell open. "Are you serious?"

Hazel began to laugh, and after another minute, Rick began to chuckle too.

"Wait," John said. "So, you're not serious?"

Hazel couldn't stop laughing, but Rick shook his head and walked over to the table. "No, no. I'm not serious. But I've heard Ranger Rick jokes too many times not to mess with people a little bit."

Hazel stopped laughing enough to get a good look at Rick. She was curious about his life as a forest ranger. He was an athletic man of about six feet. He wasn't very old, younger than

Hazel—maybe in his early thirties. A comfortable brown emanated from him, the color of rich dirt ready for planting.

"Do you live in the National Forest?" she asked.

"Sometimes," he said. "It's kind of a seasonal thing."

"I'm curious about your work," she said. "I don't know very much about what forest rangers do."

"This is a lot of what we do," he said, indicating the maps. "Helping with search and rescue. We also enforce the law in the forest. Just like Captain Tate here does in Red Gap." He clapped John on the back.

"We really appreciate your help on this Rick," John said. "I know this isn't strictly in the National Forest."

Rick shrugged. "No worries. We're happy to help." Hazel sensed the flicker of color more than she saw it. At first glance, Rick was still surrounded by brown, but then a flash of brilliant green leapt out and this time Hazel saw it. It was a streak for just a moment that shot up from his chest to the top of his head. Hazel wished she knew what that might mean.

Rick spread the maps on the table and John leaned over to look at them. "We've searched through here and here. We found her car here. So, she at least started down this trail on Friday."

Hazel spoke up. "Her friend told me that she hadn't done any backpacking in years, so I don't think she would have been covering a lot of ground. I think..." she looked at them, hoping she wasn't butting in. "I think that she went out there to be alone."

Rick nodded, the brown surrounding him lightening to the color of cocoa. "I can understand that," he murmured. "Don't worry, Mrs. Dean, we'll find her."

Hazel smiled at him.

"She must have been heading towards the National Forest," Rick said. "Those are the only trails that would make back-packing worthwhile."

"Not if she was looking for solitude," John said. "Why would she have parked way over on the other side of Red Gap, if she was planning on hiking into the National Forest? Her original plan was to be home what? Sunday afternoon?" he looked at Hazel for confirmation. She nodded at him. John shook his head. "Her trip wasn't long enough to make it all the way to the forest, so why would she head in that direction?" He put his finger down on the map. "No, I think she went this way."

Rick looked dubious. The streak of green flashed across his face again. Hazel's eyebrow twitched. She couldn't think of what that green streak might be. "There's nothing over there," he said.

"Exactly," John said. "Solitude. Do you think you'll be able to get a helicopter for us today?"

"I'll try," he said. "It's a little tricky since, like you pointed out, this isn't precisely in the forest." His face continued to flash green.

John nodded. "I'm trying to see what kind of resources I can get out here from my side. I think I have some dogs coming, but they probably won't be here until tomorrow."

"Dogs?" Rick's brown turned pale. "That'll be great."

"In the meantime, I think we should take our search in that direction," John said, pointing again to the secluded spot on the map.

Rick shrugged. "I think you'll have better luck on this side," he said, pointing to the trails that wove together and twisted their way into the national forest.

"We'll see," John said. He flickered burnt orange, a milder version of his neon orange chevron he turned when he got truly irritated. "You go ahead and take your ATV out that way; I'm going to stick to these trails with my searchers."

Rick shrugged again. The green streaking across his face disappeared, and his shades of brown had been replaced by a yellow just this side of neon. It made Hazel's eyes uncomfortable to look at it. "Suit yourself," he said. "I'll let you know when I hear back about the helicopters."

"Thanks."

"Ma'am," he said, nodding at her as he left.

"Thanks for your help, Rick," she said, but she said it more out of her good breeding than genuine gratitude. Something about that green flash across his face made Hazel mistrust Rick. John's reasoning made perfect sense to Hazel.

"So, what's next?" She asked John when Rick was out of earshot.

"I think it's time to move our base of operations," he said, digging a walkie talkie out of his pocket. "Clyde, this is John, over."

A voice came back over almost immediately. "I read you, John, what's up, over."

"We're going to move our base of operations to Cherokee Rose Trailhead, over."

"Sounds good, Captain, over." A pause, then, "we'll start heading in that direction, over."

John nodded to himself, then he got out his phone to call the police station. He instructed the front desk to let anyone who wanted to help know that they should come to Cherokee Rose instead of Twin Pines. Then he started packing up.

"What do you want me to do?" she asked.

"Help me pack up," he said. "Then you're going to sit here and tell anyone who comes along where we've moved to."

"You can't be serious," she said. "Can't we just leave a note?"

"A note?" John smirked. "No one's going to see a note. They'll turn in a circle and then be frustrated that they don't know what's going on."

"Then they'll call the station, who will tell them where everyone is."

"Maybe," John shrugged. "Or maybe they just give up and go home."

"But I want to help," Hazel protested.

"This is helping. You don't have to do it all day, just for the next few hours."

Hazel groaned, but she got to work packing up the bad coffee and donuts for transportation to their new home. John left her one camp chair to sit in and told her to stay until noon, whereupon she should drive over and join him. Then he drove away, leaving her to sit idly.

At first, there were several people that came by, and Hazel had to admit that John was right. It was much better to have her there to meet them instead of them wandering confusedly. But after the first couple hours, the traffic dropped off and Hazel didn't know if it was because people began to check in with the station about where to go or if it was just the time of day.

Luckily, Hazel never went anywhere without a book. She got *The Secret Garden* out of her car and, settling into the camp chair as comfortably as possible, opened to her favorite part. Rereading *The Secret Garden* was a spring tradition for her. She had almost forgotten where she was, having been fully immersed in the book when a voice spoke up from behind her.

"Let me guess," Lance said. "*The Secret Garden.*"

Hazel jumped. The book fell into her lap. "Lance!" She felt exposed, like she should cover herself up, even though she had multiple layers of clothing on.

He was grinning at her. "Did I scare ya?"

"You came from the opposite direction I expected people from."

"I was on the trails," he said. "Thought I'd do some more searching this morning. But I've been gone for too long now. I better get going," Lance said. "I left my parents to their own devices. Probably wasn't the best idea, but I can't stop thinking about that poor woman."

"I thought that your brother, Dansby, was at home with your parents?" Hazel said.

"Right," Lance said. "No, he is. I just don't want to leave him all by himself for too long, you know? It can be a lot to deal with at times." A tinge of limey yellow eeked out from Lance's skin. The sight brought her right back to her adolescence. Lance telling his parents she wasn't there while she muffled giggles in the closet. Lance explaining to their homeroom teacher that they were late because of a family emergency. Lance telling people he hated that his parents had a baby while he was a teenager. Lime yellow was Lance's color for deceit.

Hazel opened her mouth, considering calling him out, but a car came rumbling into the parking lot and they both turned to see who it was.

"Oh, no," Hazel murmured.

"It's John," Lance said, smiling. "I didn't get to say hi to him last night."

John got out of the car and walked towards them. He got about ten feet away and stopped short.

"Lance Fuller?" John's aura turned a warm yellow. Hazel rolled her eyes. "I can't believe it! Hazel, it's Lance!" He exclaimed as though she would now jump into Lance's arms.

"I know," she deadpanned. "I saw him yesterday."

"Lance!" John strode over to him to shake his hand. "How have you been? It's been a long time. Have you finally come to your senses and moved back to the greatest town on Earth?"

Lance chuckled. "No, no. It's my parents... you know, they're getting on now..."

John shook his head. "No, they can't be."

"I'm afraid so," Lance laughed again, but there was no humor in it.

Hazel vacillated between feeling sorry for him and being irritated by his presence.

"Well, I'm sorry to hear that. Your parents were good friends until it got awkward there." John glared at Hazel. "But I'm glad to see you again." He glanced at Hazel then looked back at Lance. "Did you ever get married?"

Hazel choked. "Lance has been helping us look for Nina," she said to change the subject.

"That's mighty good of you; you always were willing to help a friend. A giver, that's what you were. Wasn't he, Hazel?"

"He sure was," she snarked. John didn't detect the sarcasm in her voice. She didn't remember Lance ever pushing people out of the way so he could help before.

She stared intently at him, watching for any other tell-tale emotions. He glanced at her quickly and then looked back at John with that perfect smile and little chuckle that had been so charismatic when they were kids.

He began to tell John the same story he told Hazel about coming back home to take care of his parents. Hazel wished the lie Lance was telling was about his parents' condition, but the yellowish-green on his skin disappeared when he talked about them.

Hazel considered the possibility that the color had changed in meaning over the last twenty-five years. It was possible. Her children's colors for different emotions had changed as they aged.

One might think that having a way to detect when people are lying would make life a lot easier, but in fact, Hazel found that it often complicated things. Just because you know that someone is lying doesn't mean that you know what the truth is, or even specifically what they're lying about. Humans are creative when it comes to duplicity.

Hazel's brow furrowed. Or Lance could be telling the truth and that disgusting yellowy-green color meant something different now than it did when he was teenager.

"Yeah, I could tell that it was time for us to step in," Lance said. "We didn't want to wait for some traumatizing event to happen before we got them help."

"You always were a go-getter," John said.

"Uncle John, stop telling Lance what he was," Hazel chided, irritation tinging her voice.

Lance laughed. "Oh, I don't mind," he said. "Uncle John always was good at making a person feel good about themselves."

Hazel smirked, but John blushed. Lance always had been good at flattery. "Yeah, it's a good thing we got here when we did. We had to install a couple of different special locks on the front door. Someone has to be watching Dad at all times. He'll wander off or leave on appliances...It's hard to see him like this." His gaze softened and he appeared to be looking past them for a minute.

"Sorry," he said after a minute of silence. "Don't mind me, I'm not trying to complain."

Despite her confusion about Lance's motives searching for Nina, the thought of his parents needing so much help made Hazel deeply sad. John and Grandmama did a great job raising her, but the Fullers were the ones who helped her apply to college and tutored her in calculus. They were a part of her. She was ashamed of herself for letting their relationship go when Lance left town.

"I should bring a meal by," she blurted out. "Your poor sweet mom. I just loved her in high school."

"No, you don't have to do that," Lance said. "I mean, well, I guess you can if you want, but all this stuff going on with Nina is more urgent."

John seemed to finally have gotten over the excitement of seeing Lance enough to be a policeman. "Do you know Nina, son?" he asked.

"Oh, uh, no," he said, the yellow green appearing across his skin. "I mean, I've heard of her. I think she was around Dansby's age at school."

Hazel nodded. Dansby's arrival had come as a bit of a

surprise to his parents. Lance had been fifteen when he was born. Hazel remembered what an adorable little toddler he had been. It was hard to imagine him all grown up.

"I've really got to get back," Lance said, taking steps towards his car.

"Give your parents my love," Hazel called.

"I will," he said. "I'll see you around."

He was barely out of earshot when Hazel turned to John. "No one's come by for a while. I think it's time for me to get back out in the woods."

"Actually, I have a different job for you now," John said.

Hazel slumped. "You've got to be kidding me."

"This is an important one. I need you to do some snooping."

Hazel perked back up. Snooping was a passion of hers. "You don't want to send a uniform?"

John shook his head. "This needs a more tender touch. I thought you could talk your way into the Mitchells' house and see if you can find anything about Nina's plans that she might not have told her husband. I bet Mike's still asleep, so you shouldn't have to deal with him. He told me his mom has been watching the kids. Although, I gotta tell you, that woman is nuts."

"I thought you already were there—the make-up bag and stuff."

"I just did a brief look around. I think having a cop around was scaring the kids."

Hazel nodded. "I'm on it."

John smiled at her. "I knew you would be." He reached out and patted her forearm. "You're a good person, Hazel. Your daddy would be so proud of you."

Hazel shook her head, brushing off the compliment. Good people didn't hand out books to troubled young mothers without regard for the consequences.

"I'm going to get back to the search," he said when she didn't respond. "Let me know what you find."

* * *

Hazel happened to know that dinner will get you into people's homes faster than anything else. Especially delicious, comforting, homemade dinners and indulgent desserts.

That's why she didn't drive straight over to the Mitchells' house and knock on the door. Instead, she went home and started cooking. She decided to make a lasagna and leave it uncooked so the Mitchell's could use it whenever they needed to. Her mind wandered to Lance's parents. She knew that Jason wouldn't love it, but she couldn't ignore them now. She decided to make a lasagna for the Fullers as well. It wasn't Lance she would be visiting; it would be his parents. And if she was able to decipher what he had been lying about, well, that was just a bonus.

Hazel began to dice an onion to make the base of the sauce, and the mindlessness of the action couldn't keep her thoughts at bay. Without some kind of problem to occupy her mind, she couldn't keep pretending that Nina was alive. Hazel was convinced that Nina had committed suicide, inspired by a book that Hazel had urged her to read. She had been convinced of it since the moment John told her Nina was missing. Hazel knew that she shouldn't have handed that book to the fragile girl, but she had ignored her better instincts and done what the colors told her to do. She always did what the colors told her to do. It was a mistake she wouldn't make again.

Hazel's eyes began to sting from the onions, but the tears that began to flow were real and unlocked emotions she had been working hard to keep in check. Grief, remorse and shame hit her one after the other and then again. She felt dizzy from the onslaught.

She dropped the knife onto the cutting board and turned around to lean on the kitchen counter. The tears turned ugly, and she slid to the ground. Hazel allowed herself to fall down a black hole of dark thoughts. She didn't want to get up. She didn't want to continue cooking. It all felt so hard and futile.

Then a thought that didn't feel like her own pierced the blackness. *It's not too late.* Hazel gasped out of her sobs and found herself again.

Grandmama had sometimes received what she called words from the angels. Could that be what Hazel was experiencing now? Hazel had always hoped that she might as a child. She fantasized about her mom helping her from heaven occasionally. It had never happened before, but Hazel wasn't going to be skeptical enough to dismiss the possibility now.

Besides, she didn't really know anything about Nina's fate. She could just as easily be alive as dead. What right did she have to be on the floor crying? If there was any kind of chance Nina was still alive then she needed help. Hazel cursed herself for giving into a self-indulgent moment of negativity.

She grabbed the countertop and pulled herself back up to standing. She sniffled while she finished chopping the onions and concentrated on the satisfying sizzle they made when they hit the hot pan.

Then she called Nora. Nora would be able to distract her from the hopelessness she was grappling with as well as provide her with more information about Nina's life.

"Hazel, did they find anything yet?" Nora answered breathlessly on the first ring.

"We're still looking, but I..." she paused, taking a package of ground beef out of the fridge. "Nora, you can't tell anybody about anything that we talk about."

"Yes, of course," Nora said.

"Seriously Nora, no idle chit chat. Not even your husband," Hazel said.

There was a pause while Nora considered this. "I can do that," Nora said. "I can do it, if it will help Nina."

"Thank you," Hazel said. Nora's honest self-evaluation sent a surge of affection through Hazel. "I need some information."

"Anything."

"Good. Now, exactly how close are you and Nina?" Hazel began. She added the meat to the pan of caramelized onions and began to break it up with a wooden spoon.

"We're—" Nora began, then sighed. Hazel could tell she had been tempted to exaggerate and then thought better of it. "Well, we used to be really close. In high school, it was she and I and this other girl named Jessica. We were inseparable. Nina's parents went through this messy divorce when we were juniors. Like her mom threw her dad's stuff out of the windows. They got into screaming matches in the middle of their street, the whole nine yards, like in the movies. She practically lived at my house then, and I think when she wasn't with me, she was with Jessica. At the end of that summer, after her dad had moved out of town, she got over it a little bit and stayed at her own house more. She never forgave her mom for it though. She wasn't her normal self after that, just kind of sad all the time. We did the best we could for her, Jessica and I and our parents even, but there's no way to fix that kind of thing in someone else's life is there? But at the end of our senior year, she started dating Dansby."

Hazel's throat constricted. She almost dropped the phone. The savory smell of cooking meat steamed around her, tethering her to the moment. "Dansby Fuller?" she croaked.

"Yes," Nora said, surprise tinging her voice. "How do you know him? He moved away ages ago."

"Never mind," Hazel managed to choke out. "Keep going."

"Nina was really intense about Dansby. He was a little reckless, kind of a bad boy if you know what I mean. He had this motorcycle and these intense eyes that were a little too close together. When he looked at you, he could make you feel like you were the only person in the world that had the power to save him from...whatever was eating at him. Although, honestly, he had great parents and a perfectly nice life, so I don't know what he was so tortured about. He dated around a lot, but then, our senior year, he settled on Nina. She seemed to be, well, almost starstruck by him. Like she couldn't believe that he would be interested in her of all people. You know?"

Hazel hummed the verbal equivalent of a nod. She added some garlic to the pan and continued to stir, glad she had something to do with her hands.

"She kind of pulled away from us at that point. She was too busy to hang out like she normally did. She spent all her time with Dansby. We hung out with them sometimes, but honestly, they were kind of lame to hang out with. Too much PDA, you know? They didn't seem to notice if anyone else was around, so we stopped going with them."

Hazel added crushed tomatoes and a couple jars of marinara sauce to her meat mixture and turned the heat to low. Nora's story reminded her of her high school friend Jolene. Was it when Hazel started dating Lance that their friendship had first began to cool? Hazel could have sworn it was earlier than that.

"Also..." Nora hesitated. "Dansby wasn't really, like, nice."

"What do you mean?" Hazel asked.

"He was always getting into fights. He was very confrontational. Any little thing would set him off, and he would get all up in your face. He threw punches on the regular. I know he spent the night in jail multiple times. He was irritable with Nina sometimes, but I don't *think* he ever hit her. He was just moody, you know? He would get all sullen and quiet, and then suddenly he'd say 'C'mon Nina, let's get out of here' and glare at us. Then Nina would offer us this apologetic look and take off after him."

"I see," Hazel said.

"In July, after we all graduated, Nina called me sobbing. She said her mom was moving away, all the way out to Philadelphia. Nina was beside herself. She didn't want to leave Red Gap. I was a little confused because I knew she had been accepted at Clemson, which had always been her dream. When I mentioned that she said no, she wasn't going to Clemson because she couldn't leave Dansby."

"Oh, no," Hazel murmured.

"I know," Nora went on. "I didn't know what to say. It was so out of character. I didn't mean to be judgmental, but I was surprised. I said the wrong thing like—*are you sure?* or *why?* And she blew up. She said that she was staying in Red Gap, and that there was nothing that I or her mom could do about it and she hung up on me."

"Oh, Nora, I'm so sorry," Hazel said.

Nora sighed. "I was young. I probably was being judgmental. After that, I didn't see her anymore until I was about to go off to Kennesaw myself. I went into the Chick-Fil-A, and she was working there. She turned so red when she saw me. But she told me that she and Dansby were getting married, that they had found somewhere to move in together."

Hazel shook her head. It was a familiar story, but no less sad because of its banality.

"I didn't see her the next summer," Nora explained. "I lost track of her for a few years. I was a senior when an invitation to her wedding showed up at my parents' house. She was getting married to Mike. Jessica and I went together. Nina looked so different. I don't know how to describe her— transparent, I guess. Mike is so different from Dansby. Very corporate. Well, I mean, you know, you work with him."

"I do," Hazel said. She gathered a bowl and the ingredients for the lasagna's white sauce. "No explanation necessary."

"They didn't want kids initially and then they couldn't have kids when they did want them," Nora's voice had grown uncertain. "I don't remember all the details. I was still single at the time. It wasn't until I got married that I started spending time with Nina again. We doubled a couple times, but Mike is a little difficult to be friends with. So Nina and I would just go for coffee or something. We were really close for a little while when she was pregnant the first time. I was thinking about having kids, and I was so excited for her. But then she fell flat again after the baby was born. It was all I could do to pull her out of the house to get her to come to book club. She didn't talk about anything anymore."

Nora made a frustrated noise in the back of her throat. "I wish I had pushed her more. I wish I had tried harder."

"Nora, don't blame yourself. It's not your responsibility to take care of her."

Nora snorted. "Said the pot to the kettle," she said.

Hazel ignored that comment. She began to assemble the lasagna layers in two disposable foil casserole pans. "You don't happen to have her mom's phone number, do you? Mike said they were close, talked a lot."

"Huh, that's interesting. News to me. I didn't know she had ever repaired her relationship with her mom after she moved to Pennsylvania. I mean, she was at their wedding and everything, but I didn't think they were close. I think I'm friends with her on Facebook. I could message her."

"Would you please?" Hazel asked. "I know it will be kind of weird. It doesn't sound like Mike has told her that Nina's missing. Someone should tell her in person though; we don't want to spring that on her over a Facebook message. I just need her phone number."

"Can't Captain Tate get that information and do that kind of thing?" Nora asked.

"Yes, but he's a little distracted with the search. He thought it should be Mike's responsibility."

"Oh, dear," Nora said. "What a mess."

"I'm on my way over there," Hazel said. "I'm bringing them dinner, and I'm going to look around and see if I can find anything out. Maybe hack into Nina's computer or something? Just looking for any kind of clues."

"That's good, you can check on her kids while you're there. Mike's mom is...well, she's something else." Nora's voice became pinched.

"What do you mean?" Hazel pounced.

Nora sighed. "It's nothing in particular...she just...I don't know her all that well," Nora finally said. "I shouldn't have said anything."

"But..." Hazel prompted.

"But she doesn't strike me as being a kid-centric grandma, I guess. She's a little, gosh, I don't know how to put it. Formal? Perfect? Image-focused?"

"Ah," Hazel said. "I think I know what you mean. I'll get a feel for how she's doing."

"Please tell them that I'm here if they need any help. I can take the kids if they need. I've watched them before. I think her oldest daughter will remember me, Naomi."

"I will," Hazel promised. "Thanks, Nora, you've been a big help."

"Anything for Nina," Nora said, her voice breaking a bit. "They'll find her. Won't they, Hazel?"

"Of course, they will," Hazel said, pulling out a length of aluminum foil and tearing it off. "I'll make sure of it."

SIX

The weather had turned bright. The air had that shiny clean feeling that it only has in the spring, like the cold of winter had killed off all the pests and griminess in the air and the rain rinsed it away. Now the sun had come out to warm the earth, sending the wonderful heady aroma of dirt into the air. Hazel loved this time of year. It was a day when she normally would have made Jason take a long walk with her, and she would have pointed out all the plants that she wanted to add to her garden but never would.

This afternoon though, Hazel ignored the weather and pushed down feelings of misgiving that plagued her as she drove to the Mitchells' home. Before the previous October, Hazel had assumed that no one could possibly be mad at her for bringing them a hot meal. But then she had taken a meal to a family of brothers who had suffered a loss and had an unpleasant encounter with the eldest of them. Shortly after, the man had ended up in jail. Hazel didn't think that Mike or his mom were on that path, but the feeling of unease persisted.

She took the uncooked lasagna from the back of the car and the larger plate of chocolate chip cookies. Holding them in front of her like a shield, she strode up the front walk and pressed the doorbell with a free knuckle.

She heard chaos inside, children making all kinds of child-like noises. It sounded like there was some kind of dinosaur versus alien battle going on, along with piano practice and the television. Hazel was busy listening to the happy noises and was startled when the door swung wide open.

"Hi!" said a toddler standing in the doorway by himself.

"Hi," Hazel smiled, knowing exactly what to say to this small person. "I brought you cookies!"

The child's face rearranged into an expression of absolute delight. "I wuv you!" he exclaimed, radiating a bright, sunny yellow.

An older kid appeared in the hallway behind the toddler. "I'm sorry," she said, blushing. "Jack isn't supposed to answer the door by himself. He just learned how to unlock it, and he gets a little excited."

"Cookies!" Jack cried.

"I brought you some cookies and lasagna," Hazel explained. She swallowed. "I'm uh, a friend of your mom's."

"Oh, thank you, ma'am," the girl said. She had the most elegant ballerina pink countenance. Hazel was instantly enchanted with her. "But mom's not here right now. She went on a hiking trip, and she's not back yet. Daddy said she just needed a break, but she'll be back soon."

Hazel's heart constricted. Mike didn't tell them Nina was missing.

"Mimi's here though. I'm sure she'll appreciate it." The girl leaned in and lowered her voice. "She's lying down right now. She needed a break. She told us that we are *busy*. But it didn't sound like a compliment."

Hazel pressed her lips together to keep from laughing or crying; she didn't know which. The girl didn't look older than eight. She was quite precocious, and those big brown eyes pierced Hazel's sensibilities. Hazel wondered if she might be more grown up than other girls her age, because Nina wasn't well. Hazel hoped with all her heart for a happy ending for this sweet girl. In that moment, Hazel's own mother's absence stabbed at her painfully.

"What's your name?" Hazel asked.

"Naomi," the little girl said, putting out her hand. "And you are?"

"Oh my, what beautiful manners you have. I can't quite shake your hand, Naomi, because mine are full, but I'm Hazel Dean."

"Oh, Hazel Dean!" the girl's eyes sparkled with the excitement of recognition. "I've heard of you."

"You have?" Hazel was surprised.

"Yes, my mommy and daddy were talking about you. Daddy said you are a know-it-all witch, and mommy said it's not your fault if you do know it all and that you're a sweetheart."

Hazel couldn't suppress a laugh that time. "I know your mom from my bookshop. She came to book club there. I brought you some books as well that I thought you might enjoy."

"Oh, I love to read!" Naomi said, her color changing to a dusky violet. She led the way through the house towards the kitchen. "I love it when the people and characters in them feel so real. Like they're your friends."

Hazel beamed at her. "Me too," she said. "I brought several because I didn't know about your reading levels. Have you read *The Happy Lion* or *The Oxcart Man* with your siblings before? They're some of my favorites."

Naomi shook her head. Hazel set the box holding the lasagna, cookies, and books down on the counter.

"They're a little older, but just as good as the newer books. I think you'll like them. If you're a very good reader, I brought one called *Half-Magic*. I still remember reading it when I was about your age."

Naomi could barely wait until Hazel set down the box before she dug underneath the cookies for the books.

"Thank you so much, Miss Hazel!" she squealed, hopping from one foot to the other. "I'll get my grandma," Naomi said.

"Thank you." Hazel waited until a tiny woman who didn't look old enough to be Naomi's grandmother came to the door. Everything about her was immaculate from her perfect highlights to her tailored jeans. Hazel instantly recognized her from city council meetings. Karen was a regular.

"Karen?"

"Hazel Randolph! What an honor!" Karen greeted her enthusiastically, which Hazel thought was interesting considering how confrontational their last interaction was.

"I apologize for not answering the door. I was just resting my eyes for a minute. I'm not used to having four kids around all the time!"

"I'm sorry, I'm just—" Hazel was so confused, she looked behind her as though the answers would be there. "I didn't realize that you were Mike's mom."

Karen laughed. "You didn't?"

"I had no idea."

"Yep, he's my baby," she said, glowing with pride. "My one and only."

Karen loved to bother the city council. At every meeting, she had some nitpicky criticism or melodramatic harbinger of doom she demanded they do something about. Hazel couldn't decide if knowing that she was Mike's mom made everything fall into place or made her behavior towards him even more objectionable.

At the last meeting, Karen had ranted at length about the landscaping along the highway as it ran in and out of town. She felt that just mowing the weedy lawn was not a good enough solution for Red Gap, that they should have something more sophisticated. She didn't seem to have any understanding of budget constraints, and they could not get her to leave.

Now that Hazel thought about it, Mike usually took Karen's side pretty quickly during the meetings. Hazel thought that he was just a politician, attempting to win votes. Now that she knew Karen was his mom, she considered maybe there was something deeper at work.

"I just wanted to bring by a meal," Hazel said. "You know, to help out and everything."

"That's very neighborly of you. You're so well-bred. I didn't know that you and Mike were friendly."

Hazel could feel herself blush. She sometimes wondered what she would look like if she could see her own colors. "No, but Nina is a friend."

"Oh," Karen said, the mint green surrounding her flashed a bit red. "That's nice."

Hazel's eyebrows furrowed for a moment trying to figure out what red meant. Did Karen dislike her daughter-in-law?

"Come and sit down," Karen said, motioning to a couch in the adjoining room. "We can have a bit of a chat. I'm dying for some adult conversation. Being responsible for all these kids is starting to get to me."

Hazel followed Karen to the couch, feeling a little awkward. "Is Mike in?"

"No, he's out—" Karen looked around to see if there were any kids around before finishing the sentence in a lower tone. "Searching for Nina." Hazel noticed a stronger flash of red that time.

"Is he?" Hazel asked. "When I saw him this morning, he was headed back here to sleep."

Karen sighed. "He was here for a little while, tried to lie down. But he couldn't fall asleep and was so distraught that he went back out again. He'll ruin his health like this. But there's no talking to him. He always was a fool for that girl."

"Was he?" Hazel masked her surprise.

"Oh yes, I don't know what he saw in her. It's really the only time we've ever disagreed on anything. Met her at a Chick-Fil-A when he was visiting me here from Atlanta. She was working there. She's pretty enough if you like that whole waif look. But I guess it was very in style back then. Mike was taken with her right away. Love at first sight and all that. But I could tell," she lowered her voice to a whisper. "There was just something off about her. She was...I don't know, flat."

Hazel nodded. The more she learned about Nina, the more she understood that that was a good word to describe Nina, like she was a cardboard cutout of herself instead of a real woman full of emotions and life. "Did you notice things get worse after her pregnancies?" Hazel asked.

Karen thought for a moment. "I suppose. It got really bad during Mike's campaign."

"Really? Was Nina not supportive of Mike's candidacy?"

Karen shook her head. "Not at all. She was terrified of attention. Couldn't get her to go to any parties or meet and greets. She wouldn't even campaign door to door. It was like he was running as a bachelor. I'm surprised he won, honestly. If it wasn't for the support I was able to conjure up for him at the club, I don't think it would have worked out the way it did."

Hazel kept her opinions about that to herself. Karen seemed anxious to answer Hazel's questions. Everything about her tone and posture was familiar to Hazel. She had run into people throughout her life anxious to be friendly with her because of who her family was. They were interested in being close to the power and prestige of the Randolph name. They wanted to see the inside of the old house where Hazel lived or they wanted to meet Hazel's grandmama or they imagined glittering, art deco cocktail parties they would be invited to.

With the exception of the Christmas party Grandmama threw each year, there were no lavish parties or hobnobbing with celebrities. Hazel's actual life had always been a lot less glamorous than people thought. Their wealth and political influence had evaporated during the Great Depression, when Grandmama was a child.

"If you don't mind my asking, what about Mike's dad?"

Karen's mint color shifted to more of a blue. "Oh," she said. "He passed away. A long time back now. He was a Mike too."

"I'm sorry to hear that," Hazel said.

Karen waved a hand. "I don't think about him too much anymore. To tell you the truth, we weren't exactly getting along when he passed away. I was thinking about filing for divorce."

Hazel wasn't sure what to say about that. But she kept asking questions, leveraging this woman's obvious respect for her Randolph-ness as much as she could. "How old was Mike at the time?"

Karen said, "He was in college. He must have been... nineteen? Maybe he was twenty."

"And when did he meet Nina?" Hazel asked. She must have spoken a little too quickly because Karen raised one perfectly shaped eyebrow.

"I moved here after my husband passed," she explained. "He met her that summer when he came home from school to visit."

Hazel nodded, trying not to sound too eager this time. "And where did he go to school?" she asked after a pause.

"Didn't you know?" Karen asked. "He went to Vanderbilt." She paused dramatically; the silver sparks woven back into her mint green.

Hazel recognized that Karen wanted her to act impressed. "Oh, wow," she said. "That's a great school."

Karen nodded happily. "It is. I was surprised when he wanted to move here. I thought he would settle in Nashville or

Atlanta. Maybe Charleston. But I don't think Nina would ever live anywhere besides here. Maybe now that she's..." Karen's mouth snapped shut. Her mint green turned slate. "I didn't mean... of course we're hoping that Nina is back safe and sound as soon as possible."

"Of course," Hazel choked. "Yes, that's what we're all working towards."

Karen nodded so hard a lock of her hair slipped loose from the neat chignon it was woven into. "Yes, yes," she said.

"To that end..." Hazel said. "I was wondering if maybe I could help out with some housework? Maybe clean Nina and Mike's room up a bit? You know, so it's nice when she gets home?"

Karen regained her mint color,. "A Randolph wants to clean my son's house," she murmured. "Who would have ever..." she trailed off, seeming to forget that she was still having a conversation with Hazel. A purply violet glowed from the edges of her mint green. Then she shook her head a little and nodded at Hazel. "That's so kind of you," she said. "I haven't been able to do much myself, busy with the kids and all."

"Four kids will keep you busy!" Hazel agreed. "You should have a rest while I pick up a bit." She stood up and looked around.

"Down the hall," Karen said. "Last door on your left."

"Thank you," Hazel said. She started down the hall, dodging toys and clothes that were strewn everywhere. She couldn't believe that Karen had bought her snooping excuse.

She opened the door to Nina's room. It was dark and quiet inside. An unmade bed dominated the room. There were bedside tables and a dresser but little else aside from a gigantic mound of laundry in the middle of the room. Hazel closed the door behind her and quickly made the bed. "Come on, Nina," she murmured, willing her to have left some clue.

She made her way across the room and opened a door on

the far side. It was a small walk-in closet. Hazel tried not to look at Mike's side while she looked through Nina's stuff. There wasn't a lot. Fewer than ten pairs of shoes, several pairs of jeans and a half a dozen hooded sweatshirts in neutral colors. It looked a lot like Elias' closet.

Was this normal for Nina, or had she taken half her wardrobe with her? Hazel didn't know. She found a couple of purses, but none of them had anything of interest inside. Just a smattering of pens, lip balm, old receipts, loose mints, and hair bands.

Hazel abandoned the closet and opened the other door. It was a disaster of a master bathroom. Yellowing soap scum clung to the sinks, and rings of mold surrounded the bottom of the fixtures and around the drains. The floor was scattered with hair and thick dust bunnies. Hazel didn't draw back the shower curtain but noticed that a patch of mold on the ceiling above it. She cringed and made a note that she would come back with Nora at some point to give it a proper cleaning, some time when Mike wasn't there again. Nina should come home to a nice, clean bathroom. She looked under the sink and found a nondescript spray cleaner. She sprayed everything down and then stuck her hand around the shower curtain and blindly sprayed the shower as well. She put the cleaner back under the sink.

Taking in Nina's portion of the bathroom, she could see that John was right. It looked as though Nina had walked away one morning without touching anything. Her toothbrush was resting on the edge of the sink as though Nina would pick it back up again momentarily.

Hazel looked through the drawers quickly and again found nothing that jumped out at her. Then again, she wasn't exactly sure what she was looking for. She brought Mike's words up in her mind. He thought she was having an affair in recent weeks. She was giddy and distracted. Hazel looked through the drawers again, this time looking for anything that might indicate that she had a sudden renewal of interest in her appearance.

The self-tanning kit and a set of near-new makeup took on a new meaning through this lens.

Hazel left the bathroom and opened a drawer of the bedside table. Inside was a couple of books: *Think and Grow Rich*, *The Instant Millionaire*, and *The Millionaire Next Door*. Hazel pushed the drawer shut and walked to the other side of the bed. She opened the drawer and squealed. Lying on top of a pile of candy wrappers and an ancient stuffed bear was a tablet.

Hazel snatched it and, forgetting Mike's ownership for a second, sat down on the bed and pulled the cover away from the screen. She pressed the on button and was faced with the prompt to enter a passcode. She entered 000000 and 123456 without success.

She got out her phone and called Nora again. She picked up the phone on the first ring.

"Did they find her?" Nora asked without waiting for a greeting.

"No, sweetie," Hazel said, almost whispering, and casting furtive glances at the closed door. "I'm sorry. I was just wondering; do you happen to know her kids birth dates?"

"Oh!" Nora sounded thrilled that she might be able to help. "Um... I should have it somewhere. I know the months at least. I can go back and look in my journal and see."

"You have Nina's kids birth dates in your journal?" Hazel laughed.

"Yes, of course, what's worth recording more than your childhood friend having a baby?"

Hazel smiled. "Nothing, I guess. Am I in your journal?"

"Just when you solved that mystery about who killed Cash McCleary."

Hazel felt like the wind had been knocked out of her at the

mention of Cash. She still felt vaguely responsible for his death. She took a deep breath. "If you get on Facebook, can you look up Nina's mom's birthday too?"

"Yes, of course," Nora said.

"Thanks, I'm trying to figure out her tablet pass code."

"Hmmm, you could try her birthdate - 101695"

Hazel tapped it in. "Nope," she said.

Nora burst out laughing.

"What? What's funny?" Hazel asked.

"You could try Dansby's license plate number from high school. Before they got together, she memorized it and recited it all the time. Got stuck in my head. Jessica probably remembers it too. It was Nina's password for everything for a while."

"What is it?" Hazel asked.

"PNY6552."

"I think I need six digits," Hazel looked at Nina's tablet.

"The numbers should have letters underneath them too."

"Oh yes, of course," Hazel said. Jason had accused her of needing glasses twice the week before. Hazel sighed, maybe it was time for an eye exam.

She typed in the numerical equivalent of PNY: 769, then 655. The hairs along her arms stood on end when the pass code screen flew upward and let her into Nina's tablet. "It worked!" she exclaimed, a bit shocked.

Nora laughed. "That's so funny. I wonder how many people in the world are using the same password they used in high school."

"That's terrifying, Nora," Hazel said. Hazel hadn't used any fancy technology when she was in high school. She felt like she had aged ten years in the last five minutes. "I'll call you later. I'm going to hack into Nina's Facebook."

"You mean open the app on her tablet where the password is saved?" Nora asked. "That hardly counts as hacking."

"It will when I tell Jeremiah about it later," Hazel told her.

"Ah, I see," Nora said. "Call me if there's any news."

"Of course, thank you!"

Hazel reminded herself that she was only going to look at Nina's social media to find clues about her disappearance. She wouldn't snoop into anything that didn't specifically have to do with the case, no matter how curious she was.

She opened Facebook, scrolling through Nina's feed. It was full of young moms posting about their perfect children, houses, food, workouts, or husbands. Not exactly a mental health spa. She spotted a couple of Nora's posts about beautiful clothes she had sewn for her kids or of her all dressed up and on her way on a date with her husband.

The only things that stood out on the feed were occasional stunning photos from hikers from groups like North Georgia Hikers or Appalachian Trail Hikers. Hazel didn't know how to find out how recently Nina started following those groups. Was it a recent impulse, or had she been gazing wistfully at these hikes for years without being able to go herself?

As far as clues to where she might be, Hazel scoured the recent posts from the hiking groups to see if they offered clues. None of the hikes featured were too close by. A few posts were urging others to dispose of their garbage properly with pictures of bad examples. There were also a couple links to bear poaching and a wild ginseng black market. Nothing jumped out at her as being particularly helpful for finding Nina.

Pulling out a small notebook and pen out of her purse, Hazel dutifully wrote down any specific hikes or lookouts that were posted from a week before Nina's disappearance up until the day she left. Maybe there was more there than she realized. She also jotted down the names of the hiking groups so she could look at the posts again later.

Hazel closed Facebook and switched to Messenger. Her mouth fell open, her eyes widened, and her breath caught in her throat when she saw the name of the most recent conversation: *Dansby Fuller*. The message was dated Saturday, after Nina had already left on her hike. *Where are you?* That's all Hazel could read without tapping on the conversation and reading the whole thing.

She hesitated. Was this a blatant disregard of Nina and Dansby's privacy? Most definitely. But was it necessary to find out where Nina was and what happened to her? If it was, then she shouldn't hesitate. But Dansby asking where Nina was indicated that he didn't know. The conversation wouldn't have any clues to her current whereabouts—although it did suggest that something was going on between them. But if Dansby didn't know where she was, then Mike's suspicions about her running off were wrong.

Hazel had gotten into a bit of trouble when she had made assumptions about people and then gone digging into their affairs last fall. She had ended up in handcuffs. She didn't really want a repeat of the experience.

Hazel sighed and closed the app. She had another avenue available to her. She could go over and ask Dansby about his relationship with Nina. She wanted to check on Lance's parents anyways and ask Lance what possessed him to talk about her gift out in the open the way he did.

She began to wonder what Lance knew about the whole thing. His dishonesty took on a new dimension with this new information. Had he really been out searching for Nina, or was there another reason he was in the woods? A visit to the Fullers might answer a lot of questions.

Hazel looked through a few more apps on the tablet. A lot of them were mindless games and streaming services. She opened Nina's email and saw nothing but hundreds of unopened advertisements and communications from the school. No personal emails were visible. Hazel opened up the notes app, not expecting to find anything else but was instead surprised to see that it was full of one-line sentences.

Drowning, suffocation, claustrophobia
Like moving underwater in the dark
I don't want to. I just don't want to.
The sun reaches the faces of my kids, but not my own
My heart hurts
I am neither here or gone. I am ethereal, non-corporeal, like a
ghost haunting my family.
A hole opens in my throat, it is so empty but it is choking me
All the sounds are attacking me, making me cringe and want
to hide

Hazel's eyes filled with tears as she read through the list of depressing thoughts Nina recorded on her tablet. They were her innermost, private admissions, and Hazel felt bad reading them, but she also couldn't look away. She searched, scanning for any clue or whisper of a clue about where Nina might be.

The tone of the bottom few sentences changed.

A life raft thrown into a stormy sea
The knot of desperation in my chest tightens, then loosens finally.
Tunnel vision, tunnel hearing, waiting and watching for... what?
Blinking, my vision clears. Shutter clicks of light and dark are
disorienting at first
Who am I? How did I get here?
I noticed a bird outside my window, he chirped, a harbinger of
second chances and new beginnings.

Hazel couldn't help but notice how beautiful some of the lines were. Nina had the makings of a writer. If Hazel ever saw her again... Her train of thought stopped abruptly, her eyes snagging on the last sentence.

I must go home, to the woods, to find myself again.

"Hazel?" Karen's voice calling from down the hall made Hazel jump.

She snapped a picture of the notes with her phone and then closed it and put it back in its drawer.

By the time Karen opened the door, Hazel had piled all the laundry into a basket.

"Oh my," Karen said. "It looks better in here already."

Hazel gave a short laugh; her heart was racing. "Let me just start this load of laundry and then I have to go," she said. "I'd like to come back and do more another time."

"I can start the laundry," Karen said. "You've done so much already."

Hazel shifted her weight. "It was nothing, really," she said. She followed Karen down the hall to the laundry room. She loaded and started the washing machine over Karen's protests. Then she made her way back to the front door with Karen on her heels.

"Thanks so much," Karen smiled, pausing in the foyer.

"Of course," Hazel said. "I'm glad I could help." Hazel blushed.

"Do you mind if I get a selfie with you?"," Karen asked.

"Oh," Hazel said, caught off guard. "Um, sure, I guess."

Karen grinned, wrapping an arm around Hazel's neck and pulling her down so their faces were the same height. Hazel attempted a smile and blinked at the unnecessary flash. .

"Thanks," Karen said, releasing Hazel and taking a step away to admire the picture.

At that moment, a child around five years old flew around the corner at full speed with a jar full of what looked like watered down paint. The kid collided with Karen, causing the colorful liquid to explode upwards and land all over her.

Hazel watched in horror as Karen's pleasant mint color turned instantaneously to crimson red. "How dare you, you little pill!" she screamed at the kid. "You thoughtless monster!"

The child's eyes filled up with tears, his face contorted with grief. "I'm sorry, Mimi," he choked.

Hazel watched Karen, assuming that, presented with this display of penitence, she would melt, pull the child into her arms, and apologize for losing her temper. But the crimson stayed intact and all she did was snap. "Sorry isn't going to dry clean this blouse for me!" She raised a hand and started to bring it down towards the boy.

Hazel jumped towards him and pulled him into a hug, putting her body between Karen and the boy. "It's alright, love," she crooned. "It was just an accident. What did you have in the jar?" Hazel didn't dare look up at Karen.

The little boy gasped in between sobs, getting out a choked explanation. "Water from my paintbrush. I was doing watercolor."

Hazel smiled at him. "Oh, well then, no need to be upset. Watercolor comes right out." She was directing her words more at Karen than the kid but continued to look down at him. It was awkward to witness such uncensored family interaction, but Hazel was even more worried about leaving when Karen was in such a temper.

Without releasing the boy, Hazel peeked up at Karen. She wasn't standing over them anymore. She wasn't anywhere to be seen. Hazel turned back to the little boy.

"My name's Hazel Dean; what's your name?"

"Trevor," he said, wiping a sleeve across his nose.

"How old are you, Trevor?"

"Five," he sniffled.

"Five? Wow, you're practically all grown up. I bet you could help me clean up this paint water, no problem. Can you?"

The little boy nodded his head vigorously. Hazel tiptoed into the kitchen to find some paper towels. Trevor wouldn't let go of her hand. Karen wasn't in the kitchen. They retrieved the roll, and together they cleaned up the water that was left on the floor in the front entryway. Hazel's mind raced. She knew the look on Karen's face when she lost her temper would haunt her.

"Trevor?" she said softly. "Does Mimi lose her temper a lot?"

Trevor looked at her out of the corners of his eyes without

turning his head towards her. He didn't answer, not even by nodding or shaking his head. The hairs on Hazel's arm stood on end. She looked the boy over for any bruises. Nothing jumped out at her.

"I'm sorry," Karen's voice floated above her. The sharp note in her voice had softened, but Trevor ran in the opposite direction.

Hazel looked up at Karen. Her color had turned pink instead of the deep crimson, but it wasn't back to that pleasant mint green. She had excused herself to calm down. Isn't that what you were supposed to do with kids? "Oh, you don't have to do that," Karen said.

"It's no trouble," Hazel said, throwing the paper towels into the garbage. "Trevor helped me."

Karen gave a tight smile. "I'm sorry I lost my temper," she said. "It's just been such a trying few days, and the kids are quite a lot to handle. Mike always wanted brothers or sisters; I think having a big family was his way to make up for his being an only child. But they are a lot of work when there's so many of them."

Hazel softened a bit. She didn't want to judge this woman based on her worst possible moment. She had been dealing with a lot. But what kind of person so nakedly loses their temper at a child in front of a stranger? Hazel shifted her weight. Staying any longer would be awkward but how could she leave?

"Hello?" Mike walked into the hallway from the kitchen, stopping abruptly when he saw Hazel.

"Hazel Dean," he said, coloring brown. Hazel couldn't tell if he was embarrassed or irritated. "How nice."

Hazel had never been so glad to see him before. "Hi, Mike," she said. "I just came by to drop off dinner. I was just leaving."

Mike nodded. He glanced at his mom, who was widening

her eyes and tilting her head in Hazel's direction. "Oh, uh, thanks for dinner," he said, still looking at his mother.

"Of course," Hazel said. "Feel free to call if there's anything else Jason and I can do for you."

Mike nodded. When she stepped out the front door, he surprised her by stepping out of the house and closing the door behind him. "Hazel, what should I do about the kids?" he asked, the orange around him dissolving into a storm gray. "What do I tell them?"

Hazel blinked. The aggressive, snapping man she had encountered that morning was gone. He had been replaced by someone scared and vulnerable. "I don't know, Mike," Hazel said. "They haven't found her yet, so we don't know what's going to happen. If she's okay and will be home soon, or if..."

Hazel trailed off as the gray around him darkened.

"I don't know what to say. I wish that she...well. I just wish things were different." He stared at his toes.

"Whatever you do," Hazel said. "I think you should get someone else in here to watch the kids for a while. Your mom needs a break."

Mike flinched. "Oh, no," he said. "What did she do?"

"She almost took a swipe at little Trevor for spilling some watercolors. I think her patience is running thin."

Mike nodded, his eyes glazed over, and his brow furrowed. "My mom can be difficult," he murmured, staring at nothing. "When I was young...well, you don't want to hear any of that..." he trailed off, lost in some kind of memory that turned his color to a sickly yellow.

"You need some sleep," Hazel said. "Call Nora Franks. Do you have her number?"

"Nina's old friend? No, I don't."

Hazel dug out her phone and shared Nora's contact with Mike. "Let me make sure that you got it," she said.

Mike still stared blankly just past Hazel while he dug his

phone out of his pocket. He blinked rapidly and shook his head a little bit when he unlocked it and accepted the contact. "Call her right now," Hazel said. "She's been dying to help. She has kids too; your kids will have a blast. Just make sure to tell her that you haven't told the kids anything about Nina yet."

"Alright," Mike said.

"Do it right now," Hazel said. "While I'm standing here. I can't leave until I know that your kids are going to be okay and that you and your mom are going to get some rest."

Mike looked at her again, something deeper registering behind his eyes. "Thank you, Hazel." He punched the call button and Hazel could hear Nora's voice on the other end when she picked up. When Mike asked her about taking the kids for a while, the sound of her enthusiastic response could be heard from where Hazel was standing.

"Alright," Mike said. "I'll be right over then. Could you text me your address?"

Hazel started to back down the walk. Mike hung up with Nora and called down the driveway. "Thank you, Hazel. I'm taking the kids right over."

"I'm glad to hear it," Hazel said. "I'll be in touch."

As she got into her car, she glanced across the street and was surprised to see the reporter, Ermengarde McGee parked on the road in a tiny gray Ford Focus. She caught Hazel's eye and turned beet red before quickly driving off down the street.

Hazel sighed, putting the car in gear, and headed in the direction of the Fullers' house.

SEVEN

Hazel had been to the Fullers' house thousands of times. She didn't need to look up the address or ask Siri how to get there. She thought of Lance and her brain took her there on autopilot. When she turned down his street, she recognized each lot and could recall who lived there years ago. The trees she remembered were taller or had disappeared. Old Mrs. Anderson's immaculate flower beds had become overgrown and neglected. The Hardmans' house, always a jungle of vines and hedges, was now neat and tidy. Hazel was reminded of the adage: 'the more things change, the more they stay the same.'

Catching a glimpse of herself in the rear-view mirror, she was surprised at her flat hairstyle. She half expected her bangs to brush the ceiling of the car like it used to when she was a teenager. She remembered the desperate longing that accompanied first love. Now she was able to smile at it like an adorable puppy that she didn't have to take care of because it didn't belong to her. She found herself humming a George Strait song under her breath.

Hazel gasped when she spotted the Fullers' home. It looked exactly the same.

The Crimson Fire bushes and boxwood were trimmed to the exact same dimensions they had always been. Lance had complained every Saturday about his weekly chore of trimming them in the summer. Hazel could feel the fuzzy Lamb's Ear that lined the front walk against her face just from catching a glimpse of it. She used to pick a leaf every time she passed and rub it against her cheek.

Her car bounced into the driveway, and Hazel turned it off, sitting for a few minutes lost in memories. She sighed and opened the car door to get out. As she slammed the door of her SUV shut, she couldn't help but remember the ancient Honda Civic that she drove in high school. She went around to the trunk to grab the lasagna out of the cooler. She paused in the driveway and then realized it was because usually Lance would rush out the door to meet her.

Hazel couldn't shake the feeling of being in a weird time warp. She shifted her weight, still staring at the Fullers' house. She reminded herself that she wasn't there to talk to Lance, but to question Dansby. She ran through what Nora had said about his relationship with Nina as she made her way up the front steps and knocked on the door. She waited. Then waited some more. There was no sound from behind the door.

Hazel wasn't in the habit of calling ahead of time when she dropped dinner off at someone's house. Usually if the person wasn't home, she left the food on the doorstep and texted them from the car. Sometimes when people needed a meal, they didn't really want to talk. In this case though, she realized that she had made a critical error. She really should have called first. But Lance had made it sound like his parents were basically homebound. Scheduling didn't seem like an issue.

She knocked again, louder this time and then rang the

doorbell. She thought she heard muffled voices inside and called out "Hello? Mr. and Mrs. Fuller?"

The door opened wide, and Hazel felt a wave of warm air pour out of the house.

"Why, if it isn't Miss Hazel Randolph," Mrs. Fuller exclaimed. "It's been a long time, sugar plum!"

Hazel's throat constricted. The long-buried feelings she had for Sherry Fuller came bubbling up in her heart, along with a profound grief at the changes in her. The cadence of her voice was the same, but her once-booming voice sounded more like a whisper. She was a shadow of her former self. Illness had left her frail, almost transparent, except for her sunken eyes. Her bright blue irises shined out from dark circles. She looked bruised. "Hi, Mrs. Fuller," Hazel managed to choke out.

"Well, don't stand out in the cold," she said, backing up with her walker in a reckless way that made Hazel nervous. "Come on in. I'm sure Mike would love to see you."

Hazel felt even more time warped when she stepped into the Fullers' rambler. Absolutely nothing had changed. The furniture was all the same and stood in the exact same places it had when Hazel was young. The chintz couch, the glass block wall between the kitchen and dining room, and the teal carpet made her wish that she still had her floral rompers with the gigantic lace trimmed collar.

"The house looks just the same, Mrs. Fuller!" she exclaimed.

Sherry smiled. "You and Lance always teased me about the plastic covers on the furniture, but it sure paid off!" she said.

Lance's senior picture still hung in its place of honor, but now another senior picture stood next to it. Presumably, it was Dansby. Though she had her hands full, Hazel stopped to look at the photo. Dansby was slighter than Lance, less athletic. When the picture was taken, his hair had been an unnaturally dark color and it was long and hanging in his eyes, which were dark and sullen. The smile he wore in the picture was forced, more of a grimace than a smile. If he had been friends with one of her boys, Hazel would have decided that he was insecure. She had a hard time reconciling the angsty teenage boy in the picture with the tow-headed chubby toddler she played with in high school. Just like she couldn't believe that the old woman next to her was Lance's mom. Hazel wondered if she had changed as obviously as they had.

"That's Dansby when he was a senior," Mrs. Fuller said. "I can't believe how long it's been. He grew up to be quite handsome, don't you think?" She sighed.

"He sure did," Hazel agreed. "But I don't know if he's as good looking as Lance."

Sherry laughed so hard her little body shook, and Hazel was worried that she might hurt herself. Despite how frail she looked, Sherry Fuller still had a deep and vivacious laugh.

"You've always been an honest one, haven't you, Hazel?" She sighed, catching her breath and gazing at the pictures of her offspring.

"Are they close as adults?" Hazel asked.

Sherry sobered. "Lance's been so protective of Dansby over the years." There was caution in her voice instead of pride, and it made Hazel's ears perk up.

"Has he?" she asked. "I just remember Dansby as a little toddler."

Sherry shook her head. "He was a...troubled teenager. And young adult. But Lance would never listen to anything negative about him. To him, Dansby could do no wrong. It got him into some trouble a few times. I remember one time, Lance was arrested right along with Dansby because he jumped into a fight to protect him."

"Goodness," Hazel said, unable to imagine Lance in a fist fight.

"And another time he flew all the way to South Africa to get him out of jail. They never told me what Dansby did to get himself arrested that time." She sighed again. "In fact, I get the feeling there's a lot of things they don't tell me."

"Oh, I understand how that goes," Hazel reassured, trying to steer the conversation away from topics that might upset Sherry. "I have two boys of my own now."

"I know," Mrs. Fuller said, her eyes shining. "We've always kept an eye on you. I was so excited for you when you had your kids. And we voted for you for city council in every election. *That girl will be more invested in taking care of this town than anyone else I can think of*, that's what Mike always said."

"That means so much to me," Hazel said, her eyes welling up. "You two were always so special to me. I wish..." She reached out a hand and put it on Sherry's. "I should have reached out earlier. I didn't know you were struggling with your health. I've always thought about you, over the years. But I didn't know what to do, you know, after Lance left. I just didn't want it to be awkward."

Mrs. Fuller reached out with the other hand and patted Hazel's. "You did just the right thing," she assured Hazel. "Now come on into the kitchen and put that down. What do you have there?"

Hazel followed her through the dining room and into the kitchen. She looked around for Mr. Fuller but didn't see him anywhere.

"I saw Lance at the search party for Nina Mitchell," Hazel said. "He mentioned that you and Mr. Fuller haven't been feeling like yourselves lately."

"Oh, that's an understatement!" she giggled. "They told us Mike has early onset Alzheimer's. I had cancer a few years back. It's in remission now, but it took a lot of me. Add arthritis, diabetes and osteoporosis and well, I'm not as healthy as I once was."

"Are you in a lot of pain?" Hazel asked.

Sherry grimaced. "Sometimes," she said. She fell silent, looking down at her feet.

Hazel attempted an encouraging smile. "He told me that he and Dansby had come back to help you out a bit and I wanted to help and show you my support, so I brought over dinner." *And I want to interrogate your son, who I think may be involved in Nina's disappearance,* she went on in her head. She felt terrible about not telling the whole truth, but what she said hadn't been a lie. She did want to show her support for the Fullers.

"Aren't you a dear," Mrs. Fuller smiled.

"I'll just go ahead and put it in the oven for you," Hazel said. "I made my grandmother's lasagna recipe."

"What a treat! Let me—" she paused. "Just excuse me for a minute, and I'll see if Mike is up to receiving guests."

Hazel, who was almost always in a hurry herself, found it excruciating to watch Sherry shuffle out of the room slower than a snail. She pushed down the instinct to shepherd her into a chair and go off to see about Mike herself. She began to look through cupboards to find dishes to serve lasagna on.

The kitchen was cluttered and still outfitted in honey oak cabinetry with shiny brass fixtures. But it was clean and well-organized. The fridge was stocked full of labeled take-out containers. Not much home-cooking had been going on, but at least Lance had kept up with the cleaning.

Hazel found a cheery yellow buffalo plaid tablecloth in a lower cupboard and spread it out on the table. She set it with four place settings. She wished she had thought to bring some flowers to brighten up the place a little bit. Sherry probably would have appreciated that, surrounded by boys as she was. Hazel had the sudden realization that she was looking at her own future and said a quick prayer that she would age well.

She looked at the various papers hanging on the fridge. There was an information sheet about diet guidelines for Type 2 Diabetes, a printout from the Internet about what to do if

Alzheimer's patients become agitated, and another sheet with a list of doctors' phone numbers and emergency hotlines. Hazel felt a pang of guilt about the meal she had chosen. Next time she would bring something less carby.

There were also pictures on the fridge. There was a head shot of Lance in full uniform, staring the camera down. Another one was of Dansby, a little older but still sullen, on a snowy mountain peak overlooking a green valley. There was Lance holding a small child, dressed in rags, with a big grin on both their faces. One was of Dansby climbing a burnt orange cliff face somewhere in the desert. Hazel caught a glimpse of a white veil in a picture that had been covered up by one of the medical papers and pulled it out to study it. It was a wedding photo. Lance's wedding photo. He stood arm in arm with a pretty blonde girl. Hazel studied her. Her hairstyle was simple, and she wore little make-up. They were both smiling broadly, although they were looking in opposite directions.

"Hazel?" Lance walked into the kitchen, interrupting her thoughts. Hazel jumped, putting the photo back on the fridge and turned around to face him. "What are you doing here?" he asked. He peered around her, and she saw him spot the wedding photo. He had a pale blue pallor, almost white.

"I brought that casserole by like I said I might," she explained. "Your mom went to go check on your dad to see if he was up to coming out to say hi before I left."

Lance turned a flickering orange, like a flame. "I don't think that's going to happen," he said.

"Is it that bad?" Hazel asked.

"He has some good times when he seems completely normal, but he forgets stuff then he gets frustrated. I think it scares him, you know?" Lance shook his head, then nodded at the photo on the fridge. "You didn't come to my wedding," he said.

"You didn't come to mine either," she countered.

"I was overseas."

"Oh, right," she said. "I remember that now."

He took a step around her and took the picture down. The flickering orange settled into a warm ember. "Her name is Lisa," he said. "She's wonderful. We were very happy for a while."

"How did you two meet?" Hazel asked.

Lance smiled at the picture. "Lisa and I were interns together in med school."

"Ah," Hazel said teasingly. "So, this was like a Grey's Anatomy situation."

He chuckled soundlessly. "Yeah, something like that."

"What happened?" Hazel asked.

Lance shrugged, reattaching the picture to the fridge. "Oh, you know... we were both so busy, it was hard to maintain our relationship. We wanted kids, but we couldn't find the time, and before we knew it, we were older. It was just time to part ways."

Hazel narrowed one eye. "You're not too old to have kids."

Lance laughed. "My parents had Dansby at about our age, didn't they? Yeah, I know we weren't too old. It wasn't just that. It was just... everything. We didn't have space for each other."

"How long have you been divorced?" she asked.

"About a year now," he said, glancing back at the picture again. His glowing orange cooled and hardened back into pale ice blue. "My mom was so upset."

"I can imagine," Hazel said. "What about Dansby?" she asked, changing the subject. "What's he been doing all these years?"

Hazel watched Lance's color carefully, but the ice blue didn't go away. "He graduated and then went traveling. Mom and Dad didn't hear from him for months at a time. He was a worldwide hitchhiker. It felt to me like he was looking for something. Maybe belonging, maybe God. I don't know. He should have joined the military."

"That worked out well for you, huh?"

Lance looked at her sideways. "I understand why you might be skeptical about that. I know I bailed and opted out of all those plans we made. But it was really good for me. It clarified who I was and gave me the discipline and the training and the focus to do something with my life."

"You would have still done something with your life," Hazel protested.

Lance just shrugged without answering her. His pale blue pulsed a sudden burst of muddy, mustard yellow. "I think you'd better go. Thanks for the food and everything." He started herding her back towards the front door.

"Lance," she said, planting her feet. "Look, I know it's been a long time, but I know you," she said, looking right into his eyes. "I know you quite well, and you know I can tell when you're lying and when you're acting weird. It's been years, Lance, but I can tell that something's up beyond your parents' health concerns. What the heck is going on?"

Lance's arms fell limply to his sides. "Don't ask me that, Hazel," he said, his eyes pleading.

"I have to ask you that, Lance; Nina is my friend. If your brother is somehow involved in her disappearance, I need to know. She has little kids, a family. We have to find her."

"I know," Lance said, throwing his hands up. The air around him flickered with muddy yellow and red. "I know that. Don't you think I know that? Why do you think I've been out there looking for her?"

"That isn't all you're doing, is it, Lance? What else are you doing out there in the woods? Just tell me the whole story so I can help you!"

Lance looked stricken. His eyes darted everywhere, like an animal looking for a way out of a trap. Finally, they rested on Hazel. He made a motion with his arm, like he might grab her hand, but took a step back instead. "Hazel, are you still you? Are you the same as you were all those years ago?"

"You can trust me," Hazel assured him, believing herself completely. "Let me help you, Lance."

Lance took a deep breath. "It's Dansby, he's—"

"Oh, good, Lance, you're home!" Sherry appeared in the doorway like a sneaky ninja with a walker. "I see that you've found our visitor! But you behave yourself, she's married now to a wonderful man from out on the West Coast. And she's got two wonderful teenage boys."

Lance had fallen silent, pressing his lips together. He nodded at his mom.

"And look who got out of bed for the occasion!" she went on, attempting to dramatically step to one side while pulling her walker. The effect was less than dramatic, but it didn't seem to lessen the impact Lance's father's presence had on him.

"Dad!" he said.

Physically, Bill had changed much less than Sherry. The way his family had been talking about him, Hazel expected him to be in a tatty bathrobe and slippers, his hair mussed from where it was flattened against a pillow. But that wasn't what he looked like at all. He was dressed in his typical jeans and Georgia Bulldog sweatshirt and hat. A newer variation of the same outfit she remembered him wearing most of the time when she was a kid. He had thicker glasses, but he had always been bald, and he didn't have that hunched, tired look that Sherry did. He looked at Hazel and smiled.

"Hello, young lady," he said, holding his hand out. "I'm so sorry I don't remember you. I'm having a bit of trouble with my memory lately. But I can see that you were very important to us because my wife loves you very much. I love her, you know. So, I thought I should come and thank you for your visit. It means so much to Sherry, that you've come."

Hazel put her hand in his and watched, speechless as he

brought it to his lips for a tiny kiss. She glanced at Lance and saw him grinning at his father.

"Dad, you're having a good day today," he said.

Bill turned towards him and gave him a quizzical look. "I'm sorry, I don't believe we've met before?" he looked towards Sherry for an explanation.

Hazel had to look away from the raw grief on Lance's face. She looked down at his toes but could still see the waves of cerulean cascading from him. Hazel glanced at Sherry. She had also turned a shade of blue, but hers was more like the sorrow of the deepest part of the ocean. "Mike this is our son, Lance."

Bill looked sharply at Lance. "No," he scoffed. "Lance is just a baby. This is a grown man."

The pang of sorrow that shot through Hazel was too much to bear. "I made a lasagna and some chocolate chip cookies," she blurted out. "It's in the oven but should be ready in just a few minutes."

"How wonderful," Mike said. "What a kind woman you are to think of us."

"Of course," Hazel whispered, guilt agitating the back of her mind. Why hadn't she checked in on them over the years? It wouldn't have taken much.

Mike and Sherry sat down at the table. Hazel glanced at Lance; he had turned towards the back door.

"It'll just be a couple more minutes. If you'll excuse me for a second, I should go check on something," she said.

Sherry followed Hazel's gaze over to where Lance was walking out the back door. "Thank you, Hazel," she said. "We'll do our crossword for a few minutes."

Hazel followed Lance out the door and was relieved to see that he hadn't left, he was just sitting on the back steps. It was a place they had often talked when they were young. She remembered the way the birds' songs echoed through the woods in the spring, and fireflies danced among the trees in the summer.

In fall, they would watch the leaves turn colors and come down, and in the winter, they would sit with hot chocolate hoping for snow. A thousand remembered conversations hummed inside her as she sat down next to him.

"Are you okay?" she asked quietly.

"Yeah," he said, his voice husky. "It's just sometimes he remembers and sometimes he doesn't. It's hard every time he forgets about me again. Especially when he seems to be doing well otherwise."

"He didn't really forget about you," Hazel pointed out. "Just that you grew up."

Lance barked a short laugh. "Oh, yeah, well that's so much better. He just forgot about everything that makes me, me."

"Not everything," she said, nudging him with her shoulder. "Not how much he loves you."

"Yeah," Lance whispered. "I guess."

They sat in silence for a moment, watching the late after-noon sun turn the budding leaves on the trees neon green.

"Lance?" Hazel asked, looking down at her hands.

"Yeah?"

"Where's Dansby?" she tried to speak as gently as she could, but Lance still cringed. He didn't respond right away.

"I don't know," he finally whispered.

"You don't know where he is?" Hazel felt an uneasy roiling begin in the pit of her stomach.

Lance shook his head.

"Was he here before?" *Please say no*, she thought.

"Yes."

"But he left?" Hazel's stomach lurched.

"Yeah," Lance didn't look at her.

"And he didn't say where he was going?"

Lance shook his head.

"So, he's missing?" Hazel clarified.

"I guess?" Lance didn't seem sure.

"Maybe you should start from the beginning."

"Right." The idea of this calmed him. "Yes, so I got back to town about three weeks ago. Dansby was already here. We didn't realize how bad it was. He just came here to crash between jobs. He usually works doing kayaking tours or as a hiking guide in the Himalayas or whatever. It's pretty seasonal work so he usually ends up here at some point. But it's been a while because his last job was as a scuba instructor for a resort in Costa Rica. He was there for a full year."

Hazel wanted to ask why Lance hadn't been back to check on his parents himself but bit her tongue.

"I should probably tell you, just so you can understand where I'm coming from...Well...I know you haven't seen Dansby since he was a little kid. He's a very...passionate guy. Misunderstood. Polarizing, I guess I could say. He...doesn't get along with everybody. I've had to help him out a lot over the years."

"Okay," Hazel said. She was glad that Sherry had given her some context before Lance said anything, otherwise she wouldn't have been able to make sense of the cryptic explanation.

"When he got here—this was about a month ago—he was pretty freaked out by my dad. My mom has been steadily declining for years now. When I was growing up, she always said she'd better learn to like milk because otherwise she'd end up with osteoporosis, but I guess she never did because that's exactly what happened to her. She's pretty frail now; her bones can't support her weight very well, so it causes problems. But we knew that already. Knew that she was a bit fragile and slow. It's my dad...we didn't realize. My mom never said anything—"

Lance's voice broke, and he looked down at the steps between his knees, trying to compose himself. "I feel so guilty, Hazel. I haven't been back for years. I just haven't seen them. I talk to them all the time on the phone, but I couldn't tell. And my mom... I just can't imagine how terrified she must have been. My dad's memory just comes and goes. Sometimes he remembers things and sometimes he doesn't. At least we got here before he stopped remembering her. I think it would have killed her if she had to go through that by herself. Sorry, sorry. I'm rambling."

"No, you're not." Hazel shook her head. "Keep going."

"When Dansby got here, it didn't take long for him to realize how messed up things were, and he called me and asked me to come. I'm not a neurologist or a geriatrician, but I have been around the block enough to know that this was going to be a long haul and that they would need help, especially because my mom isn't capable of taking care of my dad physically." He took a deep breath. "So, I quit my job and came out here for the long term."

"You quit your job?" Hazel asked.

"Yeah, I can get another one easily enough when we're done. And it's just me, and you know, the army paid for my medical degree, so I have plenty of money saved up. I can survive for a while without working." There was a pause. Hazel had so many questions she wanted to blurt out, but she knew that Lance probably hadn't talked to anyone about this except Dansby, and since he was the big brother, he would have felt the need to be all stoic and put together. The poor man needed to talk, and Hazel wasn't going to make him feel lonely by rushing him.

"You know, I was tempted to contact you when I got back," he admitted, looking sideways at her, and smiling just enough for his dimple to show under his stubble. "But I didn't. Because I Facebook stalked you and you looked happy and good, and I didn't want to even tempt you to complicate your life with any feelings seeing me might dredge up..."

Hazel snorted. "You still have that bizarrely high opinion of yourself, don't you?"

Lance shrugged. "My marriage was on the rocks for a long time. If you had walked back into my life..." he trailed off. Hazel didn't know what to say. The conversation felt borderline inappropriate. Jason would not be happy. He hadn't even wanted Hazel to see Lance again. She scooted away from him a little bit. "But Jason seems like a great guy and you guys seem happy together."

"We are. What about Dansby?" she asked. "My friend Nora was friends with Nina in high school and she said they were a pretty intense couple their senior year."

"I didn't know," Lance shrugged. "I wish I had been more mature when I was in my twenties. I would have tried to be more involved with Dansby. At least know what was important to him. But you know, I was overseas and all that, and I didn't check in as much as I should have. When I did, I just talked to my mom and dad. Then when Dansby got older, I was in med school, and he was a monosyllabic teenager. I don't know. I thought maybe now would be a good time for us to get to know each other as adults."

"That's a great thought," Hazel said. "Did it not work out?"

"It's hard to shake the big brother mentality," he said. "Dansby had already gotten back in touch with Nina before I even got here. It was hard not to be judgmental about it."

"What did he think about her being married?"

"He didn't seem to care at all about it, honestly. I don't know why because he seems otherwise to be a pretty moral guy. He believes in karma and all that. Became enlightened when he did a stint at a yogic monastery in India." Lance shook his head. "It was like he felt like he had a previous claim on her. Like her marriage to the other guy didn't count."

"Odd," Hazel said.

"I thought so too," he said. "But he's a grown man. There's not much that I can do about it. Dansby left on Saturday. He said he had something he had to take care of. He didn't say how long he was going to be gone. He hasn't been back since."

"Have you been in contact with him since then?"

"This is where it gets weird, Hazel," he said, exhaling slowly. "I honestly wouldn't really be that worried yet if it wasn't for Nina's disappearance. But that raised a big red flag for me. So, I called him on Monday after I heard about Nina. He didn't answer. I called several times throughout the day, and he didn't answer. I thought maybe he would respond to a text instead. So, I texted him and asked him if he was okay. He texted back and said yeah, he was fine, just couldn't really take a call. So why didn't he just text after I called him five times? I don't know." Lance rubbed his hand over his face. Hazel could see how tired he was. "I texted him that Nina was missing and got absolutely no response. I have texted him a dozen times since then and heard nothing. So yes, you're right. I wasn't just looking for Nina in the woods. I was looking for Dansby as well. I'd like to believe he had nothing to do with her disappearance, but..." He buried his ashen face in his hands, his elbows resting on each knee.

Hazel nodded. She didn't need to make him voice his suspicions about his own brother. She reached out a hand and put it on his shoulder, patting him gently. She was startled by the gentle shaking of his body. Lance was facing caring for parents whose health was failing and an MIA brother that may be wrapped up in a missing person's case. He had reached the end of his rope. He couldn't cope.

Hazel remembered when they were teenagers, they watched the movie *Backdraft*. Lance pretended to have something in his eye at the end to explain his tears and sniffling. He'd always been a sensitive guy. She would have bet that it served him well as a doctor, but this family crisis... he needed support.

"Oh, Lance," she crooned, rubbing his back. "I'm so sorry

you have to deal with all of this. Don't worry. It'll work out. Everything will work out." She murmured the comforting words that every mom has uttered to sobbing children. She didn't know what else to do, but they rang hollow in her ears. There was no guarantee everything would work out. If she had learned anything in the past year, it was that sometimes things would never be all right again.

Eventually, Lance's sobs stopped, and he grew still. He looked up at Hazel through bleary eyes. "Sorry," he said. "I didn't mean to..." He trailed off and Hazel noticed the blue sorrow surrounding him turning a dusky purple. She looked away. He grabbed her hand in both of his.

"Hazel, I'm drowning here," he whispered in a voice husky with desire as opposed to the sorrow it had been filled with before. "I need you."

Hazel's heart hammered in her chest. His stormy gray eyes were as stunning as she remembered. "You've had it rough, Lance. I'm so sorry. And I'm sorry that I haven't been checking in on your parents over the years. They mean a lot to me, and well, I should have stayed in touch. Jason and I will do all we can to help you however you need."

She was afraid spelling things out any more clearly would have hurt Lance even more, but she put a distinct emphasis on her husband's name. Lance must have understood because something changed in Lance's eyes, and he dropped her hand and her gaze at the same time. The magenta burning around him dulled. Hazel kept talking.

"I can help with taking care of your mom and dad, and when we figure out what's going on with Dansby, Jason can help him with...anything he might need help with, legally."

"That's so nice of you, Hazel," Lance sounded more in control of himself. His color turned back to that bluest of blues. "And your husband. I enjoyed talking to him last night. He's a real great guy. I can tell he treats you right, and he knows how lucky he is."

"Thanks," Hazel said. "He is *everything* I'll ever need." She put a hand back on his arm, her tone softening. "But really, Lance, we'd love to help. Please let us know if you need absolutely anything. I'll be back to visit your mom and dad again soon." She stood up and brushed herself off. She checked her watch. The boys were probably home from school already.

Lance gave her one of his signature smiles, turning a little yellow around the edges. "I do appreciate it. I'm sorry. I didn't mean to make it..."

"Don't mention it." She cut him off. "I just want to help. The lasagna comes out of the oven in ten minutes. Let your mom know I had to run to meet my kids. Tell her I'll visit again soon. Let me know if you hear from Dansby or find anything else out."

"I will," he said. She headed down the steps and around to the front of the house, feeling Lance's eyes on her until she was out of sight.

EIGHT

Hazel had stayed away too long. She knew that waiting for her at home were a couple of teenagers who had satiated their hanger with junk food and were probably close to a sugar crash. They needed protein and vegetables stat, before they became mean horrible monsters. She put away the Dansby problem in her head and started working on the dinner problem, mentally shifting through the fridge and pantry, trying to think of something to eat. She didn't even attempt to think about telling Jason about her visit to the Fullers.

She sped through the mudroom shedding her coat and rain boots without slowing and swept down the hall into the kitchen. She was halfway to the pantry when she stopped short. There was a girl in her kitchen. A beautiful, impossibly thin, blonde girl. She was standing in front of the stove with her back to the door, singing softly to herself. She was wrapped in sheaths of golden yellow that Hazel thought made her look way too comfortable in a stranger's kitchen.

Hazel edged around the perimeter of the room to get a better look at her, eyes narrowed. The girl was using Hazel's stove. Did someone tell her that she could do that? The rest of the kitchen was a complete disaster. It looked like every mixing bowl, pot and pan in the house had been used, and they were strewn all over the counters. It was impossible to tell what the girl was actually trying to make.

It took a minute for the girl to notice her presence. She eventually caught movement in her peripheral vision and whirled around, pulling out her earbuds with a big naive smile on her face. "Mrs. Dean!" she cried in delight, a highlighter yellow clung to her.

Hazel automatically smiled back. She couldn't help it.

"I'm so glad to finally meet you," the girl gushed. "I've heard so much about you. Eli doesn't realize what a wonderful upbringing he's had! Like, I keep trying to tell him how lucky he is, and he says he knows but, like, I really don't think he really gets it, you know? I mean, like, my mom is fine and every-thing, but my dad works all the time, we never see him, and when he is home he and my mom are always fighting." While she talked without taking a breath, her color turned from the neon yellow to a dark, moody brownish green. "Which is, like, kind of hard, you know? I mean, I know that they love me, and everything, but I know they don't really love each other. Like, they're going to get divorced as soon as I graduate, you know? I mean, it's not like—" A notification sounded from the cell phone laying on the kitchen counter and the girl immediately fell silent and picked up the phone as though she had been programmed to do so. Her color mellowed back into a golden tone.

"Um, I'm sorry," Hazel said. "Who are you?"

The girl pulled herself away from her phone like someone pulling their leg out of deep mud. Hazel almost heard a sucking sound. But once she looked at Hazel, the neon yellow was back. It must be the girl's color for nerves. "Oh, I'm Emma. Sorry, I should have mentioned that since we've, like, never met before, you know?"

"Yes," Hazel nodded. Something about the girl made her wary of making any sudden movements. "And you are a friend of Elias?" Hazel had never heard of anyone calling Elias anything other than Elias, but it seemed like the only logical thing that the 'Eli' the girl mentioned was her son.

The girl blushed; her neon yellow immediately turning to a rose pink. Hazel was going to get a headache from the girl's roller coaster of emotions. "Yeah, like, I guess you could say that."

Hazel's eyes widened. "Where is Elias?" Hazel asked.

"Oh, he's doing his homework somewhere," she said, making a gesture towards the rest of the house.

"Is Mr. Dean home?" Hazel asked.

The girl frowned, her color changing to a neon green instead of yellow that was just as offensive to Hazel's eyeballs. "I don't think so. I mean, I guess he could have come home and just not come into the kitchen so I didn't see him, but you'd think that if he did come home, he would have come in here. I mean it's always the first place people go when they get home. I mean, I do, and I guess you do too because you're here, you know?"

Hazel's smile was frozen on her face. "I came in to make dinner for my family. I was running a little late."

The girl reverted to the yellow highlighter. "Oh, you don't need to worry about that. I made something. Eli told me that you know that lady that went missing so we thought that you were probably out looking for her, and I told Eli that I would love to help you out and make something for everyone to eat. I figured you would be hungry when you got home, and I am an excellent cook. It's my pleasure." She flashed Hazel a beatific smile.

"Um, thank you?" Hazel said uncertainly. "Yes, I was out

helping with the search." Another notification sounded on the girl's phone, and she automatically picked it up again. Hazel opened her mouth to say that she was going to look for Elias, but she realized that the girl wouldn't hear anything she said, so she backed out of the room in search of her son.

She found him in the family room with his feet, still with shoes on, up on the arm of the white sofa. "Get your feet off of there," Hazel said. "Take off your shoes." Elias did as she asked without a word, barely looking up from the book he was reading. Hazel waited several seconds, staring at him. She peeked at the cover of the novel. *Kindred* by Octavia Butler, a compelling read. Usually, she would never interrupt her progeny when they were lost in a book, but this was an unusual circumstance.

"Elias?" she asked.

He grunted.

"Is there something you want to tell me?"

Elias blinked up at her and Hazel knew that he was registering her presence for the first time. "Emma's here," he said.

Hazel crossed her arms over her chest. "Who's Emma?"

Hazel had never explained her superpower to her children. They didn't know exactly how it all worked, but they did know that their mom seemed to be able to read their minds. Hazel watched Elias carefully, and her heart sank a bit while she watched his face flush and his aura turn a distinct fuchsia. Hazel knew she should probably feel happy for her son. Emma seemed nice enough for a seventeen-year-old girl. But all she felt was an aching sense of loss in the pit of her stomach. She didn't say anything, and she couldn't tear her eyes away from her baby. His entire life flashed before her eyes. She felt as though this was the beginning of the end of their relationship. She would always remember this moment.

"She's..." Elias swallowed. "A good friend." For Elias, it was the equivalent of gushing about how much he loved and adored her.

Hazel just nodded. "She's in my kitchen," was all she could think of to say.

"She wanted to help." Elias actually smiled at her, like she would be pleased by this.

"Ah," Hazel said. "Maybe you should go help her? Do the dishes, like a good sous chef."

Elias' face transformed into a look of panicked revelation. "Oh, yeah," he said and hefted himself off the couch and into the kitchen. Hazel wanted nothing more than to follow him in and spy on him, but she resisted, flopping onto the couch instead.

She barely got her shoes off when she heard Jason's voice down the hall in the direction of the kitchen. He sounded pleasant and enthusiastic.

The couch cushions were soft and deep. Hazel let her eyes flutter closed. They stung as darkness enveloped them. It was a delicious feeling. Then she became aware of someone quite close to her and opened her eyes again.

Jason's face was right above her, a little too close for her to be able to focus on it.

"Did you meet the girlfriend?" he asked, grinning so hard it looked maniacal.

Hazel was not excited about Elias' girlfriend, and she knew that she needed to tell Jason all about her conversation with Lance as soon as possible or it would feel like she was lying to him. The combination of these feelings made her scowl at him. "Yes, I met her."

"What do you think?" he asked.

"She talks too much," Hazel said. "And she's in my kitchen, making a mess. And she calls Elias Eli."

Jason's smile faltered. "I thought she was sweet."

Hazel rolled her eyes. "She's cute, I guess."

"It was nice of her to make dinner. She told me that she

knew you would be tired from searching for Nina and she wanted to help out. That's sweet."

"Yeah, okay, I guess when you say it like that," Hazel admitted. "It does sound sweet. But is she going to clean up after herself?" she pointed at Jason like she had just won the argument.

"It looks like Elias is cleaning up," he said.

She grabbed Jason's hand and pulled him down onto the couch next to her. He wrapped an arm around her, and she snuggled into the hollow space below his shoulder.

"How did the search go today?" he asked.

Hazel sighed. "John had me babysitting the parking lot instead of out searching this morning," she told him.

"I'm sure it was necessary for someone to do."

"I guess," Hazel moaned. "I just wish I hadn't been the one standing there when he realized that."

Jason chuckled. Hazel could hear the vibrations rumbling inside his chest and snuggled in a little more. "Then he sent me over to the Mitchell's to snoop," she told him.

Jason laughed even harder, causing her head to bounce around.

"What's so funny?" she asked, pulling away from him to examine his face. He overflowed with teal mirth.

"You went to Mike Mitchell's house to search for clues? Was he there?"

Hazel twisted her lips in a grimace. "I actually had a run in with him in the morning. He had been out all night, and I may have... implied... that he wasn't the best husband..."

Jason shook his head. "Oh, Hazel. Nobody needs to see your emotions in color. They're all too obvious all the time."

"I take that as a compliment," she said. "Anyways, John appeared and benched him, sent him home to sleep. But he wasn't there by the time I got there that afternoon. I had to come back and make a lasagna and cookies before I would consider trying to talk him into letting me go through his stuff."

"Sounds about right," Jason half-smiled.

"So anyways, his mom let me in, she's a piece of work by the way. But that's another story."

"Find anything interesting?"

Hazel pulled her phone out of her pocket. "A couple things, actually. One was that Dansby Fuller was Nina's high school boyfriend."

"Who's Dansby Fuller?"

"Lance's little brother," Hazel said quickly before Jason's color could fully turn to his anxious green or that bizarre orangey red. "Nora told me that he and Nina were going out in high school. It was one of those really intense relationships."

Jason shook his head. "So, your old boyfriend just so happens to be brothers with Nina's old boyfriend? That's oddly coincidental."

Hazel shrugged. "I guess."

"Your town is so incestuous."

"Not anymore, it's not," she protested.

A smile played around Jason's lips. He pressed them together tightly.

"Okay, so I walked into that one," she admitted.

"'Not anymore,'" he shook his head. "Hilarious."

"Are you done?" Hazel chided, but she was smiling too. "Can I go on?"

"Yes, yes," he said through suppressed chuckles, "by all means."

Hazel braced herself and plunged on. "I thought it would be a good idea to find out if they've been in contact since he got back to town."

"So you confronted Lance about it?" The green anxiety Hazel had dreaded seeing since she left the Fullers washed over Jason like a wave. She smiled at him and took his hand.

"I was hoping to confront Dansby, but he wasn't there. Sherry, Lance's mom, let me in. She's had cancer, diabetes, osteoporosis, and arthritis. Can you believe it? She's much older than she should be. And Mike, his dad, he has been diagnosed with Alzheimer's. The poor man. I feel just terrible for them. You remember, Lance mentioned yesterday, that's what he's doing back in town? Taking care of them?"

"I assume you went under the false pretenses of some charitable act?"

"They're not false pretenses," Hazel dropped his hand and scooted away from him. "I loved those people as a teenager. I couldn't believe how much their health has declined. It broke my heart. I assured them that we would be there to help out with whatever they need."

"I get it," he said, turning a snippety flickering gold. "You were super close with Lance's family because you were practically married to him while you were in high school."

"I was not practically married to him," Hazel snapped.

"Sure you weren't."

"Do you really want to get into how serious my high school relationship was? Do you want to think for a minute, that maybe, any of my friend's two living parents might have been of interest to me?"

Jason opened his mouth to retort, but nothing came out. He exhaled a big puff of air. "Fine," he said. "Your interest in Lance was entirely due to his happy little nuclear family."

"That's not what I said—"

"Did you find out about Dansby? Does he know where Nina is?"

Hazel sighed too. Jason had a habit of punting arguments instead of hashing things out. Sometimes it was for the best, but other times it just made things worse. Today she decided they didn't have time for a fight. "Turns out he's missing too. He disappeared around the same time as Nina did."

"You're not serious."

"I'm afraid I am."

"That doesn't sound good," Jason said. "Maybe Mike's right; he and Nina did run off with each other."

Hazel shook her head. "John doesn't think so. He said Nina didn't do any of the tell-tale things that people do before they leave their families. Leaving gifts or a note. She didn't pack her clothes or make-up or anything. It really looks like she was just packing for an overnight camping trip."

"Interesting. You don't think he kidnapped her, do you?"

"I don't know; I don't think so."

"Have you told John about this yet?" The gold flecks around him disappeared. Hazel was relieved that this development had pushed out his anger about Lance.

"No," Hazel admitted. "I just found out, and I barely got home, and Elias and the girl..."

"Hazel, listen to me. You need to tell John about Dansby. He has resources. If he can find Dansby, he might lead us right to Nina. If you believe that Nina is in any kind of danger at all, you need to call John right now."

"But..." Hazel bit her lip. "Jason, the Fullers... What is this going to do to them? They're so delicate. Surely, we can do this ourselves. There's no need to drag the police into it."

"We're not going to have a repeat of October on our hands." Jason's voice hardened. Months before, Hazel had broken into a construction office looking for proof of the owner's involvement in a violent crime. Uncle John had thoroughly enjoyed arresting her for breaking and entering. Jason had been some-what less amused. "Haven't you learned your lesson, Hazel?"

Hazel felt a pang of loss when she reflected on what she had learned during her earlier crime fighting experience. Cash had been so young when he died, so full of promise. He was poised to change his family's life for the better. All that had been cut short in an act of senseless violence brought on by the selfish acts of a half dozen different people. His brother Eugene's life had been altered forever.

"The only lesson I've learned is that if I don't fight for what's right, no one will. People need me. Maybe it's not the easiest path, maybe it's not the safest. But it's the only way I can wake up and look at myself in the mirror every morning."

"That's why we need to go to John," Jason said in the calm tone of someone who knows he's right. "He can help."

"It would destroy Mike and Sherry Fuller. I don't want their son embroiled in some kind of scandalous investigation."

"But what about Nina?" Jason asked. "What about *her* family? *Her* kids?"

Hazel bit her lip. She imagined little Naomi's face, so hopeful and trusting and wise beyond her years. "Maybe you're right," she admitted.

"Hazel," he said, grabbing her hands and covering them with his oversized ones. "It's better to go through the proper authorities. If it wasn't for Waylon Gibbons last year, I don't know what would have happened and I don't want to think about it."

Hazel nodded, remembering the fear that overwhelmed her when she and Jason were shoved into the back of a semi-truck by a few desperate thieves. Luckily, Waylon, who was a local hermit living in the woods, noticed the commotion and let John know what he suspected was going on. Waylon was a simple, gentle soul, intensely loyal to his friends and with an exhaustive knowledge of the woods. "Oh, my gosh," she said, jumping up from the couch and heading towards the door.

"What?" Jason cried, following her. "What is it?"

"I know how to find Nina. I've got to go see Waylon, right now."

Understanding dawned on Jason's face. "Yes, of course! He knows everything about those woods. He could probably track her or something. Why didn't we think of this before? I'll come with you."

They got up off the couch and started down the hall towards the garage but heard Emma and Elias's voices when they got close to the kitchen. Hazel pushed Jason back several paces away from the door. He raised an eyebrow at her. "What are we going to do about the girlfriend?" she whispered.

Jason shot her a look. "How can you still be thinking about that? We'll figure it out later. This is way more important."

Hazel rolled her eyes. "I meant right now. We can't leave them alone in the house together."

"Oh, yeah, good parenting thought," Jason said. "Um... I could just tell her she has to leave."

Hazel's eyes sparkled. Something about playing a good joke on her kids revived her a bit. "I have a better idea," she said. "We'll have Jeremiah babysit them."

Jason chuckled. "Oh, that's devious," he said. "He'll drive them nuts."

NINE

Jeremiah was all too happy to accept the assignment: *Don't leave Elias and Emma alone for more than five minutes at a time. Be as annoying as you want.*

"Really?" he asked. "You're giving me permission to annoy Elias."

"Well, more to annoy Emma," Hazel said.

Jeremiah's face fell. "You can't annoy Emma. She's too excited to be here and too determined to be nice to me."

Hazel looked at him sharply. "Did you know that Elias had a girlfriend?"

"Well, no. I didn't *know*. But I suspected. She's been hanging around him a lot. I can't tell if Elias really likes her or if he is just too shy to tell her to go away."

Hazel laughed but remembered the hopeful look on Elias' face when he was talking to her about Emma. "I think he really does like her," she said. "So, I guess don't annoy them too much. Just make sure that they don't start kissing or anything. And make sure she's out of the house before ten."

"Don't worry," Jeremiah said. "If you tell her a rule, she'll follow it. She'll also make sure that everyone else within hearing distance follows it too. She's kind of annoying like that."

Hazel smiled at her younger son and gave him a kiss on the cheek. His lip curled in disgust, and he immediately wiped his face with his sleeve. "I hope you didn't get lipstick on me," he whined.

"I don't even wear lipstick," Hazel said, rolling her eyes. "We shouldn't be too late, but please make sure you go to sleep at a reasonable hour. It's a school night."

"Okay," he shrugged. Hazel walked halfway out his bedroom door. "Hey, mom," he said. She stopped in the doorway and turned to face him.

"I hope that Waylon can find your friend," he said.

Hazel's heart skipped a beat at her son's unexpected thoughtfulness. She smiled at him. "Me too, honey," she said.

She walked down the stairs and through the hallway where she could hear Jason giving instructions to Elias in the kitchen.

"Curfew is at ten on school nights," Jason reminded him as she came to stand inside the doorway. "Emma needs to head home before then."

Elias nodded.

"You're so lucky your parents care enough about you to give you a curfew, Eli," Emma said. "My parents couldn't care less where I am or how late I stay out. I could be doing all kinds of terrible things, and they would never notice or care..."

Jason and Hazel could still hear her jabbering when they walked out into the garage.

"Come on," Jason said. "You can't say she's not sweet."

Hazel's face scrunched together in a disgusted grimace. "I'll say she's saccharine."

"Oh, ouch," he said. They pulled out of the driveway and headed down the mountain towards the highway. Jason was quiet for a while before he spoke again.

* * *

"So," Jason said conversationally. "Did you ever learn more about why Waylon lives out in the woods by himself?"

"Not really. He thoroughly enjoys having visitors and I wouldn't say he's particularly suspicious. He just feels safe in the woods. I do know that he's worried that the authorities will force him out of his home if they find out about him. There's no chance that the building wouldn't be condemned, and he does live on state forest land."

"I bet the structure's old enough that he would be able to keep living on that plot. I could look into it. We could help him fix up the house if he's worried about that."

Hazel wasn't sure that Waylon would accept that kind of help. She shrugged. "I haven't brought it up. I'm just happy he trusted me enough to give me the GPS coordinates. It's so much easier to visit now." She fell quiet thinking about her strange friend. "I think he's just happy out there, all by himself. He doesn't like crowds."

"You've invented a tragic back story for him, haven't you?"

"You know me too well," Hazel laughed. "I imagine he was ridiculed in school when he was a kid. Maybe he was held back a couple of times and was bigger than all the other kids and his sweet nature made him a natural target of teasing. Then one day he accidentally broke something or hurt someone and felt so ashamed of himself that he never left the woods again."

Jason shook his head. "You read way too much."

"That's impossible," Hazel scoffed. She knew he was trying to flatter her to make sure she wasn't mad, but she didn't mind too much.

It didn't take very long to drive as close as possible to Waylon's house, but the road only went so far. They parked the car and got flashlights out to make the short hike the rest of the way. Hazel had stumbled across his run-down shack while she was searching for the missing truck of her murdered friend the previous year. If she had passed it during the day, she would never have guessed that someone lived there, but it was night-time and the interior light had given Waylon away.

It was after dark by the time they got there, well after what she would normally consider polite visiting hours. Hazel led Jason around to the back of the house. The porch was dilapidated and falling apart, unused by Waylon except as a red herring to anyone that may pass by. She knocked on the back door, then waited.

Jason raised an eyebrow at her. "Maybe he's not home."

Hazel knocked again, a bit louder. There was still no answer. "Waylon?" she called. "It's just me, Hazel, and my husband Jason."

The door flew open. "Hazel!" Waylon cried with delight. He stepped aside and waved them into the house. "Please come in; I will make cocoa!"

He led them through the door into his kitchen where he put the kettle on before sitting down at the rickety table. "I am sorry I did not answer right away," he said, "There have been lots of people off the trails in the woods the last few days. Very busy."

"Yes!" Hazel said, taking the seat across from him. Jason settled onto a tall stool, which was the only other place in the room to sit. "Waylon, that's just what we came here to talk to you about."

Waylon's face grew serious. "Are people not following the rules again?"

Hazel smiled at him. "Not this time. There was a lady out hiking, and she got lost. Lots of people are out looking for her. No one has been able to find her."

Waylon shook his head, frowning. "It has happened before. I remember. Sometimes people get hurt. Sometimes they can't find their way back. But it is not the woods' fault."

"We thought maybe you could help," Hazel said. She half expected him to jump right up and get his coat. She assumed he would be thrilled to be useful. Instead, he looked past her at the corner of the room, peering into the darkness without a word. Hazel looked at Jason. He shrugged back at her and followed Waylon's gaze, but Hazel knew that he wasn't looking at anything in particular. His regular shiny white had dulled to a sandy gray.

"Waylon?" she said. "I just thought, since you know the woods so well…"

He still didn't respond or blink. His color didn't flicker.

Hazel exhaled a deep breath. "I brought you another book," she said. Waylon's eyebrow twitched. He turned towards her slightly. Hazel took the book out of her bag and handed it to him. He stared at the cover without saying anything. It showed a landscape of pine covered mountains with a pile of rocks in the foreground and a robot standing on top of the rocks. "It's about a robot who gets stranded on a deserted island and becomes a part of the wildlife community."

"*Wild Robot*," Waylon said, reading the title.

"How did you like *Hatchet*?" Hazel asked. Waylon turned his head to look at her and a smile broke out on his face. The gray gave way to a bright white instantly.

"It was a very good book," he said. "The boy is at first not so smart and then he learns. It is a very good book."

Hazel nodded. "Then you'll love *Wild Robot*."

Waylon looked back down at the book, opening the cover to look at the first chapter.

"Look, Waylon," Hazel said, sitting down across from him at the table. "I'm really worried about this lost woman. Her name is Nina; she has four little kids."

Waylon's head snapped towards her; his smile evaporated. He held very still, almost like an animal before it ran away suddenly. Hazel was about to say more, but she thought better of it. So the three of them sat in silence for several long minutes.

"I will help you, Hazel Dean," Waylon said. "One day my mother went out into the woods. She did not come back. I will help the children find their mother."

Hazel gasped, looking back up at Waylon. A tear ran down one of his cheeks. She squeezed his hand. "Thank you, Waylon Gibbons," she said. "Thank you."

"It will be hard at night," he said, getting up and releasing her hands. She got up too.

"I know," she said. "But we don't have any time to lose. It's been two days."

Waylon nodded. "You will not like to hear this," he said. "But we should go in the morning."

"Why not now?" she asked. "Nina might be hurt. Every second counts."

"We could go now, but we will not find anything. I need light to look for her signs."

Hazel fought her deep disappointment. She knew he was right, but somehow it felt like it would still be possible now and that getting the head start would make up for the handicap. She needed to do something. She could feel herself start to panic. Her eyes darted around the room.

"Hazel," Jason said. "He's right. We'll go at first light. I'll take the day. We'll find her. In the morning, we'll find her. Waylon will know how to look."

Waylon nodded. "I will meet you there."

"The search is starting at the Cherokee Rose Trail head. Do you know it?"

"I can find it," Waylon assured her. "I will be there. First light."

Hazel nodded.

"Come on, Hazel," Jason said. "You need some rest."

Hazel felt that rest was the last thing she needed. What she needed was to find Nina before it was too late. If it wasn't already too late, Hazel knew she would never forgive herself. How could she go home to her warm house and climb into her cozy bed and get good, uninterrupted sleep when Nina was out here in the cold? She said goodbye to Waylon and then followed Jason down the steps and back out to the car.

He opened the door and climbed in, but she left her hand on the handle, staring into the darkness. The woods were alive with sounds. The eerie almost-human cry of an owl rang out closer than she'd imagined, making her jump. The bellowing mating call of a frog echoed through the trees. Hazel was accustomed to thinking of these sounds as positive harbingers of spring, but tonight, they felt ominous.

Jason opened his door and stuck his head out of the car. "You coming?" he asked.

Hazel looked at him. Her face must have been filled with something because he got all the way out of the car and walked over to her. He opened her door and guided her gently into the seat. "We'll find her tomorrow," he said. "It's all we can do."

Hazel stared out the window as they bounced down the gravel road. Maybe she would see a flash of color in the darkness. Maybe Nina's emotions were so strong, they would glow at night like a light and Hazel would be able to see them and find her.

"Jason, can we please just drive by the other trail head?"

"It's dark, Hazel. What are you expecting to find?"

"I don't know," she said. "I just feel like we should." Everyone in her family knew that if she said she "just felt" something, it meant they should take notice. In the past she had found lost things, avoided car accidents, run into old friends, and happened to have just what they needed in their car all because Hazel had "just felt" something.

Jason nodded. "Alright," he said. "We'll take a little detour." When they reached the highway, he turned back towards town.

Hazel kept her eyes on the woods to their right, searching the trees for anything that looked like it didn't belong there. Jason slowed down as the highway snaked through downtown, stubbornly following the reduced speed limit. The streets were vacant except for the one restaurant in town that was open past eight o'clock. The shops were all closed.

"You know the speed limit is for tourists, right?" she said. "So, they'll slow down and see how cute it is and want to stop?"

"I think you might have mentioned that before, once or twice," he said, slowing down a little more.

Jason reached over and felt for her hand.

"I suppose when you drive so slowly, it's easy to also hold hands," Hazel deadpanned.

He smirked again.

They made it through downtown and Jason stepped on the gas again, releasing Hazel's hand and putting it back on the steering wheel. It didn't take long before they were back in the woods again. Hazel turned away from Jason and kept her eyes glued to the window, just in case.

Eventually, they turned onto the dirt road leading to the trail head that John had zeroed in on that morning, as being the most likely path Nina would take. It was a long unpaved portion and Jason couldn't go more than ten miles an hour most of the time. Occasionally, there would be a huge dip in the road, that in the dark Jason couldn't see until they were on top of it. Hazel had the sudden realization that she needed to use the bathroom and every bump in the road was excruciating. She still tried to look out of the window through the trees, but it was much more difficult to see anything than it had been on the smooth paved road.

Finally, they made it to the end of the road. There was no parking lot here, no pavilion. It was too remote for that. There wasn't even a covered sign with a map and some notices like there were at many of the area's trail heads. There was just a widening at the end of the road. Hazel was a little surprised to see a forest ranger's ATV sitting in the lot.

Jason parked the car and Hazel grabbed a flashlight and jumped out, running for the trees.

"Where are you going?" Jason called after her with alarm.

"I have to pee!" she yelled over her shoulder.

She could hear him laughing.

By the time she came back, Jason was examining the ATV.

"What do you think they're doing here?" she frowned.

"Maybe they're helping with the search effort," Jason shrugged.

"But Ranger Rick told John that they wouldn't be searching in this area. He disagreed with John's assessment that she would come this way and he wanted to focus their efforts on the direction of the national forest."

"Huh," Jason said. "Maybe he changed his mind."

"Maybe," Hazel remembered the green flashes across Rick's face earlier. "Maybe there's something else going on here."

Jason chuckled. "I think you might be jaded by some past experiences."

"Could be," Hazel shrugged.

"Well, you can ask him if we bump into him. If it's even him. It could be a different ranger, right? Maybe it's just a coincidence."

"I suppose that's possible," she answered, not believing it for a second.

"Did you want to look around a bit?" he looked at his watch. "I can give us fifteen minutes."

"Alright," she said. She looked around, unsure of what she wanted to see. The breeze pulled at her, and she shivered. "Let's try this way," she said, moving in the direction the wind blew.

Fifteen minutes wasn't even enough time to go a mile and back, but Hazel stumbled forward in the dark. She scanned the distance for flashes of color. But saw nothing. She continued forward with Jason at her heels, but as the minutes passed, she began to think that her intuition had failed her. There was nothing to see in the darkness.

Jason cleared his throat behind her.

"Okay, let's go," she said. If only they lived on a wide plain, instead of the slopes and valleys that made up their surroundings, then finding Nina would be no problem. As it was, it was impossible to see more than forty feet ahead of them. She spun around and stomped back down the slope they had climbed for the previous ten minutes. But as she looked up, she caught something in the valley below her. She turned off the flashlight.

"What?" Jason asked. "Do you see something?"

"Look," Hazel said, pointing.

Jason's eyes followed her finger down the hill. He squinted through the trees.

"Do you see it?" Hazel asked.

"I think I do," he said, his voice betrayed a note of surprise. "That patch of light? Looks like a flashlight. It can't be Nina though, that close to the trail head. Someone would have found her by now."

Hazel shrugged. "Maybe it's Ranger Rick. Let's find out."

She started to pick her way down the hill, slowly.

"Aren't you going to use the flashlight?" Jason suggested.

"No, I'd like to surprise him," she replied. "I want to know what he's doing out here."

By the time they made it down the hill, the light had migrated towards the parking lot. They were close enough that they could hear multiple men's voices. Hazel started walking faster, wanting to intercept them before they made it back to the parking lot and noticed Jason's car.

"Is that all of it then?" an accented voice said. Hazel had always been terrible with accents. Was it an Australian accent? English? Irish? Maybe Jason would have a better guess.

"Should be," another voice replied, and Hazel allowed

herself a smug smile when she recognized it as belonging to Rick. "If there's any left, it wouldn't be enough for anyone to notice."

"Good. We were lucky then," said the unfamiliar voice.

The voices were quiet again. Hazel realized that they would be on top of them right as they entered the parking lot and stopped, grabbing Jason's hand to stop him too. They would appear just after the men noticed their car. It would be perfect.

"Are you sure about this?" Jason whispered in her ear. She put a finger to his lips.

She waited.

"Hey," the accent said. "Was that car here before?"

"Oh, shoot," Rick said.

Hazel tugged on Jason, and they emerged from the bushes opposite the ranger and his friend.

"Hello?" Hazel called, as though they were far enough away that you'd need to shout through the darkness to be heard. "Hello, is someone there?"

Neither of the men spoke.

Hazel walked around the car and approached them, motioning for Jason to follow her. She noticed that they were both carrying crates loaded with some kind of plant. "Ranger Rick? Is that you?" she called.

"Hi, Mrs. Dean," Rick said a little warily.

"I'm surprised to see you here," she said. "I thought you'd be looking for Nina elsewhere after our conversation this morning."

"Yeah, well, I figured that if John felt so strongly about it..." he trailed off. Hazel had a hard time discerning any colors he exuded in the dark.

"This is my husband Jason," she said, putting out her arm towards her husband.

"Hello," Jason said, stepping forward with a hand

outstretched. "What do you have there? Need a hand?" Without waiting for an answer, Jason took the crate out of Rick's hands.

"Oh…" Rick said, "Um, thanks."

"Just in the back here then?" Jason asked.

"That'd be fine," Rick said.

"Who's your friend?" Hazel asked, as the accented man loaded his crate on top of the one Jason set down.

"This is my buddy, Stephen," Rick said. "We were in school together."

"Lovely to meet you," Hazel said. "What brings you to our tiny corner of the world?"

"I'm just here visiting an old friend. I come 'round and check on the boy every so often. Worries me that he's cut himself off from civilization with this job, eh?"

Hazel raised her eyebrows. The gift of gab indeed. Definitely Irish. "How nice."

"Yeah, I thought I'd try and help out a bit, especially with this business of a missing girl."

"That's very kind of you," Hazel said.

"Well, it was nice to meet you both," Jason said. "Hazel and I need to be going now. I'm sure we'll see you around."

"Yes, good night then," Rick said.

"Goodbye," Hazel said, backing towards the car. "Hopefully next time I see you, you'll have those dogs for us. Tomorrow, right?"

"I hope so," Rick called after her.

Hazel got into the car and exchanged a loaded look with Jason but didn't want to discuss what had happened until it was certain they wouldn't be overheard.

It appeared Jason felt the same way because, without a word, he turned the key in the ignition and drove away.

TEN

"What was in the crate?" Hazel blurted out the question as soon as they had turned onto the highway. She wasn't sure what kept her quiet until then—probably nothing more than superstition.

"I tried to look, Hazel," Jason said. "But they made sure the flashlights were pointing away from the crates. All I could see was leaves and roots."

"Marijuana?" she asked.

Jason scoffed. "Too cold."

"They could have heat lamps," Hazel suggested.

"In the middle of the forest?"

"Maybe a greenhouse somewhere."

"I guess..." Jason mulled it over. "Maybe. I just don't think it was marijuana."

"Why not? I thought you said you couldn't see it."

"I saw the shape at least. I don't know. Why would they need the whole root if it was marijuana?"

"I don't know," Hazel shrugged. "Don't they use the roots for something? Is that what hemp is?"

"No, hemp is made from the leaf. But the root can probably

be used for something. Unless it's poisonous. I've never heard of it before though."

"Oh, well," she snarked. "If you've never heard of it."

He shot her a look.

"Sorry," she said, regretting her sarcasm. She reached out for his hand. He let her take it. "Sorry, I forgot we were in a fragile place for a sec. I'm grateful for your superior worldly knowledge."

"Thanks," he said. "In any case, it might be marijuana, but I would bet not."

"Okay," she said. "Good to know. They're clearly up to something, whatever it is. Maybe I should call John."

"Yes," Jason nodded. "You should call John. You also need to tell him about Dansby Fuller going missing and his connection to Nina."

Hazel frowned. She still didn't know if she wanted to do that. It would be so much easier on Sherry and Mike if she could quietly rule out the possibility of Dansby's involvement herself. She didn't respond to Jason's advice. Instead, she took out her phone and gave John a call.

John's phone went straight to voice mail. "Hi, John," Hazel said. "It's Hazel. I was just up at the Cherokee Rose trail head, and I saw something we should probably investigate. It's not exactly related to Nina, but it might be. I don't know. Give me a call back when you get a minute." She hung up.

She felt Jason's eyes on her and looked up from her phone to meet his gaze. "What?" she asked when he didn't say anything.

"Why didn't you just tell him what we saw in the message?" he asked.

"Just say it straight out? What if they have access to his voice mail or something?"

Jason half smiled. Hazel had a hard time making out his

color in the gloom, but it was either an amused bubble gum pink or his regular work-mode tan.

"Are you laughing at me? Crazier things have happened!"

Jason nodded, raising his eyebrows. "They have," he said, then sobered. "You didn't mention Dansby either."

"I'd just prefer to talk to him, rather than leave rambling messages," she sighed. "I guess he went to bed early. I think he was out all night last night."

Jason nodded. "They were talking about him at work today. Judge Proust is worried about him, living alone and all that. He takes care of everyone else and doesn't have anyone taking care of him."

"We take care of him!" Hazel exclaimed.

"You do a little bit, but that's not what she meant. She meant that he needs a wife or something."

Hazel laughed. "I can't imagine that."

Jason chuckled as he pulled into their driveway. "Me either, honestly. Do you think Emma will still be here? It's barely after ten." Hazel was irritated by the hopeful note in Jason's voice.

"She'd better not be," she growled.

The girlfriend was nowhere to be seen when they got home, and Jeremiah had told them that he never even caught her holding hands with Elias, so that was good. Jason and Hazel ate bowls of the baked potato soup Emma had made. He was full of praise, but Hazel found plenty to criticize.

It didn't take long for everyone to retreat to their bedrooms and fall asleep, but Hazel lay in bed staring at the ceiling. Jason snored next to her. She pushed him until he turned onto his side and the snoring stopped.

Hazel tossed and turned and finally sat straight up in bed, pulling her tablet onto her lap. She brought up a web browser. She had been meaning to look up post-partum depression since her conversation with Nora the previous day.

Hazel read half a dozen articles about it in the glow of the blue light from her tablet. The more she read, the more she was sure that Nina struggled with it. Hazel pulled the cover over the screen and placed it on the bedside table.

She thought back to the night she gave Nina *Anna Karenina* at book club. When everyone else got up to help themselves to treats, Nina had remained sitting in her chair. Hazel saw a swirl of emotions surrounding her in cool tones, like midnight blue, royal purple, black, deep turquoise. Such a display of emotions wasn't uncommon. Hazel often saw them at weddings, funerals, high school graduations—anytime life served up a particularly poignant moment. Hazel had wondered if Nina might be pregnant again.

A flicker of color past Nina's head had caught her eye. Hazel moved past her and down the hallway made of bookshelves until she found the tome swirling in the same colors that Nina was. When Hazel picked it up and saw the title, *Anna Karenina*, she was confused. *Anna Karenina* was an epic Russian novel about marriage. Towards the beginning, an argument between two friends sets the tone and theme for the rest of the novel. Childhood friends Stiva and Levin had reunited to share a large meal. One of the friends, Stiva, has been unfaithful to his wife. Levin thinks this is wrong.

"Excuse me," he says. "But I decidedly do not understand how... just as I don't understand how I could pass by a bakery, as full as I am now and steal a sweet roll."

"Why not?" says Stiva. "Sometimes a sweet roll is so fragrant that you can't help yourself."

This conversation stood out in Hazel's mind when she took the book down from the shelf. Perhaps Nina was considering having an affair, but Hazel knew better than to try and guess why people needed the books they did.

While Hazel spoke to her, Nina's swirl of colors whirled even more violently, a flash of pink or orange occasionally breaking through the dark tumult of color. Hazel knew Nina needed *something*, but what, she wasn't sure. She had hoped the book would be it. But now, days after Nina's disappearance, she knew that she hadn't done enough for the young mother. Hazel erred on the side of protecting people's solitude in their moments of extreme emotion. It's what she herself would want. But in hindsight, Hazel felt like she had abandoned Nina that night.

Hazel frowned, willing her thoughts away from Nina and reflecting on the last few days instead. Ranger Rick's behavior made her uneasy. Hazel had a hard time believing that he could have been involved with Nina's disappearance, but it wasn't out of the realm of possibility.

She picked her tablet up again. A visit to the Chatta-hoochee-Oconee National Forest website directed her to their Facebook page. While the organization didn't post any identi-fying information about their rangers, a person named Rick made frequent and knowledgeable comments. His profile picture wasn't a headshot; it was a picture of an avatar-style black bear, but when Hazel pursued the link to his profile, her suspicions were confirmed. Ranger Rick's last name was Lewis, and Hazel was thrilled to find that his account wasn't private. She scrolled through all his photos, which were exclusively of him in the woods at various seasons of the year. The only exception was a picture of Christmas with a man and a woman, who looked like they must be his parents, and of a girl about his age that was probably his sister. It certainly wasn't his girl-friend. He didn't appear to be involved in any romantic entan-glements.

His posts included tips and tricks about hiking, preachy sounding cautions about forest fires, and diatribes about dangers to the environment. Hazel noted he was an advocate for legalizing marijuana in Georgia. He also regularly extolled the virtues of various herbs and plants for one's health.

Hazel scanned his list of friends for one named Stephen.

There were three, each with a different spelling. Hazel squinted at their profile pictures, but she hadn't gotten the best glimpse of Stephen that night and they all looked the same to her. She followed each link and was disappointed that the first two had private accounts. The third couldn't have been the right one. He had posted a picture that night of himself at a Broadway show in New York City. A dead end. She would have to wait and talk to John about it.

Hazel glanced at the clock. It was after one in the morning. She knew she was headed toward emotional instability due to lack of sleep. Tears of frustration clouded her vision but didn't spill over. She took a deep breath and was about to set down her tablet but something nagging at the back of her mind made her type 'Karen Mitchell' into the search bar.

The first hit took her to a list of Facebook profiles for Karen Mitchells. The internet did its creepy all-knowing thing and put Mike's mom towards the top of the list. Hazel clicked on her profile and scrolled through Karen's posts. There was a picture of Karen golfing, one of her drinking a cocktail, gardening, arranging some flowers, playing tennis, eating a tiny salad. In every one, she had the same practiced smile, same tilt of the head, her body turned slightly away from the camera and one foot slightly in front of the other and on tip toe to elongate her leg and make her waist look slimmer.

"Who's taking all these pictures?" Hazel whispered into the dark.

She scrolled down far enough she found Mike's inauguration to city council. There was an album of pictures. When Hazel opened it, her screen filled with images of what appeared to be the interior of Karen's home, all decked out with fancy flower arrangements and an elegant banner that said *Congratulations, Mike*. One of the pictures showed a long buffet table covered in silver serving dishes over a white tablecloth. Two bow-tied attendants stood behind it. Karen had gone to a lot of trouble, but it didn't look like more than ten people had attended the event.

There were pictures of Karen one on one with a half a dozen gentlemen all in the sixty to eighty age range. There were a few women in some of the more general shots, but none that had taken a posed photo with Karen. The final picture was just of Karen and Mike. *So proud of my baby, the city councilman!* The caption read.

Hazel searched all the pictures for Nina or any of the kids but found no evidence that they attended the party. Hazel guessed that Karen didn't want children at the fancy party and that Nina stayed home with them rather than finding a babysitter. Maybe she was relieved to have an excuse to skip it, or maybe she spent the evening marinating in resentment.

Hazel scrolled all the way down through the years of Karen's activity on Facebook until it abruptly stopped, sometime in 2014. There were pictures of each of Mike's kids when they were born, and every couple years there was an identical shot of Karen holding a bundle of blankets with a barely visible baby inside. The only other photos of her grandkids were idyllic, staged Christmas shots, all of them in matching pajamas baking sugar cookies or snuggled in front of the fire with a book. Underneath the captions said things like *Mimi is the best, #blessed,* or *Mimi's at Christmastime.* Hazel didn't find any evidence of Nina's existence on Karen's entire Facebook account.

Thoughts chased themselves in her head, swirled up with a tangle of colors. Green flashes on Rick's face, Karen's snapping red, Mike's metallic sparks, Lance's muddy yellow, and Nina's mire of pigmented misery.

Hazel closed her tablet and set it down on the bedside table. She lay back on her pillow and tried to relax, not expecting to be able to sleep. Her eyes remained stubbornly focused, even behind her eyelids.

Eventually, through sheer force of will, she slipped into unconsciousness. She spent the night dreaming that she overslept and missed Waylon, waking with a start every forty-five minutes or so. Relief flooded her when she woke up to see the glow of predawn creeping around the edges of the window shades.

ELEVEN

"John, call me back," She left another message. "I have a lot of stuff that I need to tell you. I think it will help with finding Nina."

"Why isn't he answering the phone at six am?" she asked.

Jason shook his head, his eyebrows crinkled together. His alarm clock had gone off only a few minutes before, and he was talking a little slower than normal. His thick hair was smushed flat against the back of his head from the way he was sleeping. "I don't know," he yawned. "It seems weird that he wouldn't have responded either time. Maybe they found Nina. Try the station."

Hazel shook her head. "They won't be able to do anything for me. I'll try Brandon." She got up and paced around the bedroom listening to the phone ring.

"Miss Hazel!" Brandon said. "We were just going to call you."

Hazel's eyebrows shot up. "Who's we?" she asked. "What's going on."

"We got a tip about Nina's campsite," he said.

"What?" Hazel shrieked.

"We were told that it had been abandoned."

"Where are you?" Hazel demanded. "I'll be right there."

Brandon's voice got lower. "Miss Hazel, this isn't exactly according to protocol. I shouldn't really tell you anything. John wanted to call you as a courtesy, to give you some hope, but this is an ongoing investigation."

"Brandon," Hazel's voice lowered as well. "I'm on the city council for heaven's sake, doesn't that get me into the loop on stuff like this?"

"Well, I don't know..." he trailed off.

"What about Jason? He's the DA; is he allowed to know about ongoing investigations?"

"I suppose..."

Hazel shoved the phone into Jason's hands. "Find out where they are," she pleaded through clenched teeth.

"Hi, Brandon," Jason said into the phone, flashing a smile even though Brandon couldn't see him. "This is Jason Dean."

Hazel couldn't hear what Brandon was saying on the other end of the conversation. She held her breath.

"I completely understand," Jason said. "Yes, of course. I wouldn't want you to do anything that you don't feel is right."

Another long pause.

"You know Miss Hazel," Jason said. "She's relentless. Yeah, well. I knew what I was getting into." He grinned at Hazel. Then listened for another minute.

"Well, I really appreciate that, Brandon."

Hazel clapped her hands together and flashed a thumbs up at her husband. He turned away from her slightly. Brandon was still talking.

"Yes, I'll take responsibility. I understand. Alright, we'll see you in a bit." He hung up the phone and handed it back to Hazel. "He'll ping a location for you in a minute. He said he's the only one with service out there. It's pretty remote, well away from any official hiking trails."

"How do you do that?" Hazel asked.

"What?"

"Get people to agree with you?"

"Well, Hazel," Jason began to glow a mustard yellow. "It's all about listening to people. Not just forcing your own way, knocking people around. You've got to be a quarterback instead of a linebacker."

"A linebacker?" she folded her arms over her chest.

"You have to admit it's an apt comparison."

Hazel's phone made an alert noise. Brandon had shared his location with her. "Whatever," she said. "Let's go. Our bags are in the car."

"Breakfast? Children?" Jason asked.

"If we wait too long, they'll be done. And we'll miss Waylon."

Jason sighed. "I can't let you go without me. I promised Brandon."

"Then you'd better come," she said. "Because I'm headed out."

"Linebacker..." Jason mumbled.

"What was that?"

"Nothing... We'd better leave Elias and Jeremiah a note. Just in case they notice we're not around. I can't believe that we're at a point in life where our kids just get themselves ready for school and leave without us."

"Yes, our lives dramatically improved when Elias got his driver's license," Hazel remarked.

"I guess so," Jason said. "But I also miss when they were little."

"I know," Hazel said, tugging gently on his arm. "But let's count our blessings and get out of here."

Jason let out a deep sigh. "I'm right behind you," he said.

They got in the car and headed back to the trail they had left less than ten hours previously. "Feels a little *deja vu*," Jason mumbled.

The sun was already well above the horizon. It lit the morning with a golden glow. The trees lining main street had begun to blossom in fluffy white puffs. Spring was about to explode out of the sleeping earth. It felt wrong, when Nina's life hung in the balance, for nature to continue its beautiful dance.

"I love these trees," Hazel said.

"I do too," Jason said. "Spring is the best season in Georgia."

Brandon had instructed them to drive down the south-bound access road once they reached the Cherokee Rose trail head. It would get them closer to where the campsite was, and they wouldn't have to hike in as far. They drove until they were perpendicular to the ping on the map. John's SUV was parked in the same spot.

Hazel noticed a tree with an interesting trunk on the right, downhill side of the road. It bent sideways for a couple feet before it turned again to reach for the sky, like a living sideways letter Z. Jason turned off the car, and they got out, prepared to hike the rest of the way in.

"Look at this tree," Hazel pointed to its gnarled trunk.

"That's fascinating," Jason said. "I wonder what happened that made it grow that way. Some kind of trauma." He shook his head. "I wonder how old it is. The stories trees could tell."

Hazel popped the trunk and handed Jason a backpack. "Do you think they'll have dismantled the campsite by the time we get there?" she asked.

"Tell me there's not a gun in this backpack," Jason said, holding the pack away from him at arm's length.

"There's not a gun in that backpack," Hazel said, grinning.

"Hazel, seriously," Jason's deep green anxiety washed over him. "Are we packing heat?"

Hazel laughed. Teasing Jason about his discomfort with

firearms never got old. Neither did his Hollywood-style lingo for things he had little experience with. "No, I promise. No gun. It didn't seem like that kind of outing."

The green drained away from her husband's face. "Oh, good," he said.

Hazel was already stomping her way through the underbrush.

"Are we going to get poison ivy?" he asked.

"Maybe," Hazel said. "But you're wearing pants, you should be okay. At least you've learned not to wear big chunky hiking boots. You shouldn't get any blisters this time around."

"Yeah," Jason said, climbing over a fallen log while trying not to touch it. "That's good, I guess."

"Let's go, Jason," she urged. "We're kind of in a hurry."

"Alright, alright," he said.

They hiked in silence, the only noises were Jason's labored breathing and the song of morning birds. The sun was up properly now, glaring sharply through branches swollen with budding leaves and flowers. The woods would be stunning in another two weeks. Hazel tried not to think about it.

Twenty minutes into their hike, Hazel noticed a deer trail. It was subtle, like one of those mirage art pieces where the only way to see the picture was to unfocus your eyes. Hazel saw the trail through the grass and birch trees that the deer must have frequented. She checked the map. They were almost on top of the location Brandon had given them. "Let's go this way," she said.

"Do you see them?" Jason asked.

"Not exactly," she said. "I think Nina might have come this way."

"Really?" Jason asked.

"Yeah," Hazel said, picking her way down the deer path. She didn't want to disturb things too much for the deer. Less than a half mile down the path, Hazel heard the low rumbling voice that could only have been her Uncle John's.

"I hear them," Jason said, right as the trail widened into a clearing and John appeared in front of them.

"Hazel? Jason? What are you doing here?" he demanded, with a look of surprised recognition. "How did you find us?"

"Well, you're parked just down the road, Uncle John," Hazel said smoothly.

John groaned: "Hazel, you can't be here."

"And why is that? Is there something special about this place?" Hazel asked, widening her eyes to affect innocence.

John looked at Brandon, who shrugged back at him. John let out at deep sigh. "Fine," he said. "Mark my words, Hazel Randolph, someday you're going to learn your lesson about meddling in things that don't concern you."

"Maybe," Hazel gave a small toss of her head.

"I can't believe you were a party to this, Jason," John turned on him. "You should know better."

"You know Hazel," Jason half-smiled. "She's relentless. And she feels responsible for Nina's disappearance for some reason..." he glared at her to show his disapproval of that line of thinking.

"Well, Hazel," John went on. "If you must know, we believe this was Nina's campsite. We just finished photographing it, and we were about to take it down and back to the station as evidence before you arrived..."

"Do you mind if we take a look?" Hazel turned towards the tent.

"I guess you can look, but don't touch," John said pointing a finger at her.

The backpacking tent was still set up and zipped. A ring of rocks with some charred wood in the middle was arranged about eight feet away. "You found it zipped up like this?" she asked.

"Yeah," Brandon chimed in. Hazel approached the tent and unzipped the entrance. She waited for a snarl of protest from John, but he didn't say anything. Hazel crouched down and stuck her head inside the tent. A sleeping bag was all laid out inside of it.

"Wherever Nina is, she didn't break down her camp before she left," Brandon explained. "She must be close by."

"How did you find it?" Jason asked.

Hazel scanned the items that had been left in the tent. Nina's pack itself was missing, but her cell phone was there, lying on the sleeping bag along with a book. Hazel's heart leapt into her throat. The book glowed the same purple color it had the day she had given it to Nina. She reached out and grabbed it. *Anna Karenina* by Leo Tolstoy. It felt sodden in her hands.

"It was Lance," John said. "He always was a resourceful kid."

Hazel froze for a second, flinching, then she withdrew her head and arms from the tent and stood back up.

"When was this?" Jason asked. He didn't try to hide the growl in his voice, but if John noticed it, he didn't react.

"Just this morning," he said. "Called it in to the station around five-thirty."

"That's awfully early," Jason said, slinky orange coiled around him. "What was he doing out at that hour?"

"Jason..." Hazel pleaded. He shot her a glare.

"Just trying to be a good guy, I expect," John said.

Jason's glare intensified, the orange deepening and engulfing more of him. "Or maybe he was looking for his lost brother."

Brandon's head snapped towards Jason, but John didn't respond. His eyes widened at the book in Hazel's hand. "Hey, I said don't touch anything," John reprimanded.

"You said you already took pictures." Hazel was grateful for the delay in John's reaction. She hoped that Jason would calm down.

She looked down at the thick book and held it out a little bit towards John. It had been soaked, and the pages were completely waterlogged. Hazel gingerly turned the pages. The print had run or faded on the edges of a lot of them. "What a shame," Hazel said.

"That's a hefty book to have taken on a backpacking trip," John commented.

Hazel nodded. "Yes, it's close to three pounds. Good thing I didn't give her the hardcover."

"Wait, what do you mean his lost brother?" John turned back toward Jason. Hazel cringed.

"Dansby Fuller is missing too," Jason said with a smug half smile. Streaks of yellow wove themselves through the aggressive orange surrounding him. "I wonder why Lance has failed to mention it to you."

"How do you know that?" John snarled, his own shade of orange irritation flaring up. The two colors clashed. Jason's was a rich, dark color, and John's was neon and glaring. It hurt Hazel's eyes to look at it.

She exchanged glances with Brandon. Jason and John worked together as the DA and police captain. They had the added dimension of a father/son-in-law relationship, since John had been Hazel's father figure growing up. There were often fireworks and shouting matches between them, and Brandon was no stranger to their dynamic. Hazel knew though that Jason was usually the more level-headed of the two, and that wouldn't be the case if they were discussing the Fullers.

"I talked to Lance last night, Uncle John," Hazel said. "He said that Dansby went missing about the same time as Nina."

John turned towards her, and his orange softened. "Do you think the disappearances are related?"

Hazel gave a small nod. "When I was at Nina's house yesterday, I was able to get onto her tablet and look at her Facebook account. Dansby and Nina had been messaging each other in the last few weeks. It looks like they were thinking about renewing a romantic relationship."

Brandon swore behind her. It occurred to Hazel for the first time that he wasn't that much younger than Nina and Dansby and Nora. She turned around. "Did you know them in high school?" she asked.

He flushed. "Well, no, not really. They were seniors when I was a freshman. But I knew *of* them. Everybody did. There was a pool going about whether or not she would be pregnant before they finished high school."

Hazel's mouth fell open. "Shame on you," she chided.

"I know it was awful," Brandon put his hands out, palms to the sky. "We were just stupid kids."

"I'll say," Hazel agreed.

"The point is," Brandon went on, talking around her to John. "They had a very intense relationship in high school."

"Okay," John said. "Let's get all this stuff back to the station, and then we'll see if we can't find Dansby through credit cards and whatnot. Let's not jump to any conclusions. We're just gathering facts for now."

"There's one other thing," Hazel said.

John looked at her with raised eyebrows.

"Jason and I came out here last night, just to look around. It was a little after dark, maybe nine thirty? We ran into Ranger Rick and a friend of his. They were carrying crates filled with some kind of plant down from the mountain. We overheard them talking about how they were lucky that you hadn't discovered it earlier that day while you were searching for Nina."

John's color changed again as he processed what she was saying. It turned dark, silver gray and then crystallized and turned hard. Hazel felt like if she reached out and flicked it with her fingers, it would shatter and crash around him. "You've got to be kidding me," he said.

Hazel shook her head. "Jason didn't think it looked like marijuana, if that helps."

John raised a bushy eyebrow in Jason's direction. "Well, I guess he would know." Hazel could practically read his mind. Something about hippie west coast drug addicts.

"I'll take care of it," he said, the lines around his eyes stood out against his pale skin, and Hazel had a sudden realization that Uncle John was aging. The idea made her think of the Fullers, and a spike of fear shot through her. If John were to lose his memory, it could be catastrophic. She shook the idea from her head and forced herself to focus on the task at hand.

"Let's go," John said, turning to Brandon.

"We'll help," Hazel added, glancing at Jason. His color had died down to a smoldering coal. He saw her looking at him and nodded. Hazel thought the exertion would help him work through his emotions.

"What did you find in the way of footprints?" John asked.

Brandon shook his head. "Nothin', sir. The storm must have erased anything that had been here."

John circled the remnants of the campfire, staring at the ground. "These must be Lance and your prints?"

"Yes, sir," Brandon said.

Hazel followed them on the ground with her finger. Around the campfire, up to the door of the tent, to and from the deer path. They were deep, muddy prints, made by big men after a heavy rain. Nina's prints would have been more shallow because she was a small woman, plus the ground would have been dry when she set up the tent. Finding them seemed pretty hopeless. Hazel walked the tree line at the edge of the clearing, looking for anything unusual on the ground. She just knew that Nina had to be close by.

"Go ahead and pack everything up," John instructed, handing gloves to Jason and Brandon. "Be real careful, just in case."

The men set to work rolling up the sleeping bag and breaking down the tent, but Hazel continued to search the ground.

"What about this?" Hazel asked. She saw the faintest pattern in the mud under a bush that had a little bit of shelter from the rain. John came over to study where she was pointing but after a minute he shook his head. "I don't think so," he said. "It looks like just some eddies in the dirt from where the water ran by."

Hazel nodded. Another fifteen minutes of searching yielded nothing. Hazel gathered the book and the phone and followed Brandon, John, and Jason, who carried the rest of the camping gear onto the deer path. Hazel was startled when John yelled, "Freeze," from up ahead of her.

She took a step to the side to peer around the men in front of her and saw a very frightened young woman ten feet ahead of them on the path. "What are you doing?" John demanded.

"I was out searching for the missing woman," the girl said. She had her hands above her head even though John hadn't pulled out his gun.

"All the way out here?" John asked. "What made you come out this way?"

"I wasn't, I mean, I was close, but then I heard voices, so I started in this direction."

Something about the voice was familiar to Hazel. She took a few steps closer. "Ermengarde McGee?" she asked.

The girl swore colorfully enough that it shocked Hazel. "Hi, Mrs. Dean," she said. "It's actually just McGee, remember?"

"What are you doing here?" Hazel demanded. "This is the local reporter," she explained to John without waiting for McGee to answer. John swore.

"My goodness, people," Hazel said. "Language."

"Are you following us?" John demanded.

McGee shrugged. "Is following people illegal?"

"Young lady," John said in his stern, paternal voice. "I hope you realize the damage you could cause by publishing details about an ongoing investigation. Don't they teach you anything in journalism school?"

"But this is a missing person case. If you don't utilize the press, you're doing yourself a disservice."

"That may be true in the suburbs," John said with obvious effort to remain calm. "But the squirrels are not going to read your articles and call us with tips. Now, you need to turn around, go right back down to your car and drive away. Otherwise, I will arrest you."

McGee tilted her chin up in a gesture of defiance, but she turned and walked back down the mountain in front of them. Hazel realized with cold dread how much the reporter might have overheard them discuss.

When the cars came into view, Hazel saw that the little gray Ford Focus she had noticed McGee in the day before at the Mitchells' house was parked behind her and Jason. Hazel marveled that the girl had got herself down the bumpy road in the tiny car. If she wanted to be an effective reporter in this area, she would probably have to switch to some kind of truck or sporty SUV with four-wheel drive. The little car would be wrecked driving down these dirt roads.

McGee turned around to look at them, but John just pointed at her car until she got into it. Then they watched without moving while she did a seven-point turn, then drove off down the dirt road. Only then did they walk down to load John's car with Nina's stuff.

"We'll move the main search hub up here," John told Brandon, as they loaded things into the Explorer. He slammed the door shut and stood staring at it for a moment.

"Something doesn't feel right here," he said finally, speaking to Brandon in a low tone. Hazel took a few steps closer so she could hear. John's whisper wasn't what it used to be. He was delusional if he thought she and Jason couldn't hear what he was saying. "If she just got lost, she would have had her campsite packed up and on her back. It looks like the girl just walked away from her tent and disappeared." He shook his head.

"I would guess she took her backpack with her," Brandon said.

"Or at least it wasn't at the campsite when you got there," John said. He glanced at his watch. "We've gotta go. The rangers are meeting us at the station to go over the procedures for the chopper and dogs. With any luck, we'll find the girl by the end of the day."

When they got in the car, they didn't notice that Hazel was still holding Nina's book and cell phone. Hazel didn't say anything about it. She and Jason walked back to the car and climbed in while John and Brandon pulled around them, bumping away down the dirt road. Once they were out of sight, Hazel grabbed the phone charger they kept in the car.

"Turn the car on!" she urged her husband.

"What the...? Hazel! Is that Nina's phone? Why isn't it in John's car with the rest of the camping gear?"

"Just turn on the car!"

Jason groaned but turned the key in the ignition. The car roared to life and the windows began to fog up immediately. Hazel plugged Nina's phone into the charger and watched it with burning eyes.

The screen remained blank and dark. Maybe it had gotten too wet during the storm. But it had been inside the tent, which was supposed to be waterproof. It couldn't have gotten wet enough to completely destroy it.

"This is not a good idea, Hazel," Jason said, massaging the bridge of his nose like he was avoiding a headache.

"We've gotta go meet Waylon," she said, not taking her eyes of the phone.

"Yeah," Jason said, putting the car into gear.

"Nina didn't just get lost," Hazel said. "Dansby's disappearance is too coincidental. I think he might have had something to do with it. Maybe they ran off together."

Jason's brow furrowed. "No," he said.

"What do you think happened to her?" she asked.

"I don't know," he said.

"Do you think she killed herself?"

Jason flinched. "I don't know, Hazel. Maybe she really did run off with Dansby. Maybe she stepped away from her tent for a walk and fell. She might be fine."

"Maybe," Hazel murmured.

"I do know," Jason said, reaching out to take her hand. "Whatever happened to her, it's not your fault."

Hazel looked at him and gave him a sad smile, but she couldn't bring herself to believe he was right.

TWELVE

"Waylon will be waiting for us at the trail head," Hazel said as they bumped back down the dirt road. "We're late."

"He'll wait," Jason assured her. "We're not far."

The morning was stunning. The sky was clear blue with puffy white clouds floating high above. Hazel had been in the woods only the previous morning, but she didn't remember seeing so many flowers blooming then. It was like they had blossomed overnight. Foliage had filled in a little more as well. The branches hanging overhead looked less stark, softer and more welcoming.

It gave Hazel a good feeling, like Nina was close. Her only concern was the temperature. It had dipped back down into the thirties the previous night, which wouldn't have been good for Nina.

They pulled to the side of the road when they reached the trail head. Hazel was surprised to see a canopy set up, one of the beat cops hanging out underneath it.

"Hi there, Otis," Jason called, as he slammed the car door.

"Hi, Mr. Dean, Miss Hazel."

"We're just here to help look for Nina Mitchell."

"Do y'all have a GPS watch or a fitness app on your phones?" he asked.

They nodded.

"Great. If you could turn it on and send us the route when you're finished, we're compiling all the information to get a complete picture of where we've already searched."

"Smart," Jason said.

"The forest ranger taught us to do that when we started the search a few days ago. I hear he got clearance to take the helicopter up today. You might hear it while you're out." Hazel felt a pang of suspicion. Was Ranger Rick helping them or trying to throw them off?

"That's great," she managed to choke out.

"I think they're going to get some dogs today too," he said, his face flushed with a pineapple yellow glow. "Thanks for your help, Mr. Dean, Mrs. Dean."

They nodded and left him behind. Hazel led Jason up a roughhewn stone staircase that was the first part of the trail. They were both winded when they reached the top, their breath turning to great puffs of steam.

"Hello, Hazel Dean."

Hazel stopped short, looking around her for Waylon. She couldn't see him but distinctly heard his voice. "Waylon?" she called.

"Oh, good, you heard it too," Jason said, letting out a held breath in another cloud of steam.

"I'm right here," Waylon said. Hazel stared into the trees where his voice was coming from but saw nothing until a flash movement caught her eye. Then he appeared, as if by magic, with a big smile on his face. Hazel's mouth fell open.

"Waylon, how did you do that?"

Waylon's emotional colors were unlike any others Hazel had ever seen. They camouflaged him, mimicking the colors in nature that surrounded him. Now he was the dappled brown and vibrant green that the trees were dressed in for spring. When she had first met him, on a dark night out in the woods full of scary noises, his desire to assure her he meant no harm showed up white: an innocent in the middle of the dark.

"You didn't see me," he grinned with childlike pleasure. "I fooled you."

"That was amazing!" she cried.

"You should have been a ninja," Jason told him.

He grinned again. "I've been waiting for you."

"Waylon," Hazel said. "They found Nina's campsite. Should we start from there? Or we can head in that direction from here? What do you think?"

"Where did she begin her hike?"

"Over at the Twin Pines trail head."

Waylon was quiet for a moment. "Show me her campsite."

Hazel was getting sick of driving down bumpy dirt roads. "Let's go," she said. "After we find Nina, I'm never driving down another dirt road again."

They passed Otis again going back to the car. Jason nodded at his surprised face. "We're just following a hunch," he explained. "We'll start our trackers over when we get down the road a little way."

Otis shifted his weight, turning canary yellow. "Um, we already have..."

"John and Brandon filled us in about the campsite," Hazel said, guessing his concern. "That's why we want to go out that way."

The yellow faded from Otis. "Oh, good," he said. "I wasn't supposed to tell anyone yet."

She gave him a smile. "Don't worry."

They spent another ten minutes in the car and fifteen on the trail to get to the campsite. It was easier to find this time.

Waylon walked to the middle of the clearing and turned in a slow circle.

"They took all of Nina's stuff back to the station, but the tent was right—"

"Here," Waylon pointed to the spot the tent had been.

Hazel looked at him and then down at the spot where the tent had been. There wasn't any matted down grass or imprint leftover from when the tent had been set up. She wasn't sure how Waylon had known. She exchanged a look with Jason.

Waylon walked around the clearing for several minutes. Jason and Hazel didn't take their eyes off him. Finally, Hazel couldn't stand it any longer. "No signs of a struggle?" she asked.

"Did someone take her?" Waylon shook his head. "No. Maybe someone came to see her, and she followed them. Maybe."

"Can you track her?"

"Look all around," he told them, gesturing at the trees that surrounded the clearing. "Listen to the earth, feel the trees, smell for unusual scents. The land will tell us where she went."

Hazel and Jason looked at each other while Waylon crouched to the ground. He leaned over and put his nose inches from the earth, inhaling and then turned his ear to the ground. He picked up a few brown mushrooms that had sprung up after the rain and popped them into his mouth.

Hazel was taken aback and didn't have time to wipe the horror off her face before Waylon noticed it.

"Wild mushrooms," he said. "They're very nutritious."

"I see," Hazel said.

"Go ahead." Waylon waved his arm around the clearing. "I need your help."

Jason shrugged at Hazel and then went to the opposite side of the clearing and copied Waylon's actions.

"Do you smell anything?" Hazel asked.

"I smell dirt," he said. "And rotting leaves. Actually, it's nice. We should get a candle."

"Oh, yes, dirt and rotting leaves. I'll look for it at Target the next time I drive into town." She wandered over to another part of the tree line and reached out a hand to feel the tree. She wasn't sure what she was looking for. She patted the tree up and down like she was frisking it, but it didn't yield any secrets about Nina's whereabouts. Whatever it was that Waylon could hear and smell, she couldn't. She doubted Jason would be able to either.

Instead, she crouched to the ground and studied it, looking for any markings in the mud, anything about it that might indicate a disturbance. She saw nothing. Hazel spent the majority of her life letting her vision interpret the world for her. Being able to see other people's emotions had made her neglect her other senses. It was too easy to just rely on sight.

She got a little closer to the ground, running her fingers along the hardening variations in the surface of the mud. She felt the different textures of the moss and the tree bark and the soft, squishy mud. She let the gluey, slick muck cover her fingers, causing them to stick together and make satisfying slurping noises. She took deep breaths to quiet her breath and her heartbeat so she could hear better.

The breeze blew lightly through the trees, creating a whoosh that amplified to a whistle with an occasional gust. Birds were twittering everywhere, causing a cacophony that was hard to hear over. Hazel closed her eyes, letting it wash over her. Jason was right—it did smell like dirt and rotting leaves, but there was more than that. It smelled green.

With her eyes closed, Hazel became more aware how the breeze caressed her face and sent her hair flying about in tickly strands. She felt the rays of the sun warm her where it fell on her skin and turned her face towards it, watching how the quality of dark behind her eyelids changed as she did.

Hazel blinked her eyes open. She understood why Nina wanted to come to the woods. It would be a good place to heal, to find renewed hope when life felt impossible.

The blanket of fluffy moss made a passable towel, and Hazel wiped the mud off her hand. The goop scraped off but left a fine layer of grit behind. As fun as it was to squish her hand into the mud, Hazel didn't like that gritty feeling. She wished for some running water to wash with.

As soon as Hazel thought of water, she realized that it was what the green scent was. She stilled herself again, closing her eyes and listening as hard as she could. She moved towards Jason, her ears straining.

"What are you doing?" he asked when she got close.

"Shh!" she hushed, moving slowly past him. "There!" she gasped. "Waylon, this way. There's running water."

She tried to move through the trees with her eyes closed, still intent on listening for the faint sound of water. After a good whipping from a shockingly flexible tree branch, she gave up and opened her eyes.

"Good job, Hazel," Waylon said, catching up to her. He smiled at her in a way that made her think that he had heard the water too and had just been trying to teach them something.

"We are in a hurry, Waylon," she reminded him, swallowing her irritation. "If Nina is hurt, then she needs medical attention as soon as possible."

Waylon nodded and strode ahead of her. Jason crashed through the trees a few steps behind her. The water wasn't as close as Hazel thought it might be. The sound of rushing water became louder and louder until Hazel realized that it must not have been a stream but a waterfall that she heard. The air grew cooler as they drew closer to the mountain side. Then they broke through the trees and an idyllic scene spread out before them.

"Wow," Jason breathed from behind Hazel.

They stood at the edge of a small lake. The waterfall crashed down across the lake from them. It wasn't astoundingly tall, but it was multi-tiered, the first drop being the largest and then with a cascade of five more smaller drops to the bottom of the valley. Despite how sheer the mountain side was, at the bottom where the smaller cascades were was a jumble of large rocks of various sizes. The waterfall ended into a small lake, slightly too big to be called a pond. Snow was visible in the crevices between the rocks where the waterfall didn't disturb it.

"I've been here before," Hazel said, reaching back into her memory.

"You have?" Jason asked. "When?"

"When I was a teenager." She glanced at him and then decided not to share that she had been there with Lance.

"Lots of people know this place," Waylon said. "It's not on any maps, but many people come here for water. I am surprised the police didn't come here right away from the campsite. I guess maybe they don't remember it."

"Yes," Hazel said, memories bubbling to the surface of her mind. "Yes, I remember. Kids partied here, drugs and stuff. So they demolished the trail in, thinking it would fix the problem. I guess it did, eventually. It doesn't look like anyone has been here for a long time. The trail came in from that direction," she pointed toward the top of the waterfall. "There's a way to climb down from the top. Well, there used to be. I don't remember the waterfall though; it was usually just a trickle."

"This is because of all the rain," Waylon said, sweeping a hand up towards the waterfall. "It isn't usually this strong." He approached the water. "The lake is always here though. It is deep."

"It looks frigid," she said. She approached the pool and put a fingertip in with her dirty hand. She pulled it out immediately, the temptation to wash her hand disappeared. "It is. It's ice cold, probably full of recent snow melt." She whipped her head around toward Jason. "You don't think she fell while she was getting water, do you? How fast would you die of hypothermia?"

"It's too murky," Waylon said. "I can't see from here."

Hazel looked around and saw him walking around the lake toward the base of the waterfall.

"But does that make sense?" Jason asked. "If she fell into the pond, she would have gone back to camp to warm up and change her clothes. She should have been able to survive something like that."

"Unless there was a reason why she couldn't get back there," Hazel said.

"But wasn't her pack missing?" Jason pointed out. "Wouldn't it be sitting right here if that's what happened?"

"Maybe it's still here," she said, looking around her. There was a bit of a clearing between the trees and the edge of the woods, almost like a beach. Fallen logs and rocks were everywhere. The pack could be hidden behind or between any of them. Hazel began weaving her way around them, looking for anything man made.

Meanwhile, her husband followed Waylon, who had walked all the way around the lake to the base of the waterfall. He carefully climbed up the rocks and steep hillside higher up the series of waterfalls. Seeing him climb the rocks reminded Hazel of how she and Lance and a few of their friends would jump from the lower rocks into the lake. Then they would spread themselves out, basking in the sun and munching on wild blueberries. She sighed, a part of her longing to go back to those simple, uncomplicated days.

She continued looking for Nina's backpack. From the size of the tent and the sleeping bag they found at her campsite, Hazel knew that it would be large with shoulder straps but also additional straps that clipped around her waist and across her chest. Hazel searched under logs and around the rocks. But her mind was by the waterfall, climbing higher with Waylon and Jason. That cold knot was back in her heart.

That's why, when her hand felt cold metal on the other side of a fallen log, it didn't register right away. She moved on, feeling the rest of the way down the log before she realized she had found something and went back to retrieve it. It was a silver lighter with a tree engraved into it. It was fancy, Hazel thought it must have been a gift. Nina didn't smoke. Did Dansby? What about Ranger Rick? She didn't know. She picked up the lighter and had a flash of a memory. Mike, standing outside the courthouse smoking before their city council meetings started. Hazel shivered and stuffed the lighter into her sweatshirt pocket.

"Mr. Jason?" Waylon called. His voice carried even over the rush of water. Hazel's eyes snapped towards him. He was on top of the highest boulder. How he climbed up there when it was so slick, Hazel couldn't guess. He was looking straight down into the water.

Hazel shivered. Goosebumps broke out all over Hazel's body. She looked down at the lake. It was clear and clean at the edge, but it became darker as it got deeper. A gust of spring wind disturbed the surface and sent ripples shimmering away from her. Hazel's eyes followed them across the lake and up to where Waylon was perched on the rocks high above it. A wave of panic cascaded over her. She gasped for air and struggled to keep her feet underneath her.

"Be careful!" she yelled, one decibel shy of a scream. They didn't hear her. They were too close to the waterfall's roar. But their voices carried across the water, and she could hear every word they said.

"Do you see something?" Jason called up to Waylon.

Waylon pointed a finger down toward the lake. Jason looked over the edge of the rock he was standing on. Hazel watched his brow furrow and then clear. He looked up searching for her. Finally, his eyes locked on to hers. In that look, Hazel knew what he had seen in the water below him. She felt dizzy. She turned away from the lake, reeling. She had been caught in a riptide of grief and horror. She stumbled to a log and collapsed onto it.

"Waylon, stay here. I'll be back in a minute," Jason said. "I need to take Hazel away."

THIRTEEN

The next hours went by in a surreal, blotchy blur. Flashes of images impressed themselves on Hazel's mind while other things passed by like soap bubbles. She knew what was happening, but her heart wouldn't accept it.

Waylon, standing above the water, looking down at the icy cold water below. A look of fear took over his face, his emotional colors still mimicking the world around him but this time in the dark colors of stone and water.

Jason, with his hand hard and unyielding against her back, pushing her away from the pool. His head clouded with forest green worry, clashing against the spring green leaf buds on the trees.

A shocking red cardinal perched on a tree branch in shades of brown and tan. It tilted its head as though it was watching her. His light chirruping noise echoed through the trees. Another cardinal replied in the distance. So, he spread his wings wide and took off into the forest.

John and Brandon came crashing through the trees, their combat boots trampling the underbrush into the mud. John flashed through the trees in shades of bright red and orange. Brandon's emotions were more grim: steel and soot.

Then Waylon's face close to hers, tears in his eyes, radiating a blue-green-black like the sky right before the sun goes down. Wasn't he down at the pool? Why was he here? He was going to find Nina.

The roar of a helicopter drowned out all birdsong with its mechanical rhythm. Its insect-like shadow blocked the sun and its warmth.

John murmuring in low tones to Jason, both wearing contrasting shades of concern. John's worry was restless and bright, Jason's dark and brooding.

And then she was on her feet again, with Jason at her elbow. She saw that their car was in sight. She had no recollection of leaving the clearing where Nina slept the last night of her life. She wouldn't have budged if she had been aware of what was going on.

All at once, everything came into sharp focus and became all too real. She felt like a rubber band that began to stretch the moment she saw that telling look on Jason's face. Now the rubber band had been released, and it snapped back to reality with devastating force.

The metallic flecks in the asphalt glinted in the sun, and the cars' chrome finishes glared at her, and her head throbbed. Everything was too colorful, including Jason. She closed her eyes against the onslaught and found her ears were full of the rushing of the helicopter even though it was long out of sight. The sound of birds was piercing. The sound of a snapping twig made her jump. She was relieved when she opened the door of her car and slammed it behind her. The car was a cocoon of silence, devoid of color.

Jason went around to the other side and got in. She didn't have the energy to tell him that the colors of his anxiety were giving her anxiety, so she just turned away from him. But she could still feel his constant worried glances in her direction.

They sat in the car for a long time. Jason clearly didn't know what to do for her. He grabbed her hand and ran his finger over her knuckles. She could barely feel it. Hazel didn't have anything to say. They watched as people came and went from the parking lot.

John and Brandon came back from the woods and Jason let go of her hand to get out and chat with them for a minute. When he got back in, he started the car and followed John and Brandon out of the parking lot.

When Jason didn't make the turn towards home, Hazel had a sudden panic. Not knowing became more unbearable than knowing. Her throat was sore and swollen, like she had been sobbing, but she didn't remember doing that. She swallowed.

"Where are we going?" she rasped.

"We're going to the station." He gave her a sympathetic look. "We're going to have to make some statements. Plus, I think John wants eyes on you. He's worried."

Hazel nodded. "Do they know..." Hazel couldn't finish the question.

"The assumption is that she was climbing up the rocks and that she slipped and fell," Jason's voice was tentative, like he wasn't sure he should be telling her anything. "Maybe she hit her head, and it knocked her unconscious, which is why she didn't get out of the water. John told me that it's all just guessing right now. They're going to do an autopsy to find the cause of death and get some forensic people out from Athens or wherever. Hopefully, at that point, they'll be able to rule out any foul play."

"Do you think Dansby was with her?"

Jason flashed orange. "Objectively?" he sighed. "There's just no way to know. We need to be patient, Hazel."

Hazel glanced at Jason. "Did they say how long they think she had been down there?"

Jason shook his head.

"She might have jumped," Hazel said, squeezing her eyes shut. She imagined Nina on top of the rocks, looking down at the lake. She couldn't imagine her jumping.

"Oh, Hazel, don't."

"Will they be able to tell? Are there ways they can tell in the autopsy?"

"Let's just not jump to conclusions," Jason said, grimacing at his choice of idiom. "We'll talk to John and see what he says."

Hazel was silent for several minutes, guilt coursing through her. She shoved her hand into the pocket of her sweatshirt and was surprised to touch something cold and hard. Her hand closed around the lighter she had found at the waterfall. When she felt it, heavy and real, in her hand, another idea presented itself to her like a lifeline. She pulled it out and held it up for Jason to see. "What about this lighter I found?"

"It might not have anything to do with Nina; another hiker might have left it there on a different occasion."

"I don't think so," Hazel said. "It didn't look like it had been sitting there all winter, it still works. And that waterfall isn't on the trail. You'd have to know about it to find it. Waylon said people knew about it."

"Maybe, Hazel, but—"

Hazel's mind was working a mile a minute now, making up for its period of catatonia. She couldn't accept that this was a senseless accident, and despite her suspicions since she found out Nina was missing, she couldn't fathom that she actually would have jumped from those rocks. "Even if she had wanted to kill herself, why would she have jumped? It's not high enough. We used to jump from those rocks for fun during the summer. Maybe she didn't jump or slip. Maybe she was murdered."

"What?" Jason looked at her with raised eyebrows. "Who would want to kill Nina?"

"Haven't you ever watched a movie before? If she was embroiled in a passionate affair with her high school boyfriend, anyone could have killed her! The lover, the husband. That crazy mother-in-law of hers. Maybe Ranger Rick to cover up his marijuana business."

Jason's face collapsed into a skeptical scowl. "It wasn't marijuana. And I can't imagine Mike—"

"People who know murderers never imagine they are murderers. Haven't you ever watched television?"

"Hazel, this isn't television; this is real life. Do you know how rare cold-blooded, premeditated murder is?"

Hazel pressed her lips together, but she allowed herself the small comfort that it was possible that Nina's death wasn't her fault.

"Hazel, I know that the last few days have been a lot for you. A lot of emotions and no sleep. The last couple hours have been even worse," Jason said in a soft voice after the silence in the car became deafening. "You need to rest. I know you want to help. The next few days are going to be hard for Mike and his family. He has a lot of decisions he's going to have to make. And if what you said about his mom is true, they're going to need some real help raising those kids, some kind of plan that will keep his mom from becoming a primary caregiver."

"Yes, of course," Hazel nodded. The thought of Trevor's sad face made her throat constrict. "The kids are the most important consideration right now."

"Let's just get this interview over with, and then you can go home and sleep. Get some rest so that you can be at your best for those kids."

Hazel nodded. "I couldn't sleep last night," she admitted.

"You are a good friend, Hazel," Jason said.

Hazel wiped the tears from her cheeks. She couldn't get emotional now. There was still too much to do.

They pulled into the parking lot, and Hazel spotted the gray Focus belonging to the reporter immediately. She sucked in a breath.

"What is it?" Jason asked.

"The reporter is here," she said.

They went into the building together, opening the doors into a frenzy of activity. John was nowhere to be seen, but Brandon stood behind the front counter and Otis was there, holding a clipboard, on the other side of the desk. A few other officers milled around Hazel knew only in passing.

"I'm sorry," Brandon said. "I know you've been through a lot. But you'll have to wait. He's in with the forest ranger right now. I'm not sure how long he'll be." He raised an eyebrow at Hazel and glanced towards McGee. Hazel understood he didn't want to say anything in front of the reporter.

She nodded, and she and Jason went to sit down on a long wooden bench that ran the length of the front window.

McGee was already sitting there, on the very edge of her seat, watching everything that was going on with wide eyes and her hands poised over the keys on a laptop. She gave Hazel a big smile.

"Did they find her?" she asked Hazel and Jason. "It got really busy here a few minutes ago."

Hazel didn't know what to say. She didn't exactly have a poker face. She generally wore her heart on her sleeve and was terrible at games like *One Night Werewolf* where you had to lie. No one even wanted to play it with her anymore. Luckily, Jason was a little more adept.

"You know, we can't really tell you anything until John does," he explained.

She nodded. "Yeah, I know. I just thought I'd ask. It never hurts."

They watched Brandon work, all with their ears perked up listening for any new information.

John appeared behind the counter. McGee was instantly on her feet.

"Captain Tate, are you ready to make a press release yet?"

"No," he said shortly. "Hazel and Jason, would you come on back here, please?"

They followed him down the hallway to his office. He closed the door behind them. Hazel and Jason remained standing; John collapsed into his chair with a deep exhale. The chevron orange irritation he often wore at work was tinged with maroon.

"That was an interesting interview," he said.

"What happened?" Hazel pounced. "Is he selling marijuana?"

"It wasn't marijuana," Jason said, looking up at the ceiling.

"I'm not going to discuss *that* ongoing investigation with you, Hazel," he said, rolling his eyes. "I think that the one is plenty."

"But they're related!" Hazel protested.

"Not for you, they're not," he said. He opened his desk drawer, took out a bottle of migraine medication and shook two into his hand.

"I'm sorry you're not feeling well, Uncle John," she said.

He looked around his desk for a water, but it was hidden behind a stack of file folders, visible to Hazel but not to him. She got up and grabbed it to hand to him.

"Thank you," he said, swallowing the pills and drinking the whole bottle. He sighed again and looked at her, the zig zags around him softened a bit. "Give me a minute," he said, closing his eyes.

Hazel shot a worried glance at Jason, who shrugged. She hadn't known her uncle as being a person who 'needed a minute.'

"Jason mentioned there was something you found at the scene." he asked.

Hazel pulled the lighter out of her pocket and handed it to him. "I found this by that little lake," she said. "I think someone might have been there with Nina. Maybe Dansby? Or Mike? Or it could have been Rick or his friends. I'm not sure." She set it down on his desk.

"Oh, Hazel," he said. "We'll dust it for prints, but... the autopsy is just a formality. It was suicide. Almost certainly."

It was exactly what Hazel suspected, but hearing John say it out loud took all the air out of her lungs. She couldn't make a sound. The sound of air was suddenly loud in her ears. Her vision tunneled, darkening around the edges. She blinked to try and clear it away.

"What makes you think that?" Jason asked.

John took on the patronizing tone that he always used with Jason when they talked about work. "Her pack was strapped to her. There were rocks inside. She was face down in the water instead of face up. The moss on the rock was intact, doesn't look like she lost her footing or tried to catch herself. This information combined with what we know about her mental state when she left on her hiking trip suggests suicide. Not to mention ninety-nine percent of deaths in the woods are either an accident or suicide."

Jason nodded. "Are you going to tell McGee? Is this going to be public knowledge?"

"I'll put her off until we get the results from the autopsy back and we know more. Hazel... look, I was wondering..."

Hazel looked at him through bleary eyes. Her body felt leaden. She was nauseous. "Yes?" she asked. It was unlike John to beat around the bush.

"I was thinking about Mike. I think this could really use a feminine touch. And seeing how there aren't any women on the force in Red Gap yet..."

Hazel stared at him.

"He wants you to tell Mike his wife is dead," Jason said. "I don't think it's a good idea, John. Hazel hasn't been handling any of this very well. She feels responsible."

"Responsible?" John scowled. "Why on earth would you feel responsible?"

Hazel opened her mouth and closed it again. She glared at Jason. It felt like he was tattling on her.

"She gave Nina that book?" Jason continued without waiting for an answer. "It's about a woman who is unhappy. Then she kills herself at the end."

"Oh, I see," John said, not sounding like he saw at all. "Now Hazel, I don't really think it's justified for you to blame yourself. It's just a book after all."

"I know," Hazel said, looking down at her shoes.

"But I understand if you don't feel comfortable talking to Mike. I'll do it myself, I just thought since you knew her, and there are kids involved..." he trailed off.

"John, I don't really think that's a great idea," Jason said. "Hazel's still trying to cope with all this. She needs a minute to process her own emotions."

"I'll do it," Hazel said. The last thing she wanted to do was process her own emotions. She needed to be doing something useful, to somehow make up for the part she played in Nina's death.

"Really, Hazel?" Jason asked. "Are you sure?"

"Yes, I'm sure. John's right; it will be better coming from me. Especially because I knew her. It's the least I can do."

"We've already been in contact with Nina's mom, Lynette. We would have been in contact with her earlier, but Mike didn't seem to have her information. She's on her way now. In light of the family support from both grandmothers, we don't need to call social services, but they have a lot of programs that can help with this sort of thing, so make sure you mention that.

Also see if they go to church. Often a church community is the best support system in times of loss."

"I remember," Hazel replied. "From when my parents died."

John flinched and went silent.

"People brought so much food we had to throw a lot of it away," Hazel remembered. The image of beautiful casseroles in the garbage was an image that brought back the grief of her parents' death. "There were flowers and toys. And kids who would stand near me without saying anything." Hazel shook her head. "But there were also so many kind, good people. I don't know what Grandmamma would have done without them." She leaned forward. "You were one of them, John. You saved us."

When he looked up to meet her eyes, she saw the shine of unshed tears. "I got there too late," he said. "I should have been there sooner."

"You were there when we needed you. Whenever we needed you."

Hazel got up out of her chair. "And now," she said. "We're going to be there for Mike and for Nina's kids. This whole community. It'll support and love them the way it supported me. Everything is going to work out." She walked around the desk and wrapped her arms around John's shoulders. "I love you," she said.

He patted her arm without saying anything. She straightened and squared her shoulders. "Please let me know when Lynette gets in; I'd love to speak with her."

Jason followed her out of John's office and back down the hall. McGee still sat on the bench where she was watching all the comings and goings of the station with wide eyes. Hazel looked away from her but knew she couldn't hide her somber mood.

As they opened the door to leave the building, she noticed

the reporter put her fingers to the keys and began to type furiously on her laptop.

FOURTEEN

"Do you want me to come with you?" Jason asked as Hazel pulled open the driver's door to her car.

"No," she shook her head. "I don't want to overwhelm him. I think it would be better if I went by myself."

"Alright, I'm going to go get some work done then. Or at least try," he grimaced. "Will you come back and pick me up later? My car is still at home."

"Yeah, I'll be back," she promised. She went to get into the car, but Jason stopped her and scooped her into his arms, hugging her tightly.

"I love you," he whispered. "I'm so glad you're safe and here with me."

Hazel closed her eyes for a moment but knew that it wasn't time for her to relax into her grief yet. "Me too," she said, pulling away from him. "I love you, too."

She climbed into the driver's seat, and he backed away. He held up a hand and watched as she drove out of the parking lot.

On the drive to the Mitchells' house, Hazel distracted herself with all kinds of thoughts. What they would eat for dinner, Elias' new girlfriend, an upcoming doctor's appointment. Anything but Nina at the bottom of that small, ice-cold lake. At one point, she glanced down and saw Nina's blank-screened phone still plugged into the car charger. A shudder shot through her.

When she arrived at the house, she pulled into the driveway and sat behind the wheel for a few minutes, finding her composure and thinking about what she would say. This would be one of the hardest things she'd ever had to do. She wondered who had broken the news about her mom and dad to her grandmother. Even though they died in a trucking accident as opposed to under mysterious circumstances, it couldn't have been much easier than this.

After one last deep breath, she climbed out of the car and made the long walk up to the front door. The sounds of children could be heard behind it again. She thought about how their lives would never be the same after this day, these next few minutes. The thought overwhelmed her, and she pushed it back down to the recesses of her mind. She had to focus on the task at hand.

She rang the doorbell. The panic she felt inside threatened to well up out of her throat. She was about to ring it again when the door swung open. Karen stood on the other side.

Hazel was relieved that she didn't have to interact with one of Nina's adorable children. She didn't know if she would have been able to maintain her composure with their innocent eyes staring up at her.

"Hi, Karen," Hazel greeted. "Is Mike around?"

"Yes, but he's sleeping," Karen replied.

"You'll want to wake him," Hazel said. "I have some news."

Karen's eyes widened, and she turned and practically ran into the house. Hazel didn't follow her. She preferred to talk to Mike in the privacy of the outdoors.

Mike looked a little bleary eyed when he came to the door, but he didn't seem sleepy. Hazel guessed that he was probably drunk. "What happened?" he demanded. Karen was one step behind him.

"Hi, Mike," Hazel said. "Would you mind stepping out here for a moment where we can talk in private?"

Mike turned around and looked at his mom. "Give us a minute," he muttered. He stepped out of the house onto the doorstep and closed the door behind him. He followed Hazel down a few steps, out of earshot of his mother.

"Mike, they found Nina," Hazel said. She was going for gentle but direct.

"Oh, thank God," Mike said. He looked like he might sink to his knees. The gray surrounding him ebbed, a little life returning to his features. "Where was she? Is she okay? She's at the hospital, right? Let's go!" he took a running step towards Hazel's car before she stopped him.

"No, Mike, no. Wait," she put a hand on his arm. Tears she couldn't stop fell onto her cheeks. "She, Nina..."

"No," he interrupted, the dull gray overwhelming him again. "No, please." His eyes were so imploring, Hazel almost didn't finish.

"She wasn't alive when they found her. She's gone."

Mike stared at her. "You can't be serious."

"I'm so sorry, Mike," she said.

The emotion he had displayed so nakedly the moment before was gone. His face went slack, his entire aura paled to ivory. He didn't say anything. He didn't look at her. He turned back towards the house and stared at it.

Hazel waited, knowing that sometimes just having someone stand next to you was all that held you up.

"How am I going to tell my kids?" he finally asked.

"You'll find a way," she assured him. "You'll know what to say." She took a deep breath. "When my parents died, my grandmama had to tell me. She held me close to her and told me that my mom and dad were back in Heaven with God and that He wanted her to take care of me. She told me my parents would always watch over me and how much they loved me. And that I would never, ever be alone."

Mike blinked at her. "I didn't know you lost your parents when you were young."

"I was angry at her and God for a while, but overall, it wasn't the worst way to have the conversation, if you believe in God. Just make sure that they know they will be taken care of."

"Honestly, I don't even know them all that well." Mike ran his hands through his hair. "I always thought that Nina would parent them when they were little, and I would step in more as they got older. Oh, Nina!" he strangled a sob.

"It's not too late to get to know them better," Hazel said.

"I've got to get my mom away from them," he said.

Hazel blinked in surprise.

"She's not the best with kids," he said. "She has a bit of a temper."

Hazel didn't know what to say.

"I never wanted my kids to have a childhood like mine," he went on. "I was an only child. Neither of my parents took much notice of me. They had other interests. I was just an accessory, so I was lonely. Then I met Nina, and we wanted a big, happy family—" he broke off, a sob tearing through his throat. Hazel put a hand on his arm, but he broke away.

"I wasn't a good husband," he said, violet dusk overtook him, obscuring his face. "I know I wasn't. I know she was unhappy. I didn't know how to make her happy. I tried at first, I did. I read that *Love Languages* book. Hers was time. I spent lots of time with her. But she didn't respond. I tried the other love languages. I had a goal for a while of doing something for her from each one every day. But nothing I did worked, and I guess I just gave up after a while. I'm such an idiot."

Hazel jumped at the sound of tires squealing on the asphalt as a beater car came tearing around the corner. She and Mike watched in confusion as it pulled onto the lawn and a man jumped out of it. He approached Mike, screaming profanities. Hazel watched him with wide eyes and then had a flash of recognition.

"Dansby," she exclaimed. "How did you—What are you doing here?" Her amazement at his sudden reappearance evaporated when the roiling blood red cloud surrounding him expanded to envelop her and Mike.

"I heard!" Dansby screamed. He completely ignored Hazel directing all his vitriol at Mike. "I know about Nina. I loved her, you worthless piece of garbage. *I* loved her. What did you ever do for her? Huh? Except knock her up and then ignore her."

"Dansby, calm down," Hazel said.

"Calm down?!" he yelled in Hazel's face and then turned back to Mike. "We were going to run away together. Did you know that? Did she tell you? You didn't deserve her. And now she's dead!" Dansby screamed, throwing himself at Mike. Before Mike could react, Dansby had connected a solid right hook.

Mike recoiled, his hand flying to his face, that Hazel could tell was already swelling. He took several steps backward. "What is your problem?" he yelled. "*I* should be punching you. It's your fault she even went into the woods to begin with. *You're* the reason she's dead."

"Me?" Dansby clenched his fists. His body was heaving and shaking. Sweat poured down his face. Hazel could see shaky rust-colored waves rolling over him, consuming him. "You ruined her life! This is all your fault! Everything, all of it, everything bad that ever happened to her is because of you."

Dansby's rusty waves overwhelmed his features in a vibrating blanket. It looked like an angry version of static on an old television set. Hazel couldn't see his face anymore, just his fists clenching and unclenching. She glanced at the front door, hoping that the yelling wouldn't be heard inside the house, that no one would come outside.

"You're just a deadbeat loser. Nina saw that, that's why she ended up with me instead of you to begin with," Mike said in a frigid voice.

She felt a knot of fear well up in the pit of her stomach. Mike didn't seem to understand how dangerous Dansby was. His desperation was obvious to her, but Mike didn't see it. She didn't dare interfere. In a slow fluid movement, so neither of them would notice her, she reached into her pocket and grabbed her phone.

A visceral scream tumbled out of Dansby, and he lunged again at Mike. This time Mike was prepared enough to dodge the blow. In his anger, Dansby had fully committed to the attack and lost his footing when he didn't connect. Mike took advantage of his momentary imbalance to land a punch in his gut.

Hazel pressed the home button to unlock the phone and tapped contacts and then John's name. It took less time than it took Dansby to recover his breath. Mike stood over him. He looked down with a smug smile on his face. "It was the luckiest day of Nina's life when I walked into that Chick-Fil-A because it kept her from waiting around forever for you. You're the one who ruined her life." Then he turned his back on Dansby to walk away.

Doubled over, Dansby swung his hair out of his eyes. He shot a look of pure hatred at Mike. Hazel had never seen anything like it. Her hand with the ringing phone in it dropped away from her ear. She backed away from Dansby.

"Mike—" Hazel yelled.

Dansby ran at full speed, attacking Mike's knees football style. Mike went down hard. His head hit the cement with a loud crack. Hazel screamed. Mike rolled slightly to one side, groaning.

"Hello? Hello? Hazel, are you there? What's wrong?" she could hear John's voice coming out of her phone.

"John, come quick," she whispered into the phone while she watched Dansby climb on top of Mike who made vain attempts to crawl away. She could tell that he was disoriented and reeling.

"Dansby Fuller attacked Mike," she hissed with desperation. She watched Dansby reach his hands around Mike's throat. "Dansby, no!" she yelled. Forgetting her concern for her own safety, she dropped her phone and ran over to the men, clutching at Dansby's arms. "Don't do this!" she cried, a panicked sob tearing at her throat. "No, Dansby, don't."

Mike's eyes were wide and terror-stricken. He clutched at Dansby's hands but couldn't get a good enough grip to rip them from his throat.

Dansby ignored her and lifted Mike slightly off the ground by his throat and then slammed him back down. Mike went limp. Hazel knew that John would get there too late. Dansby was going to kill Mike.

"Dansby, what about your mom? What about your dad?" Dansby blinked, hesitated for a moment. The staticky rust wavered. Hazel knew that she was on the right track.

"They need you, Dansby," she pleaded. "Your family needs you. You can't do this."

Dansby turned to look at Hazel, she could see him more clearly through his emotion now. "But Nina..." he trailed off, tears streaming down his face.

"I know," Hazel said. "I know. She's gone." Uttering those words was like ripping a Band-Aid off her skin and pouring lemon juice on the wound. Her voice cracked, and she began to cry.

All the fight left Dansby. The rust was flooded over by a new blanketing emotion, this one a deep, dusky violet. "Nina..." he moaned. He released his hold on Mike's throat and fell off him onto the ground sobbing. "Nina, Nina," he said over and over.

Hazel kept one eye on Dansby. His grief was contagious; Hazel was tempted to give in to it herself. To let herself sit down and sob next to Dansby. Maybe to tell him that it was her fault and let him try to kill her too. To explain about the book.

But then Hazel thought about Nina's kids. They needed Mike. She tried to see if he was okay or not. That last hit had knocked him unconscious. Blood pooled on the ground underneath his head. She tried to remember the basic first aid class she had taken twenty years previously. There was so much blood she couldn't see exactly where the wound was. She touched his head gingerly, wondering if it was even a good idea to apply pressure to a blunt force trauma wound. A bone deep helplessness overcame her. Hazel's lungs began to feel like they were being squeezed. She couldn't breathe.

"It's my fault," Dansby began to whimper. "It was me."

Hazel let go of Mike and leaned towards Dansby. She knew he wouldn't remember her, but he didn't seem to care who she was. He was completely overcome by his emotions. "No, no," she said. "It wasn't anybody's fault." She spoke to herself as much as to Dansby. "Nina was ill. She needed help that she couldn't get. It was no one's fault."

Dansby clung to her. He buried his face in her shoulder and sobbed. "I loved her," he moaned. "Oh, Nina, Nina."

His keening was interrupted by Karen's scream and the wail of police sirens.

FIFTEEN

I t took Hazel several minutes to pull herself together and extricate herself from Dansby. He was still a crumpled, sobbing heap on the driveway, the fight completely gone out of him.

Hazel crawled over to where Mike was lying unconscious and tried again to remember what needed to be done for him. That was when Karen decided to come out of the house and see what was going on.

"What are you doing?" she screamed at Hazel, pulling on her arm. "You're killing him! You're killing him!"

"I'm trying to help him," Hazel tried to explain in a calm voice, but Karen didn't hear her. She didn't even seem to register who Hazel was.

"Stay away from my baby!" she screamed at Hazel again.

Without warning, Karen took off across the street, still screaming. Hazel tried to see what had set her off. If she leaned forward far enough she could see McGee was sitting across the street with her little car. Hazel hadn't noticed her before but wondered how long she had been watching the scene. Had she followed Hazel there from the station?

"Who are you!?" Karen screamed, rushing across the street to confront her. "Is this entertaining to you?" Karen continued yelling. "Huh? Why are you sitting there watching us?" Hazel almost felt bad for the reporter as Karen picked up a few landscaping river rocks and threw them at McGee until she drove off. Then Karen came back over to where Mike was, clucking and pacing, but not touching him at all.

Hazel thought that Dansby might run off when they could hear the sirens in the distance. He had stopped crying by then and was staring into space, but he didn't budge.

Hazel had blood all over her clothes. It had soaked into the skin around her fingernails. It had left a sticky smear down the side of her arm. She had always imagined that if she was exposed to this much blood, she would vomit, but she didn't. She felt nothing. She sat on the driveway in front of Mike's house and watched as John put Dansby in the back of a squad car and paramedics loaded Mike into an ambulance.

Hazel was glad that Dansby was cuffed and in the squad car by the time Karen realized he was the responsible party. She wasn't sure if Dansby was bereft enough at that point to not retaliate if she were to start kicking him with her pointy alligator skin shoes.

Hazel felt that her insides had been completely drained. There was no emotion left inside her. Not for the first time, she wondered what she would see if she were able to use her ability on herself.

Karen, on the other hand, had enough color for both of them. She still hadn't stopped screaming. She hovered around the paramedics, sobbing and shrieking, until one of them gave her some kind of sedative. Hazel watched Karen's color go from highlighter shades of orange and pink to salmon as the drugs kicked in. She got in the back of the ambulance to go to the hospital with Mike, evidently forgetting all about her four very young grandchildren in the house.

Hazel pulled her phone out of her pocket. Unlocking it left a bloody smear across the screen. Hazel wiped her hand on her coat and tapped Lance's name.

Lance answered with a groan.

"I'm sorry. Are you asleep?" Hazel asked.

"It was a long night and day," Lance said.

"Well, it's going to be another long night," Hazel sighed. "Dansby is under arrest."

"What? Why? Where?"

"I was breaking the news to Mike about his wife when Dansby appeared out of nowhere and attacked him. Mike is unconscious and on his way to the hospital now. Dansby is in the back of a police car."

"You can't be serious."

"I am sitting on the Mitchell's driveway covered in Mike's blood."

Silence. Then, "Hazel, I'm so sorry; I feel responsible."

"I just thought you should know," she replied. "You might want to go down to the station. They'll be there soon."

"Yeah, I will."

"How are you doing? Are your parents going to be okay?"

"I don't think I'm going to tell them," Lance said. "It wouldn't be the first time I've lied about Dansby getting arrested."

"Alright," she said, feeling unsettled. "I hope everything works out okay for your family."

"Yeah, me too," he said. "Thanks, Hazel. I know that you'd do anything to help. I really appreciate it. Having a friend like you right now... well, I don't know what I'd do without you."

"Call me if you need anything," she answered.

"I will."

The conversation left Hazel feeling frustrated and helpless. She made another call.

"Hello? Hazel, what's going on?" Nora said. "Any news? I've been waiting by the phone."

"It's such a long story," Hazel said. "I'm going to have to fill you in later." She just wasn't up to giving yet another person the news about Nina's death. She would tell her in person when she came to pick up the kids. "How was watching Nina's kids yesterday?"

"It was great, actually. They're such sweet children. They have excellent manners. I wish we had gotten our kids together more often before."

"I'm so glad to hear it," Hazel said. "Is there any way you might take them again this evening? Maybe for an overnight stay?" The ambulance started its engine and its sirens. They echoed through the street as it drove away.

"Oh, no, Hazel, what's happened?" Nora's voice rose an octave.

"I can tell you when you get here. Is Sam home yet?"

"He'll be here in fifteen."

"Okay, I'll wait here until you come. Nina's mom just got into town too, so maybe I can talk her into staying the night with them. We'll see. She's a little wary of Mike and his mom, so she might be reluctant."

"We don't mind at all! Harley and Jamie will be absolutely thrilled to have a sleepover with their new friends. I'll call Sam right now and hurry him along."

"Thanks, I'll see you soon," Hazel said and hung up the phone just as John was approaching her with a reflective emergency blanket.

"Here. You're in shock," he said, wrapping it around her shoulders. "Uh, Nina's mom, Lynette, is a basket case back at the station. Brandon is sitting with her."

Hazel nodded, hearing the unasked question. "I'll connect with her back at the station. I'd really like to go home and shower first."

"I think that would be wise," John said. "You're a mess."

Hazel nodded towards the car. "What's going to happen to him?"

John shook his head. "Foolish boy. He's on the hook for aggravated assault. It looks like Mike will pull through, but if he didn't, it would be second degree murder."

"But he's going to be okay, right?" Hazel asked urgently, clutching John's arm.

"They're both lucky that the hospital is in town. If we were farther away, it would be much less hopeful. I think he'll be okay since the paramedics got here so quick."

"Thank goodness," Hazel said. "The last thing those kids need is to lose both their parents." They fell into a solemn silence, and Hazel knew that like her, John was thinking about her parents.

"How did Dansby find out about Nina?" Hazel wondered after a few moments.

John groaned, orange chevron instantly appearing around him.

"What?" Hazel asked.

In answer, John got out his phone and opened it up before handing it to her. It was a twitter feed following #wheresNinaMitchell. The most recent tweet was by EMcGeeReporter: 'Sitting at the police station watching the drama unfold. Nina's body was recovered. All signs point to suicide.'

Hazel almost threw the phone in frustration. "How dare she! You should throw her in jail."

"If only I could," John lamented. "I would love to. Unfortunately, Miss McGee hasn't actually broken any laws."

"She's acting out of some sort of deluded sense of responsibility. She thinks she's helping."

"I'll take her by to see Mike in the hospital," John said. "Off the record," he added when Hazel put up a finger. "Maybe that way, she'll realize that we're not being secretive just because we're corrupt government bureaucrats."

Hazel nodded. "I hope Nora hasn't seen it. I was going to break the news in person."

"Are you ready to go get cleaned up?" John asked. "I can drive you home if you're too shaky still."

"Miss Karen has forgotten that there are four young children in the house," Hazel said. "They need looking after. Nora's on her way, but she'll be a few minutes and I don't want to check on them in my current state." She indicated her blood splattered clothes and skin. "You're going to have to do it."

John paled. "They'll be fine for a few minutes, don't you think?"

"There are four of them, the oldest is seven. No, I don't think they'll be fine for a few minutes."

John turned around. Otis was digging through the trunk of the squad car.

"John, just go sit with the kids," Hazel said. "They don't even know their mom is missing. They think she's on an extended hiking trip. Just tell them their daddy took a little fall and that Mimi went with him to the hospital. You can tell them Nora's coming to get them for another play date. They'll love that, they were there yesterday."

John nodded, wiping his palms on his pants. "Sure," he said, beads of sweat forming on his bald head, "no big deal, just a few kids."

"You're fine with Jeremiah and Elias."

John furrowed one eyebrow at her. "That's different... they're... I don't know... mine. And there's only two of them, and they're older. Little kids are fine when their mom is around if they start crying."

"You'll be fine," Hazel said. "Go ahead."

John slowly walked up to the front door and then entered without knocking.

Hazel wished very much that she could see what happened inside the house. Instead, she watched as Otis donned a coverall including shoe covers and blue latex gloves, then put on a pair of goggles and grabbed a towel before walking towards her. When he got kind of close, he tossed her the towel. He caught her raised eyebrow and shrugged.

"Protocol," he said, then he set to work cleaning up the blood on the driveway.

Hazel tried to clean off some of the blood with the towel, but it wasn't a very absorbent one and it just smeared it around even more. He was still working on it when Nora showed up in her minivan. When she got out, Hazel realized that she probably should have prepared her better for what she looked like. When Nora got closer to Hazel, she let out a little scream.

"What happened?!" she screeched, keeping a good twelve feet away from Hazel.

"There was a...an altercation, I guess you would say. I was in the wrong place at the wrong time. Dansby Fuller came out of nowhere and attacked Mike."

Nora's mouth fell open. "No," she gasped. "Why?"

"I'm afraid so," Hazel said. "Come sit for a minute."

Nora sat a good distance away from Hazel.

"Nora, they found Nina."

Nora's hand flew to her mouth, her face crumpling like she already knew what Hazel was going to say. She turned deep, ocean blue.

"She didn't make it," Hazel stammered.

Nora didn't remove her hand from her mouth. She squeezed her eyes shut tightly and gasped. "I hoped..." she didn't finish the sentence.

"I'm so sorry, Nora," Hazel said.

Nora shook her head quickly. "I wish you hadn't told me that right now. How am I going to care for the kids like this?"

Hazel gave her a sad smile. "The reporter already posted about it on Twitter. I didn't want you to find out that way."

"Is Mike okay?"

"I don't know yet," Hazel said. "They took him to the hospital. His mom went with him; that's why I called you to come get the kids."

"Do they know what happened?"

"John's in the house sitting with them right now. I think he told them that their daddy fell and had to go to the hospital but that he would be okay. Who knows though."

"Captain Tate is in there with the kids?" Nora asked.

"Yes."

Without another word, she rushed toward the house. Hazel realized that she had better make herself scarce. Her joints were stiff and complaining as she got up off the ground and made her way to her car. She slammed the door just in time.

Nora reappeared, carrying a toddler on one hip. Her other hand stretched out behind her, holding on to a toddler, who held Trevor's hand, who held Naomi's hand. John followed, carrying child booster seats for the car. He quick stepped around them towards the van.

Hazel realized that even without her gory presence in the driveway, it still looked pretty grim. Clyde hadn't cleaned the driveway yet, and there was a pool of blood where Mike's head had lain. The kids looked hesitant in their cadence so Hazel rolled down her window so she could hear what was going on.

"Alright," Nora's sing song voice rang out. "No cheating. If everyone keeps their eyes closed while we get into the car and drive away, we'll make ice cream sundaes with Harley and Jamie at my house." The children cheered, all had big smiles on their faces. Nora took a circuitous route, leaning into the game.

"Okay," she said when they got to the van. "Here we are at the car. Now you have to use your sense of touch to climb in and find your seats. I'll buckle you up."

Once she buckled all the children in, she came around the car to her door and waved at Hazel before she got in. Then she made a telephone with her hand and mouthed the words 'call me.' Hazel waved back and nodded.

As Nora drove away, John approached Hazel.

"I'm going to drive you home," he said.

"That's not necessary," she told him.

"Yes, it is," he said. "You're in shock. You don't realize how shaken up you are."

"I'm fine," she said.

"I don't care if you are fine," John said. "I'm still driving you home. Besides, someone needs to make sure the boys don't see you like this. They'll be scarred for life."

Hazel had to admit that was a very good point, so she got out and moved to the passenger's side of the car.

John started the car and pulled a U-turn to head to her house.

"I should never have asked you to come here," he said after a few minutes of silence.

"Why not?" Hazel asked. "Were you supposed to foresee that Dansby would somehow find out about Nina then snap and attack Mike while I was standing there? Don't be ridiculous."

"I'm getting old, Hazel, old and lazy. I didn't want to have to do a distasteful part of my job, so I pawned it off on you." He shook his head. "It's shameful."

Hazel's eyebrows drew together. "I think what actually happened is that you recognized that your skill set didn't work in a delicate situation, and you used the resources available to you to make sure that your job was executed well. It's the kind of thing people put on their resumes."

John half-smiled. "Maybe you're right. But I feel like a coward."

Hazel patted his arm. "You're not a coward, Uncle John. How did it go with the kids?"

John smiled. "The younger ones were pretty star-struck that I was a policeman. They wanted to see my handcuffs. I cuffed each of them, but they're so little their hands slipped out. I showed them my walkie-talkie and my badge. Thought I probably shouldn't get out the gun though."

"Yes, that was probably for the best," Hazel said.

"The oldest one though, the little girl, I think she realizes that something weird is going on. She was very quiet and seemed nervous. She perked up a little bit when Nora got there, but I'm worried about her. She reminded me of you. You know, when you were little."

"Really? Was I that sweet?"

John looked at her sideways.

"Sounds like you were a hit." Hazel said.

John turned bubblegum pink. "Oh, I don't know about that..."

"Have you ever thought about doing some kind of kids' event down at the station?"

"Actually, I did think about it when your boys were younger, but it never turned into anything."

"Maybe it's a project Brandon could help you with." Hazel mused.

"Yeah, that could be good," John said, smiling to himself.

John slowed down as he went up the hill to Hazel's house. "Let's make sure your boys aren't out in the yard before we pull in," he said, slowing down even more as he approached the driveway. It was the second day in a row Hazel hadn't been around to parent her children. She wondered what kind of destruction awaited her in the house. Elias' car was sitting in the driveway, and Jeremiah had left his bike on its side on the front lawn. John pulled the car in right behind Elias'.

"You stay right here," John said. "I'll pull them into the

backyard to play some football or something. Wait ten minutes and then come in through the garage. Do you have any towels in there or anything? Don't touch anything."

"I know how to handle messes, John. I'm a mom, remember?"

John grimaced at her and then stepped out of the car. Hazel did as he asked and waited a full ten minutes because she really didn't want her kids to see her all blood-splattered. She didn't even like them watching movies with blood splatter.

She tiptoed into the garage and found an old rain slicker she could use as a robe. She stripped out of her bloody clothes and put them into a plastic grocery bag. She tied it off and hung it on a hook. She would deal with them later. She slipped into the rain slicker and tied the belt, then slowly opened the door and tiptoed into the mud room.

She froze, listening carefully. She didn't hear anything. She slipped down the hall, past the kitchen and through the family room to the back stairs. She could hear John's voice in the backyard as she ascended the stairs so it added to her shock when she got to the top and found Elias sprawled out on the loft couch with his girlfriend. Hazel was so shocked that her brain didn't immediately recognize their activity as kissing.

At first, she thought that perhaps Emma had tripped and accidentally fallen on top of Elias. Or maybe there was some kind of medical emergency and she was giving him mouth to mouth. Then, the horror of witnessing her son's make-out session with his girlfriend sunk in.

Hazel screamed.

They flew apart as though they were the wrong sides of a magnet.

"Mom!" Elias said, the reddest he had ever been in his life.

"Hi, Mrs. Dean," Emma said, as though nothing was unusual about the situation. Her casual tone was betrayed by the bright crimson she exuded.

Hazel crossed her arms over her chest. The rain slicker made a squeaking noise. "We're going to have to come up with a few rules," she said.

"What's wrong?!" John's urgent voice called from the bottom of the stairs.

"Downstairs, now!" Hazel shouted, pointing emphatically at the stairs. Then she called to John. "Everything's fine, Elias and his girlfriend are coming down to play soccer."

The teenagers got off the couch and shuffled past her. "I like the look, Mrs. Dean," Emma said. "Very edgy, very on trend."

Hazel didn't attempt to hide her eye roll. The only thing keeping Hazel from losing her temper completely was that Elias had been so embarrassed he neglected to notice the blood soaked into Hazel's hand.

SIXTEEN

With the girlfriend safely sent home for the evening and Hazel clean again, she and John drove back over to the station. John laughed uproariously when she told him about stumbling upon Elias and Emma kissing.

"Why are you laughing?" she asked heatedly. "It was horrifying."

"They were just stealing a little kiss," John said. "No harm done."

"No harm done!? Elias is young and innocent. That girl is corrupting him."

John raised a bushy gray eyebrow. "Hazel, you are not stupid, don't pretend to be."

"Making out is not harmless!" Hazel protested. "It leads to other things."

"Hazel, I caught you and Lance kissing in a parked car more times than I can count."

Hazel fell silent. Making out with Lance in the backseat of her falling apart car was the last thing she wanted to remember

at that moment. "That was different," she said with an impe-
rious sniff. "We were idiots."

John just laughed again.

"John, why did you like Lance? Why didn't you want to take
him out back and shoot him?"

John leaned back, pondering the question. "You know, I
guess it was because I always believed that the two of you
would end up getting married."

Hazel smirked. "You assumed I would marry my high
school sweetheart? Who even does that?"

"Well, your mom and dad for two."

Hazel fell silent.

"You and Lance were good for each other; you took care of
each other and encouraged each other. Neither of you could
have accomplished what you did in high school and beyond
without the other's support."

"Just like I have with Jason now," Hazel pointed out.

John shook his head and sighed. "I know you're right. Just
because he and I are so different doesn't mean I can't see that,"
he said. "It's not like you can only achieve that in a relationship
once. I believe it's a skill."

"How come you never got married, Uncle John?" Hazel asked.

Now it was John who smirked. "I don't have that kind of
skill set," he said. "I can't be bothered helping some woman
achieve her goals."

Hazel looked at him sideways. He had turned a dusky violet
highlighted by shades of crimson and indigo. She didn't believe
him. John was a romantic at heart.

"Are you okay to put this Lynette woman up tonight?" John
asked.

"Sure, yeah, I figured that's what would end up happening
when she said she was coming to town."

They pulled into the station. The parking lot was packed.

Hazel followed John in, wondering what she would find inside. John walked through the lobby to his office without pausing, but Hazel stood at the door and took in the room.

The first thing she noticed was a chubby, peroxide blonde woman talking to McGee. She hoped that it wasn't Lynette; nosy reporters were the last thing Nina's mom would need. Hazel took a step towards them to chase the reporter off, but the next thing she saw distracted her completely.

Lance was standing at the counter trying to talk to Brandon, but he was beyond talking. Encased in waves of midnight blue and sea green, he shot loud, terse sentences bordering on aggressive at Brandon. Brandon caught Hazel's eye and sent her an expression that said 'help!'

Hazel approached her old friend. "Lance?" she said, reaching out to touch him gently on the shoulder. He whirled around. His hair was a mess, he had deep circles under his eyes, which had a wild look to them.

"Hazel!" he exclaimed, grabbing her into a desperate hug. "I'm so glad you're here. You can fix this."

"What's going on?"

"It's Dansby," he said, rubbing his face. "They won't let me take him home."

Brandon looked apologetic. "Hazel, it's the rules. He was arrested for aggravated assault. The judge will set bail at the arraignment, but that's not going to be until tomorrow at least. And—" Brandon looked at Lance and shut his mouth but he gave Hazel a shrug.

"Lance," she said. "You need a lawyer."

"Do you think your husband might help us?" Lance asked. He was still holding on to Hazel's arm like he might fall if he let go. "The only other lawyer I know is Jolene. Are you two still friends?"

"Have you been in contact with Jolene?" Hazel asked.

Lance shook his head. "I haven't talked to anybody. I just

came straight here when I got off the phone with you, but they won't let me see him."

Hazel grabbed his hands in both of hers. "Lance, look at me," she said. He focused on her face with tortured gray eyes. "If you can't see Dansby, then you need to go home," Hazel told him. "You need to sleep, and you need to be with your parents. There's nothing you can do here today. Wait until tomorrow. You'll be able to see Dansby then." She shot a questioning look at Brandon who shrugged again.

"You might be able to see him then," she hedged. "At least you'll be able to at the arraignment." She looked at Brandon for help again. He nodded that time.

"I hate to leave him here all alone," Lance worried.

"He won't know that you've left," she said. "Did you see him pass by? Were you here when he got here?"

"Hazel, it was awful. There was so much blood. Was that Nina's husband's blood?"

Hazel nodded.

"What're we going to do?" Lance said, his focus drifting from her face.

"Lance," Hazel's voice came out clipped and assertive. "Go home. Go to sleep."

"Okay, okay," he said, shaking his head quickly as though to clear it. "You're probably right."

Hazel patted his back gently and guided him towards the door. "Come by the bookshop tomorrow. I'll try to come to the arraignment with you, and I'll talk to Jason about it."

He turned towards her, taking her shoulders in his hands and leaned down to kiss her on the cheek. "Thank you, Hazel," he said in her ear. She could smell his breath and his unwashed hair. It was so familiar. Her breath caught in her throat. "I was an idiot. Back then. When I let you marry someone else. I wish..."

Hazel shook her head. He was so close that her cheek brushed the stubble on his chin. "Stop," she said.

He dropped her shoulders and took a step back. Smoky violet pulsed on his chest but the rest of him was crimson.

"Right," he said, blindly felt for the door handle before he turned around. "I'm sorry. Thanks for everything." With the last word, he turned and fled.

Hazel's heart was pounding. Her hand came up to her cheek where Lance had kissed her. It felt hot. She looked around her and noticed that everyone in the room was looking at her except the woman she suspected was Nina's mom. She needed to recover before she became the victim of the rumor mill.

Hazel moved to stand over McGee and the blonde stranger, who radiated a cloud of smoky dark blue.

"Are you Lynette?" Hazel asked.

"Who's asking?" She looked up and Hazel could see that her make-up had run all over her face, making her look like a melted wax figure.

"Hazel Dean," she said. "I was a friend of Nina's... from book club?" Hazel had no idea if Nina would have ever mentioned her before.

"Yes!" she said. "You're Nina's friend!" She jumped up and pulled Hazel into a perfumed hug. "I just can't believe all this," she began to blubber. "My baby, she was always such a sensitive girl. She was nothing like me. I didn't really understand her all that well when she was young. Now, I don't know what I'm going to do with her gone!"

"Shh," Hazel soothed, patting the woman on the back. "I'm so sorry. I'm so, so sorry." She let the woman cry on her shoulder for a while. McGee held up her phone to get a picture, but Hazel gave her a hard glare and she quickly set her phone back in her lap.

Finally, Lynette released her and pulled a tissue out of her pocket to blow her nose.

"We thought you might like to stay with us tonight," Hazel said. "Unless you want to stay with the kids. They're at our friend Nora's."

"Nora Smith?" Lynette brightened a little bit.

Hazel smiled. "Yes, well, she's Nora Franks now, but yes."

"That's wonderful; it's so nice of Nora to help. I never would have believed when they were teenagers. I can just imagine them complaining about their husbands to each other or making their kids' lunch together, having play dates. Nina and Nora. Their names ran together. Like one word. They were always together. I'm glad...I'm just so glad they had each other." Lynette shook her head, fresh tears spilling onto her cheeks. The cloud around her lightened to beautiful shade of blue. "I hope you won't judge, but I just don't think I'm up to looking after the kids tonight."

"Not at all," Hazel said. "I totally get it." Hazel glanced at McGee and then looked back to Lynette. "Let's get out of here," she said.

"Where?" Lynette asked, her brow furrowing. The cerulean blue morphed into a gunmetal gray.

"It's so public and sterile here." she gave a pointed look at McGee, who was still sitting on the bench and staring a little too intently out the window. "I own this bookshop..."

"Oh yes, Nina told me about it." Lynette's color changed again. This time to a soft violet. "I think she loved it there. I would love to see it."

"And I would love to take you there. Let's go, I'll get you Nina's favorite hot chocolate, and we can chat in peace before I take you back to my house where there are two teenage boys."

Lynette smiled and followed Hazel out the door and to her car. Hazel noticed Nina's phone, still sitting in the cup holder, and quietly pocketed it. She sent Jason a text that he should hitch a ride home with John, then she and Lynette drove in companionable silence to *Books and Chocolate*.

As she led Lynette through the store into the cafe, Hazel wondered if she would ever tire of the effect it had on people. Moving from the chaotic, overstocked shelves that reached the low ceiling to the glassed-in roof of the cafe always created a sense of wonder in her guests.

"Have a seat," Hazel offered. "That was Nina's favorite chair." She pointed to the wingback by the fireplace. "I'll make you an escapist hot chocolate. Nina always had one at book club, even in the sweltering heat of August." Hazel smiled at the memory of her friend.

"I can see why she liked it here," Lynette said, her color calming to a sky blue. She was too busy looking at everything to sit down. "It's so cozy and peaceful."

"Thank you," Hazel said, her heart swelling at the compliment.

She used a frother to mix chocolate into hot half and half, then added some sweetened condensed milk and mixed it again. She finished by topping it with fresh whipped cream and homemade marshmallows, then poured it into a handmade chunky ceramic mug and brought it to the table next to the wingback chair.

"Wow," Lynette said, coming to sit down. "That looks amazing." She settled into the chair and took a sip. "Wow," she said again. "It tastes amazing too."

Hazel sat down in the chair opposite her. "I'm trying to get a better idea of what happened with Nina," Hazel said gently. "Nora and I suspected that she might be struggling with postpartum depression. What do you think?"

"Yes, definitely," Lynette nodded. "She hasn't been herself, really, since baby number three."

"Do you know if Nina sought any help in dealing with it?"

"No, I know she didn't." Lynette set the mug down on the

table. "Sometimes she would call and say she didn't feel right. I tried to tell her to go see someone, even just talk to her OB/GYN about it, but she was worried about what Mike and his ridiculous mother would think of it, or the cost or taking the time away from her children. There was always some reason why she didn't get help."

"You two are close?"

"Yes, like the Gilmore Girls."

"Oh," Hazel tried to reconcile this with what Nora had told her. Nora had implied that the relationship between Nina and her mother had been strained because of the divorce, but she also admitted she and Nina weren't as close as they used to be. Maybe Nina had reconnected with her mom in recent years.

"We talk almost every day," Lynette went on.

"Did she tell you she was going on a backpacking trip?" Hazel asked.

"Oh, yes, of course," Lynette said airily. "I called her on Friday night when she was supposed to get home, but she didn't answer so I thought she was tied up with the kids or something."

The explanation rang true enough. "You didn't get worried when you didn't hear back from her?"

"It wasn't unusual for her to let a call go to voice mail or not get back to me right away," Lynette shrugged. "It hadn't been long enough for me to worry yet."

"You didn't check in with Mike to make sure that she got back, okay?"

"I don't interact with Mike," she said, her voice turning hard. The sky blue darkened immediately.

"I understand," Hazel said, intuiting this would be the best thing to say. "I work with him on the city council."

"Oh." Lynette moaned. "So, you know exactly what I'm talking about. He's the worst, isn't he? So self-centered. I was completely baffled when Nina married him. He's never been very attentive, if you know what I mean." She leaned back in her chair and took another sip of the hot chocolate.

"Maybe Mike wouldn't be that bad," Lynette admitted. "If it wasn't for his mom. Karen is the most controlling woman I've ever met. If she says jump, Mike will ask how high." She lowered her voice. "It's not healthy if you ask me. Nina's hinted that Karen was abusive when Mike was a child."

Hazel nodded. She had already been suspecting that. "Did Nina mention any other men in her life recently?"

"Nina? No!" Lynette laughed. "I can't imagine Nina having an affair. She doesn't have the imagination."

Hazel let the question go and moved on. "What makes you say Karen is so controlling?"

"That woman is evil," Lynette's voice went hard and flat, not a smidge of irony in her voice. Her gunmetal gray returning.

"What do you mean?" Hazel asked. Maybe Karen's temper had come out often enough that Nina had mentioned it to Lynette.

"She killed her husband," Lynette said.

"Excuse me?" Hazel said, not quite believing Lynette said what she did.

"She knocked off her husband, for the insurance money."

"How do you know?" Hazel asked, trying not to react.

"You don't have to believe me," Lynette huffed. "She didn't admit it or anything. But it's all very suspicious. The man was a triathlete. In the best shape of his life. Never been a smoker. Didn't even like alcohol. One of those health nuts, you know? Vegan or something. Then he up and dies from some liver thing? And she buys a big fancy house up in the mountains. Spends her time at your country club up there, flirting with the golf pro. I mean, come on."

"I see," Hazel tried to sound like she was seriously considering the idea.

"Plus, she was poisoning Nina."

"She was *poisoning* Nina?" Hazel couldn't help the incredulous tone.

"Every time Nina went over to her house for dinner," Lynette's voice went low and dripped with gossipy drama. "Every. Time. She came home with stomach problems. She spent all night in and out of the bathroom with terrible stomach cramps and pain. Every time. I told her to switch plates with her husband and see if his loving mother would let him eat the poison, but Nina never had the guts. Nina always did struggle to stand up for herself. Even when she was a little girl..." Lynette trailed off, taken away by memories of another place and time when her daughter was still a young, bright-eyed girl with no bad choices behind her.

"I'm so sorry about Nina," Hazel said.

Lynette sighed. "Me too." All the energy seemed to go out of her and all the saturation around her emptied until it was back to a pale blue. She stared into the fire just the same way that Nina did.

"We can stay here as long as you like," Hazel said. "I haven't been in for a couple of days, so I have some work to do. Just let me know when you're ready to go get some rest."

Lynette nodded without saying anything.

Hazel busied herself cleaning up the kitchen a bit, checking inventory and going over recipe plans for the following days. It felt good to be back in the shop, like order had been restored to the world.

"Hazel?" Jason's voice rang through the shop. She broke into a grin and walked around the counter towards him as he emerged from the shelves. Hazel thought there was nothing quite like running into one's spouse unexpectedly to light a spark between you, or maybe it was just because of the trauma she'd endured since she last saw him. She smiled right from her heart.

"Hello, darling," she said, pressing herself against him. She felt the muscles in her shoulder blades relax. He felt like home.

"John wanted to drop me off here instead of driving up the hill," Jason said apologetically.

"I'm glad you're here," Hazel said.

"And I'm just so glad you're alright," he said, putting a palm to her cheek.

Hazel almost leaned into his hand and let the tears that had been hovering behind her eyes escape but then realized that Lynette's eyes were on them. So, instead of falling apart, she took Jason's hand and led him towards her. "This is Lynette; she's Nina's mom."

Jason took her hand in a tender handshake. "I'm so sorry for your loss," he said.

"Thank you," Lynette smiled. "And thank you for having me in your home tonight. It's so kind of you."

"Of course," Jason said, even though Hazel had forgotten to mention to him that Lynette was probably coming. "We wouldn't have it any other way."

Hazel smiled, her heart filling with affection for her husband.

"I'm ready to go," Lynette said, draining the last of the hot chocolate from the mug. "I'm going to fall asleep sitting here. It's been so nice, Hazel, just what I needed. Thank you."

"I'm so glad," she said, fighting the urge to hug the woman again. She knew if she did, they might both start crying again.

They walked out the door into the chilly evening. The sun had set while they were inside the bookshop. A light fog diffused the light coming from the street lamps, causing eerie shadows around the sidewalk and street.

They all climbed into Hazel's car, with her getting into the passenger seat so that Jason would drive. Hazel didn't feel up to it. Lynette sat in the back seat behind Jason, so Hazel could still see her if she half turned around.

"Maybe tomorrow you'll feel up to sitting with the kids for a while," Hazel said, as Jason started up the car and pulled out onto the street. "I can take you to the Mitchells' house. Mike and Karen won't be there."

"Why not?" Lynette asked.

Hazel sighed. Of course, John wouldn't have told the poor woman what was going on. "He's in the hospital. Dansby Fuller attacked him."

Lynette's hand flew to her mouth, the deep blue of her grief turned into a murky green blue. "Dansby?" she whispered.

"I'm afraid so," she said.

"Maybe I should go right over there," Lynette said.

"No," Hazel said. "No, Nora's got them for tonight. Just take the evening to grieve for your daughter."

Lynette nodded, tears spilling onto her cheeks and causing streaks of skin to appear underneath makeup that had already been smudged with tears and dried again several times. She began to sob again, and the sound broke Hazel's heart.

Hazel twisted around to see Lynette in the back. Jason started the car.

"Tell me about Nina," Hazel said.

Lynette gasped. "Nina," she gasped. "Oh, Nina."

Hazel felt her own tears coming. "Nina was so quiet at book club. I could just tell she was taking everything in and that she probably had some amazing insights. But I never pushed her for them."

Lynette smiled through her sobs. "She always hated talking in groups."

"Sometimes she would sit for a long time after our discussion. After everyone left, she would be there, staring into the fire. She was so strikingly beautiful like that, with the fire lighting up her dark eyes and creamy skin. If I was an artist, I would have liked to paint her like that."

Lynette's sobs had quieted as she listened to Hazel. "She got that from her dad, that coloring," she said. "She was stunning. I wish you had known her when she was younger. She had these beautiful pink cheeks, and her eyes shone. I was so proud that she was mine." Her voice cracked.

"I think her daughter Naomi looks like her," Hazel said.

Lynette nodded. "I think so too."

"I guess that's something," Hazel said. "That she still lives through her children." She glanced at her husband and saw a single tear rolling down his cheek. He reached out and took her hand in his.

The three of them rode the rest of the way home in silence, each lost in their own feelings.

SEVENTEEN

After they had Lynette safely settled into the guest room, Jason and Hazel sat in their room upstairs talking about what had happened. Hazel had brought Nina's phone into the house and plugged it into her wall charger, and miraculously, it lit up with the low charge symbol.

"Maybe it just needed to dry out for a bit," Jason suggested.

"Jason, do you think that Nina was really going to run off with Dansby when she went into the woods?"

"I don't know," Jason shook his head. "Does it matter at this point?"

"I think it would to Mike. And maybe to Nina's kids one day."

"There's no way to know," Jason said. "It's not worth thinking about it. Let's just assume that she wasn't."

Hazel eyed Nina's phone sitting on her bedside table. The low charge symbol had disappeared, and in its place was an apple symbol. "There's one way we might be able to know..."

"You want to look at her social media? Didn't you decide it was immoral before?"

"Well, she's gone now. Privacy seems less important than finding out the truth. I only saw the first few words of Dansby's last message to Nina. It said, 'where are you?'"

"I don't know, Hazel... sounds like you might just be trying to satisfy your idle curiosity."

Hazel's phone rang and made them both jump.

"It's Uncle John," she said, looking at the caller ID.

"Uh, oh," Jason said. "You'd better answer it. You don't want him banging down the door this late on a school night. Our kids would love nothing more than for you to be arrested again."

Hazel closed her eyes and answered the call. "Hello?"

"Hazel, do you have something you'd like to share with me?" he asked in a warning tone.

"Um," she said.

"We're going through evidence and the girl's phone is missing."

"Nina," Hazel corrected.

"Nina!" John shouted into the phone. "Her phone! It's missing! You wouldn't happen to know anything about that!?" John was one person who Hazel didn't need to be in the same room with to tell what he was feeling. She could imagine those signature orange zig zags buzzing from him.

"Oh, yeah," she attempted a casual tone. "I just thought I'd give it back to Mike when I saw him again."

"Hazel?" John's voice was filled with exasperation.

"Yes, Uncle John?"

"Bring me the damn phone! Now!"

"Yes, sir," she said meekly. John ended the call and Hazel glanced at Jason.

"We're headed to the police station now?" he asked, grinning.

"Smugness is not attractive, Jason," Hazel said, as she

grabbed the phone. She looked at it in for a moment before turning to her husband. "So, I have an ethical question."

"Oh, great," Jason moaned.

"Should I find out everything I need to know about Dansby and Nina's relationship right now before I give John back the phone? Or should I wait and let him decide if it's important to do so? What if Dansby really is a person of interest, and John just didn't want to tell me? He said that suicide is almost certain. Then again, what if John doesn't look into Dansby very much because he's certain that it is suicide?"

"Are you asking me as a lawyer or as a human?" Jason was eyeing her warily.

"I don't understand the difference," she said.

"I know you don't," he said, shaking his head. "Hazel, this is a dangerous line of thought. Why don't you just hand John the phone and tell him everything you know about Dansby and Nina? Then everything will be tidy and easy for any trial that may or may not happen in the future. He's not stupid or naïve. Anything he didn't already know he could have figured out for himself based on Dansby's extreme reaction to Nina's death. Where did he even come from? I thought he was missing."

Hazel frowned. "Lance did too. But I guess he was around somewhere nearby." She shook her head. "I can't. I just can't let it go. If there's any chance it wasn't suicide, this will be important. I don't necessarily trust John to pursue it. I'm going to see what Dansby messaged to Nina the day before she disappeared."

She grabbed Nina's phone and opened it up to the messenger app.

"I've got a bad feeling about this," Jason said, but he didn't try to stop her, so she decided it was morally ambiguous enough to be justified.

The Dansby conversation Hazel had seen on Nina's iPad previously was still sitting there with its haunting first five words. *Where are you? I have to—.* What did he have to do? Hazel tapped on it anxiously.

Where are you? I have to see you. From Saturday afternoon. Well after Nina had left on her hiking trip. Relief washed over Hazel. Whatever had happened after that, Nina had not set out into the woods to run off with Dansby, or even to see him.

Hazel kicked herself for not guessing the end of that sentence. She scrolled further to see more of the messages between them.

Don't shut me out Nina. Let's not make the same mistake again. Time stamped Saturday morning.

One from Friday night, *Nina, please answer me. I'm in agony.*

Another from Friday afternoon, *Are you okay Nina?*

Friday morning: *did you get my last message? I want us to be together. Leave that awful husband of yours.*

Thursday night: *There's nothing to be confused about. I love you. I've always loved you. Leaving you is the biggest regret of my life. Don't make the same mistake twice. Come with me. Leave everything else behind. I never want you to be sad again.*

It wasn't until Hazel scrolled down to Thursday morning that she saw Nina's last message to him. *I'm so confused. I need a break. I need to think by myself for a little while. Please leave me alone for a few days.*

"Anything helpful?" Jason asked.

Hazel shook her head. "It looks like Dansby wanted to run off together, but Nina didn't respond. She wanted a couple days to think."

Jason nodded. "Leaving your kids behind is a big decision."

"I can't imagine anyone actually going through with it," Hazel scoffed.

"And yet people do all the time," Jason said.

"Not all the time."

"Hazel, mental illness puts people beyond accountability

for their choices. They don't know what they're doing. Their brains are feeding them untruths."

Hazel nodded. "Have you talked to your mom lately?"

Jason smirked. "Speaking of questionable accountability, nice segue. She's okay still. This has been one of her longer lasting relationships. She actually sounded good the last time I talked to her. Up, but not manic, you know?"

Hazel smiled. "I'm glad."

Jason sighed. "I wish I could be too. I just don't trust it. Her or this guy. And when it doesn't work out, I'll have to fix everything. Just like every other time."

"Maybe it will be different this time," Hazel suggested. "Maybe she finally found someone grounded and mature."

"Maybe," Jason grumbled, but Hazel could see a rosy violet pulse for a split second. Jason would never stop hoping for a normal, drama-less family situation for his mom. "I'm not going to hold my breath. You'd better go," he said pushing her toward the door.

"Alright," she said.

"You'll be okay to drive yourself, right?" he asked.

"Yeah," she said. "I'm feeling pretty normal at the moment." She reached out and put a hand on his face. He covered it with his own.

"I love you," he said.

"I love you too," she smiled.

She headed downstairs and found Jeremiah, all arms and legs, sprawled out on the couch.

"Where you goin' mom?" he asked. "It's kinda late for you."

"I have to head down to the police station to take something to Uncle John," she explained.

"By yourself?" he asked.

She smiled at him. "Yeah," she said.

"Can I come with you?" he asked. When they broke the news about Nina to Elias and Jeremiah, they hadn't seemed surprised or emotional. Hazel noticed color shifts on each of them, but nothing catastrophic. Hazel wasn't too concerned about their non-reactions. They were teenaged boys and they had never met Nina.

But now, Jeremiah buzzed with a restless teal. When she recognized his anxiety about her leaving, she almost burst into tears. She bit her lip.

"Of course," she said, struggling to talk without her voice cracking. "Just run up and tell dad first so he doesn't worry."

Jeremiah nodded and ran upstairs. Hazel used his absence to compose herself.

It took no time at all to drive through the deserted streets of the city. Jeremiah was worked up about some drama on the soccer team and jabbered the whole way there.

The police station was housed in the rear of the county courthouse where the city and county offices were also located.

On a whim, she parked on the courthouse side of the building and used her key from city council to let herself in. She didn't want to deal with any crowds of people that may be in the police station lobby. She could bypass it and get to John's office from the back door leading to the courthouse.

Jeremiah fell quiet as their steps echoed through the hall-way. Hazel wracked her brain trying to think of anything else she should look up on Nina's phone before she turned it over to John.

Entering the police station through the back hallway, she peeked into Captain Tate's office.

"He's not in here," Jeremiah said. "Can you just leave it on his desk?"

Hazel frowned. She wanted to say a thing or two about it to John before she left.

"Let's just see what's going on up there," she said, indicating further down the hall to the lobby.

John was the only police officer in the room, but he wasn't

alone. McGee the reporter was there. Hazel heard Jeremiah draw a sharp breath.

"Aren't you going to get tired of sitting there?" John bellowed. "I said, no comment."

"Why was Dansby Fuller arrested?" McGee was enveloped by a vivid green.

"Are you deaf? No comment!"

"Oh, dear," Hazel muttered. She froze, wondering if she should just go back out the way she came in, but it was too late. Jeremiah strode over to where John and McGee were arguing. He glowed pinkish violet.

"Perhaps I can be of assistance," he said, stretching up to his full height. "I would be happy to comment." Hazel's hand went to her forehead. John and McGee stopped and blinked at him for a minute. His sudden appearance put a complete stop to their conversation. At least until McGee spotted Hazel.

"Mrs. Dean!" the reporter yelled, running towards her, vaulting the half wall that separated the police from the civilians.

"Hey," John shouted. "You can't come back here!"

Jeremiah crumpled a little as she went by without acknowledging him. The violet surrounding him dulled and darkened.

"Mrs. Dean," the reporter came right up next to her, invading her personal space. Hazel took a step back. "Mrs. Dean, I heard you were at the scene when Dansby Fuller attacked Mike Mitchell. What do you think provoked the attack? What can you tell me about what happened?"

Hazel blinked at her. "You mean you saw I was at the scene because you've been following me around everywhere? Have you not learned your lesson?" she asked.

McGee stepped back, blinking. Her brow furrowed.

Hazel looked past the reporter at John. His orange chevrons were going nuts. "Miss McGee," he said through clenched teeth. "You're going to have to come back into this portion of the room or I will arrest you for trespassing."

Miss McGee backed up through the swinging door in the half wall but didn't break eye contact with Hazel. "Mrs. Dean, please. What happened?"

"I have no comment," Hazel told her.

The green faded a bit in its vibrancy, but it didn't disappear. "Well, this is a public building," she said. "Well, it is on this side of the wall anyways. I'm not going anywhere until I learn what's going on here. I was right, wasn't I? He met her while she was hiking? Did Dansby murder her?"

John hadn't had a lot of occasion to interact with the press before. Journalists had historically ignored their tiny town. He stared at McGee with his mouth hanging slightly open, his brow furrowed and his jaw working. The orange zigzags that fell from him didn't let up an iota. But she was right—he couldn't actually kick her out.

"Um, John?" she said. "I have that thing you wanted."

"Just put it on my desk," he said without looking away from McGee. For her part, she was staring right back at him. She didn't appear to be afraid of John, an indication of her naivete.

"Are you sure?" Hazel asked. "I think it requires your immediate attention." She tried to imbue her words with meaning, but John didn't get the hint. He was too busy glaring at Miss McGee. On the other hand, you could practically see McGee's ears perk up.

"Don't worry, I'll get to it," he said. "Brandon is coming back to relieve me on the front desk. I'll get to it then."

"Okay," Hazel said, "Are you sure?"

"I'm sure," John said. Hazel wondered what kind of scene played out in his mind if he left McGee by herself for a moment. Maybe she would hack into the computer system or start rifling through drawers or find a gun and force him to tell her about the progress in the case.

Hazel nodded. "Okay," she called to John. "We'll leave you to it then. Have fun with your reporter stare down."

John grunted, settling into a chair, and crossing his arms over his chest.

"Bye, Mrs. Dean," McGee called cheerfully. "And what was your name? Jarod?"

"Jeremiah," he corrected her, the violet igniting again. Hazel tugged on his shirt sleeve, and he shuffled back down the hallway without taking his eyes off McGee.

Hazel made her way back to John's office and set Nina's phone carefully on his desk.

"What's that?" Jeremiah asked.

"A phone," she said. She found that the best tactic to avoid her kids' curiosity was to be as mundanely truthful as possible.

"Why won't John tell McGee anything about the investigation?" he asked. "She's just trying to do her job."

Hazel sighed. "Miss McGee published something earlier today that hurt a lot of people. She means well, but she doesn't seem to understand the consequences of publicizing things the community isn't ready for."

Jeremiah furrowed his eyebrows. His aura turned a deep green. "In school they taught us that public access to information is a hallmark of a healthy democracy. The press is an important part of our political system."

Hazel sighed again and closed her eyes for a minute. She wasn't in the right mood to have a political philosophy conversation with her fifteen-year-old. "Can we talk about this another time?" she asked. "I need to get home and get some sleep."

Jeremiah opened his mouth to say more, then shut it again and nodded. "Okay, mom," he said.

Hazel patted his arm. "You're a good boy."

He smiled, and then motioned for her to go ahead of him out of John's office.

* * *

With the sense of urgency about finding Nina gone, Hazel found herself hitting the snooze button long after the sun had come up. Her eyes were swollen from crying herself to sleep, and it made them even more reluctant to open and face the day. Jason got out of bed twenty minutes before her. She finally forced herself to make it downstairs in time to say goodbye to Jeremiah. He and Jason were eating eggs while Elias sat at the bar, refusing to make eye contact with anyone.

Jason gave her a kiss. "I'm going to take Jeremiah to school on my way into the office this morning," he said. "I'll let you know as soon as I hear any kind of a whisper about the autopsy report."

Jeremiah opened his mouth, but Jason glared at him, and he closed it again. Hazel wondered what they had been talking about before she came downstairs. She couldn't believe that it was just the previous morning that they met Waylon in the woods.

Hazel made a mental note to bring him a treat later. She didn't think she had even spoken to him after they found Nina's body. He had come all that way to help them and braved inter-acting with the police. He deserved some recognition. She wondered how he was feeling, if the situation had brought up any bad memories for him.

Jeremiah wrapped his awkward, too long arms around her. "Bye, Mom, love you," he said. He loosened his hold and attempted to pull away, but she refused to let go of him. She was almost afraid to. She remembered when he was a tiny baby she could hold with just one arm. Now he towered over her. He was unusually patient with her display of affection, but after a minute, he squirmed in her arms. She didn't let him wiggle away.

"I've gotta go to school, Mom," he whined.

"Are you sure?" she asked.

"I really do," he told her. "I've got a test, and if I don't make it to soccer practice, then I'll lose my spot in the game on Saturday."

"Okay," Hazel said, releasing her son. "But tonight, we're going to have some real family time. Jeopardy and baked goods. No girlfriends allowed."

Elias flinched.

"Jeopardy is getting old, Mom," Jeremiah said. "Maybe we should try The Chase instead?"

"Don't blaspheme," Hazel told him.

"Yeah, yeah. Let's go, Dad." He gathered his multitude of school bags and headed out the door.

"I'll talk to you soon," Jason promised, kissing her one more time before he left. "Have a nice talk with Elias," he whispered in her ear.

Hazel nodded. Once Jason had left the room, she opened the fridge and pulled out a container of yogurt.

"How are you doing, Elias?" she asked.

He shrugged, looking down at his bowl of oatmeal.

"I never got to tell you how sorry I was about yesterday afternoon," Hazel said, pulling a bowl out of the cupboard.

Elias turned red, still not looking away from his oatmeal.

Hazel felt herself fill with resolve. "Look, I'm sorry if you are a bit embarrassed, but I think it's important for us to have honest conversations. You're a senior in high school, for crying out loud; it's not completely inappropriate for you to have a girlfriend." Hazel got the granola out of the pantry.

Elias continued to exude crimson and be completely silent.

"I wonder why you didn't mention her earlier?" Hazel phrased her statement as a question.

Elias shrugged.

Hazel had heard many of her friends complain about their non-communicative teenagers. Elias' quietness didn't bother

her as a rule; maybe because she was able to see his emotions and knew plenty about what he was feeling without him having to tell her. Now, sitting across from him, all she could see was that he was intensely embarrassed.

Frustration welled up inside of her, but she tried to push it back down. "I can tell that you don't want to talk about this." She paused and was seized with a sudden stroke of inspiration. She got up and walked around the kitchen island and pulled Elias into a hug. He stiffened, but she didn't let go.

"It's been a rough couple days for me," she murmured. "The woman who died, Nina, she has four little kids. The biggest one is only seven. I'm just..." she sighed. "I just love you so much. It's a privilege for me to be your mom. You are a good boy. I'm sorry I've struggled with Emma's appearance. I just wasn't prepared, and like I said, I've been going through a lot of emotions. But I love you, and if you really like this girl, then I'm sure she must be something really special."

She could feel Elias soften as she spoke. The red glow surrounding him relaxed into more of a pink, and when she was done, he reached around her and hugged her back. "Thanks, Mom," he said.

Hazel went back around to finish her breakfast, and they sat in companionable silence until it was time for him to go to school.

* * *

A few hours later, Lynette and Hazel were in the car on the way to meet Nora and Nina's kids at the Mitchells' home. The weather had turned dreary again, and the temperature had dropped. Lynette shivered in the passenger seat, but Hazel didn't think that the ice blue that settled around her had anything to do with the cold.

Hazel had texted Karen before they left, asking how Mike

was doing and explaining that Lynette was there and would be taking over childcare responsibilities for the next while.

Her phone buzzed as they were driving, and she handed it to Lynette. "Is it Karen? What did she say?"

Lynette looked at the phone. "Mike stabilized and regained consciousness last night. No thanks to your inept attempt at first aid. They are running a million tests. I'll let you know when we hear anything definite."

Hazel waited a minute for Lynette to continue reading. "Is that it?"

"Yeah."

"She didn't mention the kids at all?"

Lynette shook her head. Hazel scowled.

"I don't know what we should tell them," Hazel said. "Mike hadn't even told them that Nina went missing. Now their mom is... gone, and their dad is in the hospital." Hazel shook her head. "Those poor babies. How often do you see them usually?"

"Not as often as I'd like," Lynette said, the blue around her darkening a bit. Hazel interpreted that to mean never.

"I'm just not the right person to tell them," Hazel said. "I just met them the other day."

Hazel remembered how gentle and loving her grandmother was when her parents died. Grandmama pulled Hazel into her lap, even though she was too old for that kind of thing and let her hold the antique teddy bear she had always coveted. She stroked Hazel's hair and told her that her parents had gone up to heaven and that Jesus was taking care of them. She let Hazel cry and sob and slobber all over her, while tears streamed down her own cheeks. Hazel couldn't imagine having to go through that without someone to love on her and share her pain.

"I don't know if I am either," Lynette said, her face paling and her color changing to flat gray.

"They need someone who loves them," Hazel said. "Is that you?"

Lynette's eyes filled with tears. "Of course, I love them," she said. "I would do anything for them. I'm just not used to being the one that's here. I surrendered; you know. I surrendered to Karen." A sob escaped from her throat. "I feel like this is all my fault."

"You're not the only one," Hazel murmured. "Mike and Dansby both talked about it being their fault yesterday." She didn't mention her own sense of responsibility.

"Poor Nina," Lynette said, settling back to an ice blue. "Her life was full of people who let her down."

The sad thought hung in the air between them.

"I've got to stop and get gas," Hazel said, with surprise. The gas indicator light was on. Something so pedestrian and normal seemed so impossible in the circumstances.

If Lynette felt the same way, she offered no comment.

Red Gap had two gas stations, one located on the east of town and the other on the west. They were on the eastern side of town, closer to the woods, so it wasn't a long detour to stop for gas.

Hazel pulled in and got out of her car. She had paid and just set up the pump when she caught a glimpse of a woman who looked just like Karen standing by the corner of the convenience store.

Hazel ducked behind the pump and peered around it. She couldn't imagine that Karen would be out and about. She had just texted Hazel from the hospital, hadn't she? But there was no mistaking Karen. She was immaculately made up and gesticulating in the same way she often did at city council meetings.

Whoever she was talking to was hidden from Hazel's view, around the corner of the building. Hazel watched and strained her ears trying to pick up what Karen was saying. She looked agitated, Hazel could see a puff of crimson from where she was standing, but she wasn't screaming. Hazel could only make out sounds, not words.

The gas pump automatically shut off. Hazel replaced it in its holder without taking her eyes off Karen. She glanced back at Lynette, then over at Karen again.

Hazel didn't know how long she could justify standing there spying on Karen, and she didn't know what she was even watching for anyways. Surely the woman was allowed to run some errands while her son was being taken care of by medical professionals in the hospital. It was just that she had so carelessly forgotten about her grandkids that irked Hazel.

She huffed, as though Karen could hear her, and got back into the car. As she turned the key in the ignition and began to inch forward, Karen walked away from the building and got into an SUV.

A man began walking across the parking lot to a pickup truck at one of the other pumps. Hazel did a double take, almost hitting another car as she pulled out of the gas station.

The man Karen had been talking to was Ranger Rick. He was out of uniform, but Hazel would recognize his loping gait anywhere. He looked like he belonged in the forest. Hazel couldn't imagine what the buttoned-up socialite would have to say to a rugged back woodsman. Perhaps she was giving him a piece of her mind about something to do with the national forest.

While she was puzzling over it, Lynette spoke up again. "We're almost there, huh?" Hazel glanced over at her. She was kneading her hands together in her lap and she had turned a pale turquoise.

"Listen, Lynette," Hazel said. "Karen... well, you seem to understand why she isn't the best person to be helping with the kids too much. I saw how she interacted with them. I just... But they need *you* now. You can't surrender. You need to fight for them."

"I know," Lynette nodded. The color around her didn't change in tone, but it seemed to harden and become more solid somehow. "I already quit my job. I'm moving up here."

Hazel's mouth fell open. "Wow," she finally said.

"Yeah, I know," Lynette said. "It seems impulsive. But I've actually been thinking about it for a while. This last year or so, Nina has just seemed so depressed. I thought if I moved back into town and she had someone to help that wasn't Karen, it might help."

Hazel nodded, but her heart felt like lead. Now there was no way to know how much it would have helped.

"That's really nice, Lynette," she murmured.

Lynette nodded, wiping tears away from her eyes. "I wish I had done it earlier. But—" she attempted to smile. "Better late than never, right?"

Hazel smiled back. "I think so," she said. Her heart swelled with affection for Lynette. Maybe she was a little rough around the edges, a little over the top. But her heart was in the right place.

"Alright, here we are," Hazel said as she pulled behind Nora's van in the Mitchell's driveway. "Let's go see your grandkids."

EIGHTEEN

Hazel grabbed her book bag and walked down Main Street to her shop. It didn't take very long for the kids to warm up to Lynette. They were all snuggled on the couch together reading a story when Hazel left. She didn't know how Lynette was going to tell them about their parents, but she trusted that she would make them feel as loved and safe as possible. Lynette was a good woman.

As Hazel drove away from the Mitchells' house, the exhaustion of the previous days pulled on her. She craved the comfort of her bookstore. She had been away from it for too long. She turned her music up and drove straight there. She liked parking at the lot at the end of the street and strolling past the cute shops and restaurants. Her building was the last one on the street before it broke off from the highway and turned right.

When she got to her door, she took out her key and let herself in. It was warm and cozy inside. The old-fashioned coat rack standing by the entrance stood waiting for her to hang her book bag and coat. The books shone with their bright, cheerful colors, seeming to welcome her home.

"Hello, my friends," she said. She got out her wood polish to shine the front desk and breathed in the cheerful scent of orange oil.

She realized with a pang that Nina would never come through the front door of the bookshop for book club again. Hazel would never again press a mug of hot chocolate into her hands with an understanding smile. Nina would never come into the shop the week before Christmas asking for book recommendations for her kids as they were growing up. She would never fret if they were struggling to learn to read or rant about the lack of books for a precocious twelve-year-old. She would never stop and ask Hazel what on earth she was supposed to do when the pitch of her teenage son's changing voice literally made her cringe. She would never commiserate about her high schooler's mood swings. Nina would miss all those moments in her children's lives.

A blanket of melancholy enveloped Hazel. She reached into her book bag and pulled out the copy of *Anna Karenina* that she had found in Nina's tent. John may have noticed that Nina's phone was missing, but he hadn't said anything about the book. Hazel would set it aside in a place of honor and keep it in Nina's memory.

She made her way to the back of the shop, trailing her fingers against the spines of the books. They were old friends, and just being near them lent her comfort. She made her way to her favorite chair by the fireplace, incidentally the one that Nina had been sitting in at book club the previous week. It felt like a lifetime ago.

She wondered if Nina had been a margin-scribbler. She wondered how far Nina had gotten through the heavy tome. She flipped through the pages, slowly at first, then skipping big sections. Hazel's favorite parts of the book were when Levin waxed romantic about country life in his idealistic way. Despite the famous first line, Tolstoy couldn't hide his bias in favor of traditional family life for long.

She wondered what Nina had thought while she was reading it. Did she get far enough to see the depressing consequences of Anna's affair? Hazel didn't know whether to hope that she had or hadn't. There were no clues to be seen; Nina hadn't put a single mark in the margins of the novel.

Hazel flipped through each page until she got to the last one. This copy of *Anna Karenina* didn't have any notes or explanations from the translator in the back. The last page faced the back cover, and there, in heavily water damaged ink, were small cramped handwritten words. Hazel's eyes scanned over them without being able to make out what they said at first glance, but at the bottom in larger, loopy letters, she saw Nina's signature.

Hazel's eyes widened. Could this be Nina's suicide note? Hazel got out of her chair and went to reach over the bakery's counter to where she had hidden some reading glasses. She didn't need them all the time; in fact, she had done her best to hide their existence, but for the level of illegibility Nina's handwriting had suffered in the rainstorm, she was going to need them.

She went back and grabbed the book, then sat down in a different, straighter chair with more light with a higher table next to it. She put on her glasses and leaned over it, carefully creasing the cardstock back cover so she didn't have to hold it open while she attempted to make out what it said.

Time ticked by. Each word required careful study to determine where the pen originally pushed down on the page versus where the ink had run. Sometimes Hazel had to rethink a word she had puzzled out because it didn't make sense in the context of the other words. Sometimes a whole sentence came out at once, relatively unscathed by the water damage.

Finally, with her neck aching and her eyes watering, she looked over what she had managed to make out.

· · ·

I feel like I have finally woken up from a long sleep. I have felt like a victim of my own life for a long time. I've been out of control, drifting, allowing things to happen to me. The woods have always been a place of clarity for me, and I am kicking myself for not thinking to come out here before. I don't feel exactly like myself again, but I feel like I've caught a glimpse or a picture of what I used to be. I used to be happy, I did. And in this place full of renewal and new life it has restored my hope that I can be happy again.

Dansby is not the answer. He is what he always was, an intense distraction from real life, a way of refusing to face the things that I need to face. A way to escape. This time, thank God, the obligation I have to my children kept me from jumping feet first into the vortex that is Dansby Fuller.

My children! Of course, my children. If anything has the potential to bring joy, isn't it them? I'd forgotten, but now I remember the wonder of Naomi. How beautiful she was as an infant. How much her baby smiles thrilled me, how proud I was of the simplest things, how I would stare at her endlessly. How could I forget?

I need help. I am going back, and I am getting help. I'll ask Nora or Hazel if they know of anyone. Hazel would know; she knows everyone. It's hard for me to have hope that help will help me, but I will do it. I will take steps ahead with hope and love in my heart. And I will do it for my kids. I'm going to report Karen, too.

I'm writing all this down in case I forget again. I have to be able to remember what I'm feeling right now—when my head burst through to the surface for just a moment and I took deep gasps of pure, sweet air.

All I have to do now is tell Dansby. I'm not looking forward to it, but it has to be done. I'll tell him I still love Mike. He won't believe me, but so what? It's the only way. And maybe, one day, it will be true.

. . .

Tears streamed down Hazel's cheeks. She sat, stunned, staring at the page, at Nina's neat and simple handwriting. It felt like she was sitting across from her in the shop. Sipping on her hot chocolate, finally getting all her feelings out and into the heart of a friend. If only she had been able to do it that night after book club. Everything might have been different. Hazel stroked the page. "You will be so missed, my dear friend," she murmured. "So much more than you ever realized."

But Hazel understood her need to get away, to delve into nature, to sort out her emotions.

Hazel couldn't imagine Nina, after writing this, climbing to the top of a waterfall, and jumping to her death. So how, then, did she die?

John had said that there was no disturbance to the moss and other foliage around the rocks that Nina must have fallen from. That's how they ruled out an accident. If she hadn't jumped on purpose and she hadn't slipped and fallen, that only left one other option.

Someone must have thrown her over the edge.

Hazel heard the jingling sound of the bell indicating that someone had come into the shop. She set aside the book and the paper she had written Nina's message on and made her way through the stacks to the front of the shop.

"Hello?" a voice called.

"Coming!" Hazel said. She burst through the bookshelves, surprised to find Lance standing there.

"Wow, Hazel," Lance said, turning in a circle with wide eyes. "You've done well. I would never have guessed this was the same building. Remember how rebellious we felt sneaking into this old place?" He put his hand against one of the stone pillars original to the building. He looked genuinely pleased enough but Hazel noticed a thin layer of greenish gray surrounding him. She recognized it as his pain color and knew he was hurting for his brother.

"I do remember," she said, smiling. "I always wanted to fix it when I grew up."

"And now you have," he beamed at her. "It's perfect for a bookstore. Can I see the rest?"

"Of course!" Hazel couldn't think of anything she loved more than showing people around the store. It had taken her years to renovate it and fix its multitude of hazards. And another couple of years to stock her inventory up to the level that she wanted. "These are the stacks," she gestured at the rows of oak bookshelves that stretched to the low ceiling. She started down the middle row with Lance on her heels.

"A little chaotic, isn't it?" he chuckled. "I see that your housekeeping abilities haven't improved."

"Hey, my house is immaculate," Hazel lied. "And I prefer the word 'cozy.'"

They got to the end of the bookshelf where the ceiling rose. About ten feet ahead of them it turned to glass, sloping upwards into a dome and then down to the ground in Victorian greenhouse style. Hazel had worked endlessly with a designer from Atlanta to get it just right. She grinned when she saw Lance's mouth fall open.

"Isn't the effect marvelous?" she gushed. "I really wanted it to open up back here and take advantage of the view."

"How is it not sweltering in the summer?" he asked.

Hazel smiled, holding up a finger. "Ah!" She walked behind a counter and pressed a few buttons on a control panel. The glass darkened until it was opaque.

"Whoa," Lance said.

"It's smart glass," Hazel explained. "It will actually change on its own throughout the day. It keeps glare out and prevents it from getting too warm, which would be bad for the chocolate. I never could have built the chocolate shop like this if it wasn't for this stuff."

"That's the coolest thing I've ever seen. It must have cost a fortune."

Hazel shrugged. "Well, you know my trust fund, from the settlement with my parents' accident? Jason doesn't want to use it for living expenses. We agreed we could use it for college for Elias and Jeremiah—those are my boys—but for day-to-day expenses, Jason wants to cover that with his job."

Lance nodded. "I can understand that," he said. "So, you used it to build all this?"

"I think it was a good use of the money."

He grinned. "Me too."

"Hot chocolate?" Hazel asked.

"You don't happen to have anything spiked?" he asked.

Hazel gave an apologetic grimace.

"I didn't really think so," he said. "Just thought I'd ask. How about just some coffee?"

Hazel nodded, pouring him a mug. He grabbed it and settled into an armchair.

"It is cozy," he said.

"Thanks." Hazel came back around the counter and sat in a chair next to his. "It is in the summer, too. I did all this research on how to make summer cozy. We hang fairy lights and put all kinds of LED candles around. Lots of fresh flowers, mostly from people's gardens. I serve all these iced beverages and s'more flavored things. There's a patio out there," she pointed to a set of double doors almost invisible in the glass. "I don't keep the doors open though because of the bugs. I thought about getting the patio screened in, but I think it would ruin the view."

Lance nodded. "I think you're right. This place is amazing, Hazel, a real accomplishment." He reached out and squeezed her hand. "You've made a great life for yourself, haven't you?"

Hazel tried not to relish the praise. "I try," she shrugged with a half-smile. "Did they schedule the arraignment?"

"Yes, but it's not until tomorrow. I went and saw your husband before I came here. He doesn't think that there's a good chance they'll let Dansby out on bail."

"Oh, no, I'm so sorry."

"But he was helpful," Lance hurried on, like he had to apologize for Jason. "He's going to try to advise they do because Dansby's a caregiver for my parents, but because of me being around, it's a long shot."

"But that's so much for you to handle all alone."

He gave her a sad smile. "He also told me that I'm going to have to hire a lawyer that's not him. Some kind of conflict or something."

Hazel's mouth fell open. "He did? Why would he do that?"

"I don't think he likes me all that much." Lance's color flashed a buttery yellow. "I wanted to let you know that I've reached out to Jolene. She's going to represent Dansby."

"Humph," Hazel said at the mention of her high school frenemy. "Well, I suppose you have to have someone. How are your parents handling things?"

He set his coffee aside. "I can't bear to tell my mom. I wish my dad was here. Well, you know, really here. I mean, I feel guilty for wishing my dad was here, since he technically still is. It's the weirdest feeling. To miss someone who's still here."

Hazel was emotionally exhausted, which was the only explanation she had for tearing up in that moment. "You're carrying such a heavy burden all alone," she said.

He reached across the table and put a hand over hers, rubbing his thumb across her knuckles. "I'm not alone. I have you."

She looked down at his hand and then up at him with a pained expression. "Lance..." she said.

Lance got up before she could finish. "Thank you," he said. "I won't bother you anymore. I'm going to get back to mom and dad."

Hazel got up too. She saw Nina's book lying on the table across the room. She realized that the note might bring the Fullers some comfort. It would be nice for Dansby to know that Nina didn't really kill herself and maybe that would help him be more composed during the trial. Which could help with his sentencing. "Hold on a minute," she said. She walked over and grabbed the book and the paper she had translated the note onto. "I could tell that Dansby is really broken up about Nina's death. I found this in the back of a book she had with her on the hike."

She handed him the paper. "It's a note," she said.

Lance scanned it.

"She didn't kill herself," Hazel said. "I don't know what happened to her, but she didn't kill herself."

Lance handed the note back to her. She set the note and the book down on the table and put a hand on his arm. "I thought maybe you could tell Dansby when you see him. It might bring him some peace to know that she didn't choose this."

"Look, I'd better get going." He turned to go but stopped. "Can I get a coffee to go? My mom had this fall, and it's going to be a long night." His gray green flickered for a moment, an extra flash of pain.

"Oh, no Lance, your mom fell?" Hazel took his coffee cup to the counter and poured it into a to go cup and then filled the rest with the pot.

"Yeah, it's been a rough couple of days for sure. At least I know where Dansby is now..." She turned back around and walked back towards him to hand him the coffee cup. She pressed it into his hands and then was stunned to spot a book in the middle of the smoke gray section that had taken on a greenish tone that matched the color surrounding Lance.

Hazel walked over pulled the book from the shelf. "Lance..." she said, taking in the cover.

"Yeah?"

"I think this book wants to go home with you." She held it out to him.

"*The Great Gatsby*?" he asked, reading the title. "Didn't we read this in high school?"

"We were supposed to," she laughed. "I have since then, have you?"

He shook his head.

"Maybe it will be helpful..." Hazel trailed off. The short classic book featured a main character who pined for a lost love to the point that he created a whole new identity to have a chance at winning her back. She frowned. Why would Lance need to read that one?

He took it from her and turned it over in his hands, flipping through the pages. "Thanks," he said. He set the book and the coffee back down on the table. Something in his green-gray demeanor flickered and a deep violet rose to the surface. Without warning or hesitation, he gathered Hazel up in his arms and pressed his lips to hers with desperation.

Hazel was staggered by how normal it felt. It didn't feel like betraying Jason; it felt like going home. She was so surprised by that feeling, that she didn't break away from him as fast as she should have.

After a second longer hesitation than she should have had, she pushed him away. "Lance!" she gasped. Her heart was hammering in her chest.

"Let's go, Hazel," he said. "Let's run away together. We belong together. We always have. I'm the one that ruined it. I know it was my fault. I need you. I was such an idiot, all those years ago. I wanted to make sure I knew what I was missing out on. I was too naive to realize that you are the most beautiful, interesting, and caring woman that I will ever meet. I should have known that you weren't going to be available by the time I figured that out."

"Lance, you're under a lot of pressure lately. You don't know what you're saying."

"I do, I swear. I've thought about it so many times before. Not just since I've been back in Red Gap. Before that. Before Lisa and I split up. I know it was awful of me, but I always compared her with you, and she always came up short."

"Lance, stop it."

"Not this time, Hazel. Tell me it hasn't been the same for you. Tell me that you love Jason more than you loved me. I don't believe it's possible."

Hazel's face stung as though she had been slapped. "It is possible because it's true. We were just kids, Lance; we didn't even know what love was. What I have with Jason—"

"Yes, we did. We were in love, and we were made for each other. Everything that has happened to us since we broke up was just exposition."

Hazel shook her head. "No," she refuted.

He took her face in his hands. "Hazel, I know that you care for me."

Tears pricked her eyes again. "I do, Lance, of course I do. But it's not like that."

"I don't believe you," he said, searching her eyes with his. "Why else would you have given me *Gatsby*?"

"Lance, please," she grabbed his forearms, trying to pull his hands away from her face. "The book was the same color as you. That's what I do. I give people the books that match their color."

Lance kissed her again, hard. Like he was trying to erase what she was saying. This time it didn't feel homey and familiar. Hazel tried to push away but he just crushed her even closer, with one hand on the back of her head.

Hazel felt the familiar tightening of anxiety in her throat.

NINETEEN

"What's going on here?" a voice boomed.

Lance let go of Hazel and took a step away from her. Hazel gasped for air, sinking into a chair.

John was standing between them and the stacks. Hazel wished they had heard the bell when he walked in. Maybe then Lance would have left her alone.

"I was just leaving," Lance said, gathering up his things.

"Like hell you were," John said. "Hazel?"

Hazel looked at John and watched understanding cross his face.

"What are you doing to my little girl, Lance Fuller?"

"Sir, respectfully, I would have to tell you that we are adults now, and my relationship with Hazel is none of your business."

"Is that so?" John growled.

Lance paled. "I know you wish Hazel had married me instead of Jason."

"You know that, do you?"

"Yes, sir," Lance said.

"Well, then I thank you, son. Because your behavior today

has completely broken me of that notion. You are less than half the man that Jason Dean is. He is filled to the gills with honor and integrity. Which is a lot more than I can say for the likes of you. He is an excellent husband and father, and I am tickled pink that he's married to my Hazel."

Hazel's heart filled with emotion as John talked about Jason. It was nice to finally hear the old curmudgeon admit those things. But with every word Lance shrunk a little more. "John," she said. "Lance is going through a lot right now. I'm sure under normal circumstances—"

"Which is why I'm going to let him leave here without giving him a good beating. Get out of here, son. And don't come back."

Lance turned toward Hazel. "Hazel, I'm sorry. I don't know—"

"Just go, Lance," she said.

He gave her one more apologetic glance and disappeared down the stacks.

John eyed Hazel. "Are you okay?" he asked.

"Yes, I'm fine," she said. "Just a little embarrassed."

John chuckled. "Don't know your own desirability, eh? Well, I know that's through no fault of Jason's."

Hazel blushed. "I just thought it was all ancient history."

"Look," John said. "I know that I liked Lance a lot when you were younger and I give Jason a hard time, but... Jason is an okay guy, I guess."

Hazel's lips twitched. "'An okay guy, I guess?' Sounded like a lot more than that a minute ago."

"Okay, fine," John threw his hands up. "He's a good man. He's a good husband and a good father, I know you and Lance have some history and that you think I always wished that you had married him, but I don't. I don't wish that. Jason is good for you. I... he's not terrible to have around. Don't do anything that will jeopardize your relationship."

Hazel blanched. "I have no intention of jeopardizing my relationship, believe me. Lance is going through a lot of emotional turmoil and I think it made him a little delusional. I'm glad you walked in when you did.

"Oh," John said, all his bluster evaporating. "Well, good." Hazel grinned. "I'm going to tell Jason you said that he is a good husband and father."

John's lip curled up. "If you must," he sniffed, waving a hand to indicate that he was done with that subject.

"What brings you to the shop, John?" Hazel asked. "Did you get the autopsy results back yet?"

"No, we don't have the results back from the autopsy report yet. But I was wondering if you might be able to shed some light on a few head-scratchers. Since you were friends with the gir—" he cleared his throat. "Since you and Nina were friends."

That familiar stab of guilt poked at Hazel. "We weren't as close as I would have liked," Hazel said. "Do you want any coffee or anything?"

"Are there any more blondies?" he asked.

"Yes, but they're not fresh. They've been in the fridge."

"That's fine," he shrugged.

Hazel got him a blondie and poured a cup of coffee and went to join him at the cafe table. He had chosen the same one that she had been sitting at with Lance. She settled into her chair and was about to move Nina's copy of *Anna Karenina* from the tabletop to underneath her chair. But then she clutched it tightly in her hands.

"Listen, John, I know that you think that Nina took her own life, but I may have found something that will change your mind."

John exhaled. "Hazel, what happened to that phone I asked you to bring by last night? We were able to get a warrant and access her messenger account this morning but it would have been much easier if we had just been able to use her phone."

Hazel wasn't following. "I put it on your desk last night as I was leaving."

John's face softened. "Are you sure Hazel? I know you've been under a lot of stress. Could you have possibly put it in your purse without thinking?"

"No, I'm certain. I left it on your desk and then Jeremiah and I left."

"What was with Jeremiah last night anyways?" John asked.

Hazel groaned. "He has some kind of crush on that reporter-" She broke off and her mouth fell open. "Jeremiah!"

"Jeremiah what?" John said.

"No," Hazel said, shaking her head. "He wouldn't be that stupid."

John raised an eyebrow. "How stupid?"

"You don't think..." She paused, pursing her lips. "I'm worried he might have pocketed the phone to give to McGee. As some gambit for attention."

John groaned. "I'll look into it," he said, and then moved on. "We got the warrant for the messenger account because of the lighter you found at the scene."

"The lighter?" Hazel said, still distracted thinking about Jeremiah's reckless behavior.

John's face was grim. "We were able to pull a couple finger-prints from the lighter you found at the scene. They belong to Dansby. It places him at the scene. When we gained access to Nina's messages, it appeared that he was pressuring her to leave her husband. It doesn't look good for Dansby, Hazel."

Hazel felt a little dizzy. She closed her eyes to steady herself.

"Unfortunately, this also makes Mike a suspect. He could have found out about their relationship and killed her in a fit of rage."

Hazel shook her head. "I thought of him before, but he was truly surprised and lost when I told him that she had died. I don't think it was him."

"Hazel, I know you pride yourself on your ability to read other people and tell when they're lying, but you might be surprised by some of these guys. And even if he genuinely is lost and grief-stricken, that doesn't mean he didn't kill her."

"I guess," Hazel said.

"It doesn't matter right now, because he's in the hospital and he's not going anywhere. What I need to know from you is anything else you've found out in your escapades that I need to know before we really start looking into this as a murder case."

Hazel took a deep breath. The way John said it made it sound so formal, and she realized with a jolt that her quest for Truth, with a capital T, meant something different to John and to Jason. To her, it was a matter of principle, of making sense of the world when things didn't make sense. For them, it was the beginning of a long chain of events with irrevocable consequences. In this case, a chain of events that could ruin not only Dansby's life, but Sherry, Bill and Lance's lives as well.

She thought, for just a moment, about what would happen if she didn't share Nina's note with John. But she dismissed the thought as fast as it popped into her head. Staying quiet to protect her friends was weak and cowardly. Truth trumped easy, every time.

John had interpreted her short silence to mean that she didn't have anything to tell him.

"If Dansby were to confess, the sentence would be much easier on their family. I came by here to ask if you would talk to Lance about it, but in light of what I've just witnessed I guess I'd better do it." John said. "I'll explain the situation to him. Get him to advise his brother. I'd talk to Jolene, but that woman's as sour as a raw slice of rhubarb." He paused then mumbled. "It would have been much better coming from you though."

"*If* Dansby did kill Nina, which seems to still be a big if. Lance just asked me to help persuade the judge to let Dansby out on bail. I don't think that's going to happen now."

"No," John shook his head, his jowls gave a slight jiggle. "Not unless more information comes to light that exonerates him."

"I do have something I want to show you," Hazel said. "I still had Nina's book, the one she took on her hike, and I was flipping through it this morning and discovered a note she had written in the back. It was a bit water damaged, but I was able to make out what it said." She put the book on the table and flipped to the back cover where she expected to find the note tucked between the cover and the last page.

Instead, the note and the back cover were missing.

Her stomach lurched. "It's gone," she said.

"The note?" John asked, "what happened to it."

"Oh, no; oh, no," Hazel said, putting a hand to her forehead.

"What is it?" John asked, rising from his chair.

"Lance thinks... he must be..." the implications ran through Hazel's mind faster than her mouth could articulate them.

"What about Lance?" John asked. "Hazel, are you alright?"

Her tumbling thoughts seemed like they were falling all around her, and when the last one landed with a thud, there was nothing left but silence. She looked up at John. "Nina wrote something in the back of *Anna Karenina*. It said that she was going to go back home to her family and try to make her marriage work and get help for her depression. She said that all she had left to do was to tell Dansby about her decision.

"When Lance was here, I told him about it. I knew that Dansby was devastated about Nina, and I thought if he knew that she didn't kill herself, then he would have some peace. I didn't think...I still don't think...I showed Lance the note. Then he asked for coffee to go. I went over to pour him a cup...he must have..."

John swore. "Let's go," he said.

Hazel got up and followed him out of the bookshop, barely remembering to lock the door behind her. John's car was parked by the curb right out front. Hazel got into the passenger seat and John hopped in the driver's seat turning on his siren.

He made a dramatic U-turn and went flying down the road. "Remember his parents aren't well!" Hazel shouted over the siren. "Let me get him out of the house. Turn off the siren. I don't want to scare them."

"In a minute!" John yelled back. He tore through the streets, leaning on his horn.

When they turned off the busier road into the Fullers' neighborhood, John turned off the siren and slowed down.

"Thank you," Hazel said. "His parents are sweet. They have no idea what's going on."

John nodded. "I'll park over here where I won't be conspicuous. You go on ahead. I'll wait outside. You'll just have to get him out of the house."

Hazel got out of John's car, her nerves making her knees feel a little wobbly as she approached Lance's front door. She stood and took a deep breath and then knocked. And waited. No one came to the door. Hazel wondered if Lance hadn't gone home. But he had specifically told her he was going to go home and check on his parents.

She knocked again and rang the bell. She remembered that Lance told her his mom had fallen. Maybe he wasn't there, and she couldn't get to the door because she was down with her injury. Hazel was about to give up and tell John they'd have to look for Lance somewhere else when Sherry answered the door.

"Hi, Mrs. Fuller," Hazel said.

"Hazel! Lovely to see you again," she said. "Sorry it takes me a long time to get to the front door."

"That's okay," Hazel said. "I heard about your fall. I hope you are feeling well."

Mrs. Fuller's face filled with confusion and a sherbet orange tint. "Fall?" she said. "I didn't have a fall."

Hazel paled. "You didn't?"

"No, whatever gave you that idea?"

"Lance told me..." Hazel trailed off and attempted a smile. "It's not important. I'm glad to hear that I misunderstood."

"Me too!" she chuckled. "We can't have me falling."

"Is he here by chance?" Hazel asked. "Lance?"

"I'm afraid not, dear. He's still out looking for Dansby. I'll tell you that boy is going to be the death of me. Out all hours, no consideration for anyone. He's been like that ever since he hit puberty. We thought he would grow out of it, but he never did," she shook her head then shrugged. "But what can you do except love them?"

Hazel smiled, that familiar sense of melancholy wrapped itself around her heart again. What indeed? "Well, thanks anyways, Mrs. Fuller. I will see you soon."

Hazel walked away from the house and motioned to John to get back in the car. "He's not here," she said.

"Well, then, where is he?" John asked.

"She doesn't know. You don't think he'd be dumb enough..." Hazel said.

"Either the station or the scene of the crime? You think?"

"I think he wants to see Dansby. It's all he's talked about the last couple times I've seen him."

"Let's try the station then."

John waited until they had pulled out of the parking lot and then turned his siren back on and swerved out into traffic. Hazel clung to the handle on the ceiling, but it was more because of her emotional state than because John was taking the turns too fast.

They made it back to the station faster than Hazel thought possible, and John jumped out and ran inside without stopping to wait for her. Hazel looked around the parking lot for Lance's car. She didn't see it there. A second later, John ran back out of the station.

"He's not here," Jason said. "Brandon said he just got a call from Jolene about setting up a visit with Dansby for Lance. Maybe he's at her office."

"Yes!" Hazel said. It made sense. It was also not great. If Lance had passed the note along to Jolene, there was no way they were getting it back without a warrant. She wondered if he would have been calculated enough to think to do that.

John reached up to turn on the siren again, but Hazel put out her hand to stop him. "No, John, call the judge. We're going to need a warrant."

"Obviously..." he said, reaching for his phone as though he had been going for that all along. He spoke to the judge for a couple minutes and then got off the phone. "She says that we need evidence that Lance has been in contact with Jolene since he was at your bookshop before she'll issue the warrant."

Hazel groaned. "That's so much driving back and forth. What if they destroy it before then?"

"We'll just have to hope that they won't want to do that for some reason." John pulled out of the parking lot, turning his siren on again.

Hazel was again amazed how fast you could get somewhere when you didn't have to obey any traffic laws, and everyone got out of your way. In less than ten minutes, they were in front of Jolene's office.

"Do you see Lance's car?" John asked.

Hazel looked around but didn't see it. She shook her head. "No, but that doesn't necessarily mean that he's not here."

"Right, why don't you go inside and check it out? Get a text message ready to send me before you go in, and if he's in there hit send and I'll run and get the warrant. If he's not, then I'll just wait for you here."

Hazel made a face but nodded her head. "Okay, I guess. I can just tell Jolene I'm looking for Lance."

"You guys used to be best friends, what happened?" John asked.

Hazel was already halfway out of the car. "No time to explain," she told him. She had never been to Jolene's office before. It was in a 1980s era building off Main Street, completely devoid of personality. Just a blank building with four rows of tinted windows, one for each floor. Typical of Jolene to want to work in such a soul-crushing building.

Hazel ran through the front doors and scanned the directory. Jolene Kelly's office was on the fourth floor. Of course. Hazel pushed the elevator's button, but when the doors didn't immediately pop open, she started up the stairs. When she got to the top, she ran-walked the hall, scanning each name plate. Finally, she found Jolene's door and burst in.

Hazel found herself in a small lobby. There was no front desk, only a few chairs and an open door into an office beyond. Hazel inched towards the open door. She could hear voices beyond. Hazel dug her phone out of her pocket and prepared to text John, then inched her head around the door frame. There was no one there, just an empty hallway and the voices were a little louder.

Hazel hugged the wall and slid into the hallway, edging in the direction of the voices. She couldn't make out what they were saying, but she hoped she might get close enough to at least recognize Lance's voice so she could confirm that he was there. The voices became more distinct. Hazel pressed her ear to the wall, but the voices were too distorted to recognize as belonging to someone specific. The only thing she could tell for sure was that there were two voices, almost certainly a man and a woman. The woman must be Jolene. "No need to be worried..." she was saying. "Panicked... stupid..."

"Now what?" the man said.

Hazel got to her hands and knees on the floor. She had reached the edge of the closed door of the office. There was no way to know if Lance was the person inside or not except for a small rectangular window built into the door at eye level. Hazel thought if she could ever so slowly stick her phone's camera just barely above the bottom of the window, she would be able to take a picture and see who it was in the office.

She took a deep breath. It would be embarrassing if she was caught, but it would be even more embarrassing if she was caught and it wasn't Lance in the office. She needed to be relatively certain it was him in there. She pushed her ear to the door again and listened for anything that might give him away.

"...deniability," Jolene said. "...can't prove... the one... took...."

Hazel couldn't hear every word, but she was almost certain that they were talking about Lance taking the note. It was enough for Hazel, so she slowly—so a sudden movement wouldn't attract attention—got up from her knees into more of a crouching position and lifted her phone up towards the window. When the camera had just barely cleared the edge, she tapped the button to take the picture. To her horror, the flash exploded with light.

She snatched her hand back and ran towards the lobby. She had made it halfway to the hallway when they caught up with her.

"Hazel?" Jolene said. "Are you spying on me?"

The man next to Hazel was not Lance. It was another man that Hazel had never met before. "Um," Hazel stammered. "I..."

"I'm calling the police," the man said.

"Don't bother," Jolene said. "She's got the police in her pocket."

"Hey!" Hazel said. "I do not. Go ahead," she said to the man. "Call the police. They'll arrest me. They've done it before."

"Yeah, a lot of good it did last time," Jolene smirked.

The man looked from Jolene to Hazel. Then he threw his hands up in the air and headed back down the hall to Jolene's office. "Why are you here?" Jolene asked. "If you don't tell me, I will call the police and they'll be forced to arrest you for trespassing. Again. Now I heard that last time there was quite a public scene between you and your husband. I wish I had been there. But I'd be willing to catch the second showing."

"I'm looking for Lance," Hazel said. "I thought he might be meeting with you."

Jolene nodded. Her face was impassive, but there were spots of emerald green orbiting her. "I thought as much." She tossed her hair and turned away from Hazel. "He's not here. I haven't seen him since yesterday at the station. Now, Hazel, I knew that you were selfish, but stringing Lance along like this is downright cruel."

"I'm not stringing him along," Hazel protested. "I'm trying to help his family."

"Right…" Jolene said, "because you don't constantly need to be the center of attention at all."

"Are you going to call the police or not?" Hazel demanded.

Jolene shook her head. "As amusing as that would be, I don't have the time for it today. Now, run along."

Hazel hated that she couldn't think of anything to say or do after that except turn on her heel and leave.

TWENTY

"He's not there," Hazel told John when she got back in the car. "Jolene claims she hasn't seen him since last night."

John groaned. "Well, he's got to be somewhere. Maybe he skipped town?"

"No," Hazel shook her head. "He wouldn't leave his brother. He feels responsible for him and like he's been letting him down the last twenty years."

"What a mess," John said, shaking his head. "He still might be innocent in all this. Maybe there's another explanation for what happened to that note."

Hazel's phone played Jason's signature ring tone.

"Hi, Jason," she said. "I'm kind of in the middle of something."

"That's fine. I'll be quick. I wanted to tell you that your instincts about Karen were correct."

"You got her records?" she exclaimed. At least there was some good news. If they could find something on Karen, then they could protect her grandchildren from her.

"I had to pull a few strings to get them in a hurry," he said.

"But since there are children involved, people were pretty coop-erative."

"What did you find out?" Hazel could feel John's curiosity. She turned away from him, towards the window.

"Karen Mitchell isn't real. We have to do some more digging."

"What do you mean she's not real?"

"It's a fake identity," Jason explained. "Her name isn't really Karen. She changed it a long time ago. From the dates we've found, her husband probably didn't even know. Also, Mike Mitchell Sr. is not Mike Mitchell Jr.'s biological father. The first time Karen Mitchell shows up in the records is when she's married to Mike. Before that, she doesn't exist, and Mike Jr. was born only three months after the wedding."

"So you think she was pregnant when she met him and assumed an identity at the beginning of their relationship?"

"That's exactly what I think. I don't know how all of this was missed when Mike Sr. passed away. You'd think that at least the life insurance people would have been all over something like this."

"Interesting," Hazel said. "Can you find out where she came from, who she was before?"

"Maybe," he sounded uncertain. "With a lot of help. We'd have to check into things like people who went missing around the time she changed her name, who match her description. But she could have come from anywhere in the country or even the world for that matter. It's kind of a needle in a haystack situation."

"Okay," she said. "Keep me posted." She ended the call and looked back over at John.

"Things just got worse," John said.

"You've got to be kidding me," Hazel groaned.

John handed her his phone. He had a browser page up with an article in an Athens newspaper. *Murder in Idyllic Red Gap*

The byline read E. McGee "She quotes the messages from Dansby," he said. "From Nina's phone."

"So, Jeremiah did hand it to her," she said. "What was he thinking?"

"We've got to find Lance before he sees this," John said. "Where do we go now?"

"Let me think for a minute," she said. In her head, she replayed all the times that she had talked to Lance over the last few days. He had come clean the other night on the back porch; she was sure that he told her everything that he knew then. It must have been after that.

She would be able to tell if Lance was lying to her. Or would she? He had just spent a half hour in her bookshop, and she hadn't seen any of his tell-tale yellow green duplicity. The only thing she saw on him was pain.

He knew that she could tell when he was lying. He didn't have all the details, but when they were kids, she told him she could see people's emotions. It had been a game they played together when they walked through the hallways at school or were at the movies. He was the only one besides her Grand-mama who knew her secret, which made it doubly painful when he abandoned her to see the world.

That afternoon, in the bookshop, he was either in so much pain about his family that it masked his deception, or he had found a work around for her gift. He was one of the only people in the world who would know to do that.

Hazel groaned in frustration. "Did Lance ever tell you that Dansby was missing too?" Hazel asked John.

"Dansby was missing?!" John exclaimed. "No, he didn't tell me that."

"He was going to," Hazel explained. "He realized that he needed help the other night when I was talking to him. I told him to go to you. He looked relieved. I thought he would talk to you the next morning."

"I was out," John said. "That's when we found the campsite."

"You mean when Lance found the campsite?" The hair on Hazel's arms stood on end.

John looked at her with wide eyes.

Hazel closed her eyes against the frustration that welled up inside her. It was on the tip of her brain. "Jason and I were not too far from there the other night when we ran into Ranger Rick and his friend. It was around ten.

We didn't stay past ten thirty. Maybe even earlier. Gosh, I wish I could remember. I wasn't paying enough attention at the time."

"What are you getting at?" John asked.

"Something happened between when I was at Lance's house that night and the following morning when he reportedly found the campsite. Something that changed his plan. And I think..." Hazel could hardly bring herself to admit it. "I think he's been lying to me ever since then."

"You don't think he killed Nina?" John asked.

"I don't know why he would," Hazel said. "He has no motive."

"Protecting his brother?" John asked.

Hazel smacked her forehead. "I know where he is," she said. "Protecting his brother, of course. He's been doing it Dansby's whole life."

"Where is he?"

"We used to go to this park, Deertail Park. Sometimes we would take Dansby there when he was a toddler, and Lance thought his mom could use a break."

John nodded. "That is just the kind of boy Lance was, always so consid—"

"Not now, John!" Hazel cried. "Let's go!"

John didn't turn his siren on this time. They didn't want Lance to hear them coming and run. The park was about ten minutes away. They drove in tense silence, each of them hoping that they were wrong, that somehow Lance wasn't involved in Nina's death after all.

Lance's car was sitting in the parking lot. Hazel jumped out almost before John stopped the car. She saw him almost immediately and began to run towards him, leaving John behind. He was sitting on a picnic table with his feet on the bench. He stared down at *The Great Gatsby*, gunmetal gray surrounded him in a transparent cloud that made it hard to see his expression. Birds were singing, the cardinals swooping from the trees to the grass and back again. Daffodils had begun to bloom in a garden bed next to the park. Their bright yellow flowers and the bright green on the trees actually complemented Lance's melancholy color quite well.

The cheerfulness of spring made the terror clutching at Hazel's throat seem surreal. The gravel path crunched beneath her feet. She knew he could hear her approach, but he didn't look up.

"I knew you'd find me here," he said. He held up *The Great Gatsby*. "I'm not Gatsby, am I? I'm Nick Carraway."

Hazel didn't know what he meant; he hadn't facilitated the affair between Dansby and Nina, so she just put out her hands in a whisper of a shrug.

"I don't know what I was thinking. The minute you found this note, I knew it was all over. I thought maybe the autopsy would miss it, maybe she had gotten all the bumps and bruises in a fall off the waterfall. But this note," he held it up for a moment and then let it fall back into his lap. "I thought about destroying it. Maybe no one would believe you. But you're Hazel Randolph, aren't you? And the book is sitting there with its back cover missing...I just panicked. I didn't know what else to do. I'm sorry I lost it for a minute there. Leaving with you just seemed like the best way out. Like in an old western. I'd put you on my horse, and we'd ride off into the sunset." He glanced at her before continuing.

"I knew you'd never leave your kids. It was stupid of me. I'm so sorry I kissed you." Lance held the note and book cover out to Hazel. "Here." She took two steps and grabbed them from him.

"Make sure Nina's kids get this eventually, and Mike should see it too," he said. "I hope... I hope that they can find some peace from it."

"You helped Dansby hide Nina's body," Hazel said. Her voice was quiet, gentle but full of remorse and anguish.

Lance squeezed his eyes shut and nodded. "Late that night, after you brought us the lasagna, he called. He was desperate. He was inconsolable. He said he needed help. I couldn't get anything out of him that made any sense. He just kept telling me I had to go down there. I had to go to the waterfall by the hidden lake." He finally looked at Hazel. He didn't seem to register John's presence, even though he had caught up to Hazel and was standing beside her.

"You and I went there a few times, do you remember?" He asked. "It's where some of the kids would go to party when we were young. They blocked off the easy path after we graduated, but I showed Dansby how to get there when he was about fourteen and I was home on leave for a minute. I wanted him to think I was cool."

"When I got there, he was there, and she was...she was..." Lance jumped off the table but only made it half way to the trash can before he threw up. Hazel jumped back. He walked back and collapsed onto the bench, wiping his mouth with his sleeve. "He killed her," his voice came out hoarse, barely above a whisper. "Hazel, he killed her. How could he do that? How is it even possible!? I can't imagine. He said that he loved her. That he wanted to make her happy. That she wouldn't let him. She wouldn't leave her husband. He went looking for her when she didn't respond to his messages. He didn't like that. That she was ignoring him." Lance shook his head. "I don't understand."

"Why didn't you call John?"

"What could I do?" He turned toward them, his voice now urgent. "He's family," he told them. "I was never there for him when I should have been. I should have stayed here and married you and kept an eye on him. Everything is all wrong."

"No," John said, stepping around Hazel to approach Lance. "No, you're not responsible for your brother. He's his own man. Each person is only responsible for their own choices."

"But..."

"No," John said more forcefully. "No, Lance. He's a grown man. He's just as capable as you are. He needs to learn from his own mistakes. You should have come to me. You should have told me."

Lance's voice was choked with emotion, but no tears ran down his cheeks. "I know," Lance said. "I know, I should have. I just panicked. I couldn't let him go to jail. My parents..."

"Your parents will learn to live with it. How is it better for both of their sons to be involved?"

"You've come to arrest me, Uncle John?" Lance's voice came out in a strangled whisper.

"I'm afraid so, son," he said. The phone clipped to his belt began to ring. "Excuse me a minute." He turned away from them and accepted the call.

"Oh, Hazel, what are we going to do?" Lance moaned. "What will happen to my parents? I'm such an idiot. How could I have been so stupid?"

Hazel smiled sadly at him. "You were protecting your baby brother," she shrugged. She turned slightly and caught John's eye and then froze. He was a distinct shade of yellow. His eyes were wide.

"What is it, John?" Hazel asked.

"That was the autopsy report."

Hazel flinched.

"No, it's...I can't understand it..." John looked at Lance. "Tell me exactly what happened, Lance."

"I..." Lance took a shuddering breath and tried again. "When Nina disappeared, I thought it was a little bit strange because we hadn't seen Dansby for a couple days. I told Hazel before, that wasn't super unusual, but it worried me because I knew that he had reconnected with her in the past few weeks. So I wanted to help with the search effort, not knowing exactly what I thought I would find, but I thought they might be together. I certainly never thought that Dansby..." he shook his head.

"Then that night, Tuesday, Dansby called me out of the blue. I told you, he didn't tell me what happened just that he needed me. When I went down there, I found...He was there with Nina's body. She was...she was just limp and lifeless. Dansby was so worked up, sobbing and raging and telling me that I could fix her because I'm a doctor. It was dark so I couldn't see how much of a mess she was until I got close. The bruising was...extensive, and she had a big gash on her cheek.

"I never got the whole story. Dansby said he didn't mean to hurt her. He kept saying that over and over again. But she was dead. She was already dead. Long before I got there. Maybe, if he had called me earlier. If we had found her sooner...But it was too late. When I realized Dansby had killed her, I lost my mind a little. All I could think about was how we needed him at home, that he couldn't go to jail. I..."

The color of anguish that enveloped Lance made Hazel want to curl up and cry herself. It took all her self-control to keep her feet and concentrate on what Lance was telling them.

"It was my idea," he whispered through the dark haze. "I said if we put her pack on her, it was heavy enough that her body would sink. I knew that John was already thinking it was a suicide."

Hazel's head snapped toward John, who looked down at his feet.

"I told Dansby that we should throw her body in the lake, from the top of the waterfall. Then no one would know it was him. They would think the bruising was from the fall. He didn't want to do it. He didn't want her to be in the lake. It was too cold, he said. So I did it myself."

Hazel swallowed a gasp.

"I know, I know," Lance clenched his eyes shut with a shudder. "Dansby was a wreck. We went home, and we both took some sleeping meds. He'd been in the woods for days now. We both needed some rest. I woke up to your call, Hazel, telling me that he had attacked Mike."

He held his wrists out to John. "Please arrest me. I can never make up for what I've done." He buried his head in his hands again.

Hazel almost went down. She felt her knees go weak.

"How?" she cried. "How did you lie to me like that?"

Lance looked up at her with deep, red rimmed eyes and then held out his hand. "Thumb tack," he said. Hazel could see a dozen puncture wounds decorating his palm.

John gave Hazel a questioning look, but she didn't know how to explain that Lance had physically injured himself to mask the deception she would have been able to see.

"Oh, Lance," she murmured. "I told you to let us help you."

He didn't say anything, just continued to look at her with those sad eyes.

"Lance," John broke the silence. "What you have done is very serious and there will be penalties for it, but I am afraid that you are mistaken about what happened between your brother and Mrs. Mitchell."

Lance's head snapped up. "What?"

"What do you mean?" Hazel couldn't imagine what John was implying.

"That phone call was the autopsy report. Mrs. Mitchell didn't die from a beating or strangulation or whatever Dansby did to her."

"She didn't?" he gasped.

"No," John said. "She died of liver failure."

* * *

Hazel vowed never to set foot in the police station again after that day. All she wanted to do, was go back to the shop and lose herself in *Persuasion* and escapist hot chocolate. But the complete autopsy results were in a file on John's desk, and she wanted to see what was inside more than anything.

In a giant breach of protocol, John had invited Lance into his office as well before he was thrown in jail.

Now they sat in the chairs facing his desk in tense silence while John glanced over the contents of the file. They all looked up when they heard running feet down the hallway and Jason appeared in the doorway, red faced and breathing hard. Lance flinched when he came in.

"I came..." he said, putting his hands on his knees. "I heard..." He trailed off when he saw Lance sitting next to Hazel. Hazel was relieved when instead of turning tiger orange, he flushed to a shade of hot pink she knew was embarrassment. He must have gotten the anger out of his system. Hazel smiled at him.

"What's wrong with you?" John snorted. "Run a marathon?" John laughed at his own joke while everyone else blinked at him.

Lance was hunched in a chair with a glazed look on his face. Hazel saw that he was still in the deepest despair. His bad choices had robbed him of any relief he might feel to know that Dansby didn't kill Nina.

Hazel had come to the end of her patience. "What is it, John? What does it say?"

"She did have some bruises and cuts, consistent with being in a fight. They found all kinds of dirt and stuff under her fingernails but also skin, which I assume will prove to be Dansby's. However, the cause of death was liver failure. It was a progressive condition. She must have first felt the effects just partway into her hike and then she would have been too weak to have made it back on schedule."

"Oh, no," Hazel said.

"I'm surprised you didn't notice how yellow she was when you found her, Dr. Fuller," John said. "I noticed it when we pulled her from the water, but I thought it was because she had been in the lake for a couple days."

"It was dark," Lance stuttered. "I was...I thought it was bruising. I'm sorry, I'm having a hard time processing. Dansby didn't kill her?"

John shook his head. "He did cause some injuries but none of them were fatal."

"Oh thank God," Lance exclaimed.

John frowned. "But that doesn't excuse his behavior."

"Of course not," Lance said, instantly chastened. "Of course, it doesn't."

"We'll need to question him, but you told me that he and Nina hadn't planned to meet up, is that right?"

Lance nodded.

"He had found her the same evening that he called you?"

"Yes, they had just had the fight and she collapsed. I don't know how long he waited before he called me. Maybe if we had been looking in the right places, we would have been able to find her before he did." Lance paused, overcome with emotion for a moment. Hazel felt the same way. If they had found her the first day they could have treated her and she might have survived.

"When Dansby called me, I couldn't understand why she hadn't come home before that," Lance continued. "But if she was suffering from liver failure she would have been disoriented and fatigued. She was probably dehydrated too since she hadn't planned to be gone so long. That's probably why she was at the waterfall."

"Poor Nina," Hazel murmured, wiping tears from her eyes. "If she was that unwell, it must have taken every ounce of will power to tell Dansby she wanted to end their relationship."

Lance shook his head. "I don't understand why Dansby couldn't tell that something was wrong."

"That brother of yours needs some serious anger management therapy," John growled. "Otherwise, he really will kill someone at some point. As for right now we're going to charge him with anything we can make stick. You're looking at some jail time yourself, son."

Lance's face crumpled even more, and he looked down at his hands.

"But John," Jason had recovered his breath. "What caused the liver failure?"

"Yes," Hazel jumped in. "No one mentioned that she was a drinker. I didn't find any alcohol stashed in her house."

John took a plastic evidence bag out of the file and laid it on the table for them to examine. Inside, were several small brown mushrooms.

"Mushrooms?" Jason asked.

"They were in her pack," John said. "These ones are just fine, but there are death caps growing all over the place. The quick onset of liver failure is consistent with consumption of death cap mushrooms."

Hazel's hand flew to her throat. "So... so..."

"It was just an accident," Jason said.

John nodded. "She foraged the wrong mushrooms."

Lance buried his face in his hands and broke down in sobs.

No one made a move to comfort him. Hazel was stunned. "So if we had found her sooner?" she choked out.

John shook his head. "There's no way to know. It depends on how long ago she ingested it and how good her body was at putting up a fight. Don't torture yourself with what-ifs, Hazel."

Hazel remembered Waylon picking a mushroom and popping it into his mouth. She shuddered.

The four of them sat there, regarding the innocent looking mushrooms. Each of the men wore their own shade of frustration. John glaring at the evidence bag, simmered in a deep red-purple. Jason wore a sad smile, emanating a soft, baby blue. Lance was engulfed by a black cloud tinged at the edges with stone gray regret.

TWENTY-ONE

J ason didn't scream or yell the way Hazel thought he would. He sat motionless on the bench at the foot of their bed, staring at her with blank eyes. If she couldn't have seen his emotions she might have thought that he felt nothing, but he was surrounded by a swirling array of tiger orange, verdant green, deep blue and puce.

Hazel sat down next to him and grabbed his hands. "I'm so sorry Jason but I wanted to be completely honest with you."

Jason began to nod slowly. "I know," he said.

Hazel knew how wrong it was for her to expect a pat on the back for her integrity, so she swallowed all the other things she wanted to say. "I'm so sorry I kissed him back," she said, squeezing his hand in response to a stabbing pain in her heart. She had already explained about how Lance had been the one to kiss her, how she had hesitated just for a moment before she pulled away. She didn't need to tell him again. It was the only thing she could apologize for. She hadn't done anything else wrong.

Jason finally blinked. He reached over to pat her shoulder without looking at her. The gesture broke her heart. Her sweet husband felt the need to comfort her in the wake of her infidelity. It felt so wrong. Hazel saw that his face was wet with tears. A sob welled up in her throat. The idea that she had hurt him was torturous.

The grieved silence was too much for her and Hazel gave in to the temptation to talk.

"I never meant to hurt you. I didn't realize...I didn't think. It felt so far away, all those feelings we had for each other. I thought it felt that way for him too. I wouldn't have seen him much, but I felt terrible about his parents and Dansby." Hazel would have felt better if Jason was up pacing around the room and yelling out his abject desolation.

"Shh," Jason finally turned towards her. He took her face in his hands and looked into her eyes.

"Jason, I—" another sob interrupted what she didn't know how to say.

"You still have feelings for him," he said without taking his eyes from hers. "I know you do."

"No!" she protested. "That's ridiculous. What am I doing wrong? I was just trying to be nice!"

He smiled sadly at her.

"Jason," Hazel said, throwing her arms around him and burying her head in his chest. "You don't need to be jealous of Lance. I love you, not him."

"Of course, I'm jealous," he said, patting her back. "Lance was your first love. There will always be a part of you that still loves him."

"I don't believe in that nonsense," Hazel argued, pulling away from him.

"But I do," Jason had said, swallowing.

"Love isn't some ethereal chemistry," Hazel protested. "It's a choice. It's a verb. I choose you, Jason. I chose you a long time ago and I keep choosing you, everyday when I wake up in the morning. You are my first, my best decision every day." She caught a breath before another sob escaped from her throat. She looked at her husband. He was so open and earnest, so genuine. Hurting him felt like kicking a puppy. She felt like a monster. She looked away. "Are you—" she could hardly bring herself to say the words. She took a deep breath. "I understand if you need a couple days."

He blinked at her, like he didn't understand.

"You know, if you want, I could take the kids and stay with John or something..." she trailed off, unable to make eye contact with him.

"What?" he yelped, panic engulfing him. "Why would I do that?"

"I don't know, if you're too angry or disgusted to be around me."

"Oh Hazel," he said, gathering her into his arms. "I'm just hurt, I'm not angry," he murmured into her hair. "Well, not at you anyway. I'm not going anywhere."

They held each other for a long time, and an understanding grew between them. Hazel didn't stay anything until Jason's color had soothed to a soft, muted orange.

"Jason," she asked tentatively. "Is it because of your mom? That you were so jealous?"

Jason's brow furrowed, the orange darkening again. "I don't think I can talk about it," he said.

"I know," Hazel said. "But I think it might help if you did."

He looked at her, turning violet dusk. He grabbed her hand and put it to his lips. "I'm sure lots of things are because of my mom," he said. "I don't know how to sort them all out. But yeah, maybe not knowing who my dad is, maybe having a constant revolving door of men in my house growing up, I'm sure that has something to do with my insecurities."

"Oh, Jason," Hazel said. "I will never leave you."

"I don't think that you can know that."

"Of course, I can."

Jason gave her a pained smile. "I know that you believe that. And that's good enough for me." He kissed her and then gave her one last big hug. "Enough about me," he said, getting up and walking to the dresser where Nina's note was lying.

"You're going to give this to Mike, right?" he asked. "I think he needs to read it."

Hazel nodded. "I think so too."

"What does this mean?" he asked, reading it yet again. "That she was going to report Karen? We still haven't found anything on her."

"I've thought about that," Hazel had said. "I'm not positive. She almost hit her grandkid when I was there. It could be that. I dismissed Lynette's story about Karen killing her husband, but could that be it? Maybe Nina knew something about it. You don't think it could actually be true, do you?"

The space between Jason's eyebrows furrowed. "I don't know," he said, tan blanketing him. "It seems farfetched, but stranger things have been true. Let me work on it more tomorrow," he said. "I'll call in a few favors. I think that we need to get this cleared up if either of us are going to be able to sleep at night thinking about those kids."

"I do feel better knowing Lynette is going to stay," Hazel said. "But yeah, it would be nice if we didn't have to keep wondering."

"Okay," he said. "I'll look into it more at work tomorrow."

Hazel and Jason were up late talking. They went over everything that had happened over the previous week and laughed and cried together. They eventually fell asleep in each others' arms, snuggling much closer than usual.

Dealing with Jeremiah was a little more straightforward. He was grounded forever. Hazel put Jason in charge of giving Jeremiah a lecture about how privacy fits into the democratic process. She took a seat and sat silently throughout the conversation. Their son glowed beet red the whole time, remaining uncharacteristically quiet.

Hazel hoped that he was embarrassed enough to have learned his lesson, since he admitted that handing McGee Nina's phone hadn't gotten him any special attention from the reporter.

"I'm swearing off women for a while," he said.

Jason's color flashed a bemused cotton candy pink, and Hazel saw him press his lips together to keep from laughing.

Hazel gave her son a pat on the arm and a pitying smile before they left him alone.

* * *

After a couple days in the hospital, Mike was released into Karen's care. Lynette planned to stay at his house with the kids and take them by each day for a quick visit, but he would stay at his mom's house until he recovered more fully and could handle kids jumping on him.

Hazel found herself driving to Karen's house that afternoon to visit at Mike's request. He had texted her, wanting her advice and opinions on how to move forward with his kids and their care. Hazel was relieved he had asked. It saved her the trouble of having to figure out how to help from afar.

Hazel alternated between a deep sense of loss, burning anger and anxious busyness. Knowing that Nina hadn't killed herself under the inspiration of *Anna Karenina* made her feel grounded again. At least she felt like herself, instead of second guessing her entire life philosophy.

She pulled into Karen's driveway and took a deep breath.

It was hard to transition out of the compassion she had been feeling for the Fullers and focus on the Mitchell's perspective.

Hazel felt oddly naked without a casserole or desserts to

carry, but Karen had specifically requested that she not bring food. Karen always adhered to a strict vegan diet, and she was feeding Mike the same in an attempt to facilitate his quick recovery. Hazel had several awesome vegan dessert recipes, but she swallowed her tongue and resolved to only bring a book for each of them. She guessed *The Notebook* for Karen and *The Count of Monte Cristo* for Mike, who was going to be stuck in bed for a while still.

"Hazel Randolph Dean," Karen greeted her with air kisses that Hazel didn't quite know what to do with. The same cool mint green that she had when Hazel first met her surrounded her like a halo. "Thanks for coming. Poor Mike has been worried sick about those darlings. I know that you'll be able to put his mind at ease so he can rest and recuperate."

"I'll do my best," Hazel said, attempting to smile at Karen. Hazel had grown to mistrust her in the time since they had last met. All the polished things she had first admired about Karen had turned sinister and Stepford-esque.

She followed Karen through the house filled with low glass tables, ceramic sculptures, and abstract wall art. It was the farthest thing from kid-friendly Hazel could imagine.

Mike was set up in a bedroom that looked more like his room than it did a regular guest room. A bookcase filled with t-ball, fast pitch and football trophies stood on one wall. The decorations looked like what a woman would imagine a man wanted: wallpaper and quilt in blue and green plaid, an oil painting of a mallard in flight, and dark wood furnishings. An empty blender cup and straw sat on the bedside table next to him. Hazel wondered if Mike would ever regain his strength if all he got to eat was kale smoothies.

Mike's head was bandaged in white gauze, and Hazel saw that he was black and blue all over his face and neck. His right hand was in a splint. Hazel shuddered, imagining he might have fractured his wrist when he hit Dansby. Pus yellow radiated from his skin. It looked like steam rising from his body. Hazel assumed it was his color for physical pain.

Hazel sat down in a chair next to the bed, and Karen sat in a similar chair on the other side. "How are you feeling, Mike?" Hazel asked.

"My ears are ringing, and my head is throbbing," he whispered. He kept his head very still. "They told me that I was lucky. He could have killed me. I got off with a severe concussion. They're telling me it could take years to recover."

"Oh Mike, I'm so sorry," Hazel said. "You've been through so much."

"Luckily, he has me to help him," Karen said, jumping in. Her bright tone didn't match the somber mood in the room. "Otherwise, who knows where he'd be."

"Mom, I want to talk to Hazel alone," Mike said without looking at Karen.

"Alone?" Karen's brow furrowed and the metallic sparks throughout her mint exterior flashed. "Why?"

"Just go, Mom," Mike said in a louder voice, attempting to turn toward her.

Karen jumped up. "Yes, I'll go, baby. Don't exert yourself." Her voice was sweet as tea until she turned toward Hazel. "Don't let him hurt himself," she said through gritted teeth, pointing a finger at Hazel.

"I won't," Hazel promised.

Karen backed out of the room and shut the door halfway.

"Would you close the door all the way, please?" Mike asked.

Hazel got up and pushed on the door until it clicked shut, then came and sat back down next to Mike. He didn't immediately say anything, so she sat quietly, waiting for him to speak. His Adam's apple bobbed as he swallowed.

"I've had a lot of time to think, in the last few days," he said. "I've been a little fuzzy. But the one thing I do know is that I need to...purge...certain influences from my life."

Hazel nodded, not entirely sure what he meant. But if he was referring to any kind of desire to change his life for the better, she would help however she could.

"Hazel...I," he stopped and swallowed, looking up at the ceiling before he continued. "I need help," he finally said in a barely audible voice.

"Mike," Hazel said, leaning forward. "I'm right here with you. I'm already on it."

He nodded, closing his eyes again for a moment. "There's just...It's just that..." There was a long silence. "I'm sorry, I lost my train of thought."

"It's the concussion," Hazel said. "Take your time."

"There's something important I needed to tell you."

"About your mom?" Hazel hinted.

A flash of recognition crossed his face. "Yes, that's it. My mom. Hazel, she shouldn't be with the kids all the time."

Hazel nodded. "I know. I was at your house last week. I saw how she was with the kids." Hazel turned around to check the door. It was still closed tight, but Hazel thought she had sensed someone.

"Oh yes, that's right," he said, frustration tinged his voice. "I'm getting so confused. You had me call Nora."

Hazel nodded without saying anything. Elias suffered a concussion during football season, but his symptoms hadn't been nearly as extreme. Poor Mike was having a hard time following his reasoning to the end. *The Count of Monte Cristo* wasn't going to be the right book for him. "You want me to help you keep the kids away from your mom?" she asked.

"She can't be around my kids," the words came pouring out of him now. "I don't want them to have the same experience I did growing up. Nina didn't think she was a very good mom, but she didn't know what she was talking about. My mom was a very bad mom, Hazel. She was okay as a grandma, but she can't be there all the time. I don't know what to do, I don't know if I can stop her on my own."

Hazel blinked at him. "Didn't your mom mention Lynette to you?"

Mike's eyes widened, then he blinked. "Lynette? Nina's mom?"

"Where did you think the kids have been staying this whole time?" she asked.

"I thought that Nora had them."

"Why wouldn't your mom have told you about Lynette?" Hazel wondered out loud.

"Lynette is here with the kids?" Mike asked. The pus-colored steam rising from his skin dissipated. A healthier shade of green emerged.

"Yes," Hazel confirmed. "And she's planning to stay. She already quit her job so she can move up here and help out. She told me it was something that she was already thinking about before Nina died."

Mike exhaled as though he'd been holding his breath. "That's wonderful," he said.

"It sounds like she might have rewritten her relationship with Nina in her head a little bit," Hazel said, feeling responsible for some reason. "But she has good intentions. She's a nice woman."

Mike smiled. "She has a big personality. Nina always humored her." He began to chuckle but winced with pain. "She probably would have panicked at the idea of her mom moving up here, but I think it would have been good for her overall."

Hazel smiled. She had been confused by the discrepancies between Nora's version of Nina's relationship with her mom and Lynette's version. Mike's reaction resolved her confusion, and she suddenly understood how they must have been together. "She was a good daughter."

Mike's color flashed suddenly violet. "Yes," he whispered.

"And a good mom and a good wife. I just wish that she had realized that."

"John told you about the autopsy results?" Hazel asked.

"Yes, while I was still in the hospital." Mike winced. "I guess it's some comfort. But I'll never know what she was thinking, if she really was going to leave me for Dansby."

"I have something for you," she told him, taking the transcribed note and book cover out of her purse. "It was something Nina wrote in the book that I lent her. She took it with her on the hike. I thought you might like to have it. Take your time with it. Reading is going to be hard for you right now." She slipped it into his hand and got up. "I'm going to head out." She grabbed the empty blender cup from the bedside table. "Let me get that for you. Call or text if you need anything, really."

He nodded, but his eyes were on the note in his hand. Hazel didn't want to watch his reaction when he read it. It was too private a moment for her to observe. She left the room quickly and walked back down the hall looking for Karen. "Karen?" she called. Her voice echoed through the room but there was no answer.

Thanks to the open floor plan, Hazel knew right where the kitchen was and went to wash the blender cup, so she could be useful in some way. The kitchen was shiny clean in a way that made Hazel think Karen wasn't much of a cook. The range would be the envy of any home chef but looked as though it had never been used. The only disorder was a blender on the counter with a tub of greens next to it and a few scattered, formerly frozen blueberries thawing into puddles of dark juice.

Hazel looked around the sink for some kind of cleaning implement, but all she found was paper towels. She used them to clean up the blueberries, but when she looked around for a trash can, she realized it must be hidden in one of the cabinets. Reasoning that no one could possibly object to help cleaning up the kitchen, Hazel began to open and close cupboards looking for it. The cupboard to the left of the sink had a sliding rack that held a can for garbage and one for recycling. Hazel pulled it out and threw away the paper towel. She was about to slide it back in when she noticed something in the back of the cabinet that caught her eye.

The rack had wheels that slid on a track, like a dishwasher rack, so it was easy to take off and set aside. Hazel got down on her knees and put her head into the cabinet. There, in the back, was a crate full of knobby rooted plants that was identical to the crate she saw Ranger Rick with the other night in the woods. Hazel's blood ran suddenly cold, goosebumps breaking out on her arms.

Her phone blared with Jason's ring tone, the Police song *Every Breath You Take*. It was meant to be a joke, but he had a knack for calling at moments like this when the lyric 'I'll be watching you' made her shudder instead of laugh. She jumped slightly, hitting her head on the top of the cabinet. She groaned, crawling back out of the cabinet, and pulling the phone from her pocket.

"Jason?" she sat on the floor, rubbing the top of her head.

"Hazel!" her husband sounded excited. "We finally found Karen Mitchell's previous identity!"

"You did!? What a coincidence." Hazel lowered her voice to a whisper. "What's her real name? Does she have a record?" Hazel put the trash cans back on their track and slid them back into the cupboard.

"Yes, petty theft and fraud. Her name was Vera Aurelio. When she disappeared, it was after the death of a previous spouse, but he appeared to die of natural causes. There wasn't an investigation or anything. She was pregnant at the time. No record of that baby anywhere. She shows up just a couple of months later as Karen getting married to Mike."

Hazel closed her eyes for a moment. "Let me guess. Was it liver failure?"

"How did you know?"

"That's how Mike Senior died," Hazel said, her throat going dry. "And Nina."

"Hazel, let's not jump to conclusions," Jason warned, panic tinged his voice. "Nina foraged the wrong mushrooms. Karen wasn't anywhere near her when she died, hadn't been for days."

"We don't know that."

Jason scoffed. "I'm pretty sure we do. If you want, I can have John see where her phone was during those days."

Hazel nodded. "Or I could just ask her."

Jason grimaced at her. "I was afraid you might say that," he said. "Hazel, that could be dangerous. What if she really is a killer?"

"I can't just let it go!" Hazel said. "There are kids involved. We don't have time to wait around for John."

"Don't do anything until I get there," he said, his voice pointed.

"Well, I'm already here," Hazel said. "So, you'd have to move fast."

"You're at Karen Mitchell's house?" Jason swore. Hazel blinked. Jason rarely swore. "I'll be right there," he said. "Don't do anything foolish." He hung up without waiting for a response. Hazel didn't even get a chance to tell him about the connection she had found between Karen and Ranger Rick.

She sighed and picked up the tub of greens to put it back in the fridge. She felt the need to put them away before they wilted. Then she would go find Karen and have a chat with her.

The fridge interior was just as shiny clean as the rest of the kitchen. A few clear acrylic bins held a few apples, some berries and carrots and cucumbers. Hazel thought that it was no wonder the woman was grumpy with her grandchildren if this is all she ate. She set the greens back down next to a tub of mushrooms and then froze. She picked up one of the mushrooms and examined it.

A door around the corner slammed shut. Hazel dropped the mushroom and closed the fridge just in time. Karen appeared at the far side of the kitchen with a basket full of fresh produce.

"Hi there," Karen said, heading to the sink with her vegetables. "Did Mike fall back asleep?"

"I wanted to give him some privacy," Hazel explained. "I found a note that Nina wrote before she died. I think it will bring him some peace."

Karen's mint color snapped with metallic sparks at the mention of Nina's name. "I was just going to make a vegan omelet with these fresh veggies for Mike. Why don't you have a seat, and we can chat?"

Hazel hesitated and then sat down in one of the bar stools at the kitchen island.

"How do you make a vegan omelet?" Hazel asked, curiosity getting the better of her.

"With chickpea flour," Karen said, smiling.

"Can I make one for you too?"

"Oh, no," Hazel said. "I'm not hungry."

"Nonsense," Karen said. "These vegetables are from my garden. It doesn't get any healthier than that."

"Okay," Hazel said.

Karen got out a cutting board and a large knife and began to chop tomatoes and onions. "So, what did you and Mike talk about?"

"The kids mostly."

"Oh?" Karen said. Her tone didn't change, but Hazel could see the metallic sparks flying around her.

"Karen, can I ask why you didn't tell Mike that the kids were with Lynette?"

Karen brought the knife down on a carrot with a thwack. Then she looked up at Hazel and gave her a sweet smile. "I didn't want him to have to worry about that kind of thing right now," she said. "Not while he's recovering."

"You've been working so hard to take care of him," Hazel observed.

"Yes," Karen said. "He's a special man. He has a lot of potential."

"What kind of potential?" Hazel asked.

"Well, political potential of course," she said. "I thought you would have noticed that, being on the city council with him."

Hazel had a hard time keeping a straight face. In her opinion, Mike had neither the talent nor the inclination to run for anything that would even require a party affiliation. He wasn't exactly poised to be the president one day. She didn't know what to say, so she just nodded.

"I always knew Mike was special," she said. "That he would do great things one day."

Karen walked to the fridge and got out the mushrooms. She took one out of the basket and began to slice it. Cold fingers of fear clutched Hazel's heart. She tried a different tact.

"Karen, you are in such amazing shape," Hazel said. "I can tell that you really take care of yourself."

"I do," Karen confirmed. "We're nothing without our health after all."

"You must have some sort of secret. Supplements? Herbs?" Hazel asked. "I mean aside from eating super healthy."

"What makes you think I have a secret?" Karen asked.

Hazel decided to risk it. "I heard you might have access to some non-FDA approved supplements and things like that."

Karen pursed her lips together. "I have no idea where you heard that, but it's absolutely ridiculous. I would never put anything into my body that has the potential to harm it."

She began cooking the vegetables, along with the mushroom from the fridge, in a sauté pan.

"Sorry, I must have misunderstood what Rick said," Hazel said, carefully dropping Rick's name.

Karen looked at her sharply. She poured some chickpea flour into a bowl along with some water.

"I bet you hear a lot of things don't you Miss Hazel?"

"I suppose," she said.

"People seem to open up to you," Karen went on. "Like my daughter-in-law for example."

"I—"

"And my son. I thought you two were at odds, but you seem to be getting along great the last few days."

"I would never let our political differences get in the way of helping him through this crisis."

"Everybody seems to really love you, Hazel Randolph Dean," she said, pouring the chickpea mixture over the top of the vegetables. "That must have made things pretty easy for you throughout your life. A lot of doors have been open to you."

Hazel shrugged. She was busy thinking about what she would do if Karen tried to serve Mike the omelet. She was only about eighty percent sure that the mushrooms in the fridge were the same kind that killed Nina. "Is the mushroom from your garden too?" she heard herself asking.

Karen didn't look at her. She was concentrating on the pan. "No, I actually took a foraging class years ago. Back in the eighties, before it was in style. I had a knack for it and have enjoyed it ever since."

"Well, you live in the right area for it," Hazel said.

"Yes, I do," Karen said. She slid the omelet onto a plate and pulled a fork from a drawer. She set the fork on top of the omelet and began to walk around the kitchen island.

Hazel knew that it didn't matter how unsure she was, she couldn't let Mike eat that omelet. She began to get up from the chair, intending to follow Karen into Mike's room and cause a spill or something.

"Where are you going, Hazel?" Karen asked, pushing her

back down into the chair with one hand. Her bright red finger-nails seemed to flash the same kind of warning as the red stripes on a poisonous snake.

"Oh, I thought I'd come with you to feed Mike," she said.

"Oh, no, dear." Karen set the omelet in front of Hazel. "This one is for you. Mike doesn't eat mushrooms."

Hazel looked down at the plate and felt the blood drain from her face. She tried to keep the tremble out of her voice. "I told you I'm not very hungry, Karen

Karen pouted. "You'll hurt my feelings if you don't try it," she said. "Go ahead, take a bitty little bite."

"No, thanks," Hazel said, attempting to sound casual despite the rising panic. She wondered if doctors would be able to save her if she ate the mushroom and debated taking the chance.

Karen's voice changed then. Her amicable Southern drawl gave way to a more nasal, hard accent. "Why won't you eat the omelet, Hazel?" She picked up the fork and scooped up a bite sized portion of the omelet. There was a big piece of mushroom visible in the middle.

Fear pushed everything else out of Hazel's mind. She couldn't think of an excuse. She didn't make up an answer. She just blanked out.

"You are trying to push me out of Mike's life, aren't you?" Karen asked.

"What?!" Hazel said. "No!"

"I heard you two talking about me. You don't think it's good for me to be around my grandchildren. You're telling Mike to distance his family from me."

"I didn't tell Mike to do anything," Hazel said.

Karen turned a deep crimson. The metallic sparks snapping around her looked dangerous. She took a few steps away, to another kitchen drawer, and pulled out a handgun.

"Whoa, Karen," Hazel jumped out of the chair and put her hands up. "Karen. I swear, I'm not trying to cut you out of

Mike's life. I believe that Mike can use all the support he can get right now."

"Shut up!" Karen screamed. "I thought it was all Nina's fault. I thought, once Nina was gone, everything would fall into place. It would be back on track. But you! You had to swoop in and try to fix things, and now Mike is going to stay here! In Red Gap! There's no career for him here, no advancement! Do you have any idea what I've sacrificed for him? Any clue!? No! You couldn't possibly understand. You have everything. Everything that I always wanted, you were just born with, and now you're going to take it all from him too.

"He went to *Vanderbilt*. Do you know what I had to do to make that happen? He was supposed to go somewhere from there. But then that *trollop* seduced him, and he moved to this stupid little town. He doesn't know what he wants. He was satisfied with this pathetic city council position. I told him that he could be so much more, but he didn't listen to me. He wanted to make *her* happy. He said that it was too much for *her*. That *she* couldn't handle big time politics." She began to move around the island towards Hazel. "Don't you see? She had to go. She was holding him back."

"Karen, you don't want to shoot me. You've been really clever with the mushrooms. Really, you have, but shooting someone in your kitchen is different. They'll know it was you."

"I don't care!" she screamed, angry tears streaming down her cheeks. She appeared to be in the middle of a blood red thundercloud with silver lightening bolts snapping all around her. Her emotional color extended three feet around her in every dimension.

"Mother!" Mike's voice was low and rumbly through the kitchen. He emanated a deep navy blue that radiated authority.

Karen whirled around to face him. Her color changed again to a deep violet. "Michael! What are you doing out of bed?"

"Mother, put the gun down."

"Don't you see, Mike? They're holding you back. They're all holding you back. I won't let them. I'm taking care of you, sweetie. Just like I've always done."

"Mother, put the gun down."

Hazel saw the indecision on Karen's face. Then she saw it harden. The crimson cloud was back, darker than ever and the sparks around her began to fly again. Karen began to turn towards Hazel, so she ducked behind the island. The gun went off and Hazel heard herself and Karen both scream and Mike yelp in pain. Hazel jumped up but didn't see either of them. She ran around the island and saw Mike on top of his mom, pulling the gun out of her hand.

"Are you alright? Are you alright?" Hazel shouted.

Karen began to sob.

Michael moved awkwardly, holding out the gun to Hazel. "Here, take this," he said.

Hazel grabbed the gun from his hand and turned the safety on. "Did you get shot?" she asked.

"Help," Michael said.

Hazel shoved the gun into the pocket of her blazer, then bent down to assess Mike's situation. "Are you...did you get shot?" she repeated.

"No," Mike said, patting himself down. "No, I don't think so. I think I just pulled some stitches when I tackled her. I'm so dizzy." His eyelashes fluttered.

"Oh, no, you don't," Hazel said, grabbing him by the arm and pulling with all her might. She slapped his face gently with her other hand. "Stay with me," she fretted. "I've got to get you some real food."

Karen was still sobbing on the floor. Mike regained himself enough to sling his arm around Hazel's shoulders. They stumbled their way to a chair.

"I called the police," he said. "Earlier, when she was screaming at you."

Karen heard what he said and began sobbing even louder. She still hadn't moved. She seemed to be broken. Her son taking an active role against her seemed to be more than she could handle.

"Let me get you some water," Hazel said to Mike.

Jason ran into the room as Hazel was handing Mike a glass. He stopped short in the doorway and looked around. Fresh blood seeped through Mike's bandage and Karen was a broken, devastated heap on the floor. They could hear the sirens in the distance. Then he looked around at Hazel. The sight of him made her weak with relief.

"Damn it, Hazel!" he yelled. "What did you do?"

Hazel put a hand on the back of Mike's chair to steady herself and gave him a weak, unsteady smile. "All I did was put the greens away," she said.

TWENTY-TWO

The warm spring sun came out after a terrific thunderstorm. Clouds of steam rose into the air from the sidewalk in front of Hazel's shop. She was grateful that the rain had stopped, for the sake of the event she was hosting that afternoon. The azaleas in the planter between the sidewalk and the road were blazing with pink. Hazel opened the front door of the shop wide to let fresh air in.

She stood in the front of several carts, sorting books. It went against her instincts to sort them into genre categories instead of by the colors they emitted, but she forced herself to. Their colors clashed against each other, and she had to look away, concentrating on each individual title instead of the collected groups.

She kept an ear on the door, waiting and checking her watch at frequent intervals. Finally, she took a standing sign from behind the counter, unfolded it, and set it up on the street.

Nina Mitchell Memorial Book and Bake Sale
All proceeds between 3pm to closing today will be donated to
Postpartum Support International

She wheeled the carts out the door as well and arranged them on the sidewalk. Then she set up a folding table on the other side of the door and set a chair behind it.

"Miss Hazel!" A small voice cried. Hazel looked up and saw Naomi Mitchell running down the sidewalk toward her. "Hello, Miss Hazel," she said breathlessly when she reached the entrance of the shop. "I brought some books for you." She handed Hazel a stack of children's books. A buttery yellow surrounded the little girl.

"Why, thank you, Miss Naomi," she said. "Why don't you put them right here?" she pointed to a shelf on a cart devoted to picture books.

"Will they really help people like my mom?" she asked, her voice full of earnest hope.

Hazel felt tears behind her eyes. She bit her lip. "Yes, they really will," she said.

"I'm glad," she said.

"Where's your dad?" Hazel asked.

"He's coming," she said. "He's getting the car seat out." She wrinkled her nose, her sunny color turning dark gray. "He's a lot slower than mommy was."

Hazel held out her hand, "Why don't you come help me get the treats we're going to sell today?"

She led Naomi back through the stacks and smiled when she heard a soft "wow" escape from her when they walked into the cafe. She stopped in the middle of the room and looked up through the glass ceiling to the sky. She radiated a lavender glow.

Hazel went behind the counter and put several trays of goodies on a cart. Naomi caught up with her after a minute.

"What do you have?" she asked, her eyes wide.

"Brown butter blondies, double chocolate peanut butter cookies, lemon bars, white chocolate cranberry pecan cookies, mint brownies, and magic bars."

"I can push it," Naomi chirped. "I'll be careful."

Hazel watched her push the cart carefully and oh so slowly, around the counter and through the maze of chairs and tables. By the time they reached the front of the shop, Mike and the rest of his kids were there.

"Naomi!" he scolded. "You shouldn't run off like that until I'm ready."

"Sorry," she said, looking at her toes, her color instantly turned deep blue. "I was so excited to give the books to Miss Hazel."

Hazel watched Mike melt into a deep pink. "It's alright," he said. He let go of the five-year-old's hand to pull her into a hug with one arm. The other arm carried a toddler and had an occupied car seat dangling from it. "I was just worried."

"I'm sorry, Daddy," she said putting her arms around his neck.

He set the car seat down on the ground and looked around. Hazel crouched down for a moment to tickle the baby who smiled and giggled.

"The kids seem great," Hazel said to Mike. "How are you holding up?"

"We're doing okay," he said. "Still figuring things out."

"How's your concussion?"

"Doctor says I'm pretty much back to normal. I'm just supposed to avoid any risky behaviors that could bonk my head again. I don't think Dansby's getting out of jail anytime soon though, so I should be fine."

Hazel pursed her lips together. Dansby had been charged with assault and battery and with hiding a death from the police. They had reached a plea deal that involved some significant therapy and anger management courses in addition to his jail time.

Lance, on the other hand, was sentenced one year in jail and a few thousand dollars in fines for his part in concealing

Nina's body. It was the minimum sentence. Jolene was good at what she did, just as Jason had told her.

In the meantime, Hazel contacted the Fullers' church congregation and put together a schedule for someone to check in with them each day and see how they could help. Hazel planned on going as often as she could herself as well. They all hoped that Bill's condition wouldn't deteriorate too much before Lance got out of jail.

"Hello, everyone," a cheerful voice called.

"Grandma!" Naomi and Trevor shouted and ran to her, wrapping themselves around each of her legs, shining with love.

"How has it been with Lynette?" Hazel asked softly.

Mike shrugged, turning a neutral gray. "She's great with the kids," he said.

Hazel laughed. "What a diplomatic answer. Well, that's just what you needed, isn't it?"

"Thank you, Hazel," Mike said. "For this," he indicated the sign, "and for everything. I couldn't have done any of this without you."

Hazel made a dismissive snort. "Without you, I might not be alive."

Mike smiled at her, radiating a rich turquoise. "Now what would I do without my city council nemesis?"

Hazel threw back her head and laughed. It felt good.

"Now then," Lynette said, settling into the chair behind the treats. "Let's raise some money. I'll start us off." She put twenty dollars into the cashbox and grabbed herself a lemon bar and handed a cookie to each of the cheering children.

John's SUV pulled up in front of the bookshop, and he climbed out. "I heard you're selling brown butter blondies over here," he said, looking at Lynette.

"Oh, is that what these are?" she said, tilting her head so she was looking at him through fluttering eyelashes.

Hazel watched John turn fuchsia and begin to stutter.

"Watch yourself," Mike said, nodding toward John and Lynette.

"Hazel!" Nora appeared from behind her and gave her a big hug. "How's it going so far?"

"Well," Hazel said. "I've been open for ten minutes, and we seem to be out of blondies."

"I'll go get more from the back," Nora said, disappearing into the shop.

More of Hazel's friends and neighbors began to show up until the crowd filled the shop and sidewalk and spilled out into the street.

At one point, Hazel ran into the back and found a surprise visitor.

"Waylon!" she exclaimed, almost dropping a tray of peanut butter banana cloud cookies. "How did you get back here? I've never seen you in town before."

"I wanted to buy a cookie to help the women." He held out a crumpled five-dollar bill towards her. It was an old-fashioned one Hazel hadn't seen for decades. Hazel couldn't help tears from spilling over onto her cheeks. She set down the tray and threw her arms around him.

"Thank you, Waylon," she said. "Without you, I don't know if we would have ever found her."

Waylon tentatively patted Hazel on the back and then wiggled out of her hug. "Please, take this," he said, pushing the money into her hands.

Hazel grabbed a paper lunch bag and handed it to him. "Fill it up," she said. "You can take anything in here."

His eyes got big as he looked at all the treats.

"Oh, Waylon," she said. "I don't know if I should hand out books anymore."

He glanced at her after slipping two cookies and a brownie into his bag. "Your books help people," he said.

"Do they?" she said. "Sometimes I feel like they cause more trouble than they're worth."

Waylon shook his head. "Trouble is never far," he grabbed a lemon bar. "It's not your fault."

"I don't know," she said.

Waylon set down the bag and looked Hazel in the eyes. "Your books are important," he said. "They help people know who they are. It is a great gift."

His earnest expression brought tears to Hazel's eyes. "Thank you, Waylon," she sniffled. He went back to his bag of goodies.

A sudden idea seized Hazel. "Can I introduce you to someone?"

Waylon froze.

"Don't worry, you'll like her." She ran back through the shop and found Naomi. "I'd like you meet someone," she said, taking the little girl's hand. "He's a friend of mine. He helped your mom."

Naomi nodded and the two of them walked back to the cafe.

"Waylon," Hazel said. "This is Naomi; she's Nina's daughter."

Waylon came around the counter and knelt down, so he was closer to Naomi's height.

"Miss Hazel said that you helped my mom," Naomi said.

Waylon looked up at Hazel, who nodded, and then back to Naomi.

"I tried," he said in a quiet voice.

"Thank you," Naomi said.

Waylon flushed, his cheeks turning red and his aura turning pink. "Would you like a cookie?" he asked, holding one out to her.

Naomi nodded solemnly and accepted it from him. They munched on cookies together in silence.

"I need to go," Waylon said, getting up. "It was nice to meet you, Naomi."

The little girl nodded.

"I'll see you soon, Waylon," Hazel said, taking Naomi's hand and leading her back towards the crowd. Waylon stood still, wiggling his fingers in good-bye.

Elias and Jeremiah were standing by the door when she reappeared, with Emma who immediately ran up to Hazel and hugged her. Naomi dropped Hazel's hand and ran back over to her grandmother. "This is, like, so great, what you're doing," Emma began. "I did, like, a project about depression in, like, health class. And it's, like, such a huge problem."

Hazel did her best to smile at Emma and was relieved when Jason appeared at her side.

"Hi, Emma," he said. "What's Elias looking at over there?"

Emma whirled around to go see what book Elias had in his hands, leaving them alone.

"Thank you," Hazel breathed.

Jason wrapped an arm around her. "How are you holding up?"

"I'm okay," Hazel said. "I know it's been weeks, but it's still so hard to process everything."

"I wanted to let you know that they finally caught up to Rick and his friend Stephen."

Hazel shook her head. "Who knew there was a black market in wild Appalachian ginseng?"

"The good thing is that they hooked into a whole network of people dealing in much more serious substances. They think that they'll be able to make a lot of progress now that they have Rick and Stephen in custody."

"And Karen?" Hazel asked, lowering her voice.

"Rick and Stephen confirmed that she was one of their middlemen. She hooked into an extreme naturalistic health racket. She can claim ignorance about where Rick was getting the ginseng though, so it won't be enough to charge her. But that's fine. We don't need the smuggling racket. With your testimony and the mushrooms John got from the fridge, we can build a solid case even if she doesn't confess. But I think she will. The judge isn't setting bail; she'll be locked up until her trial. Then we'll have a nice long time to build a case against her for her husband's murder as well."

Hazel shivered. "It's all so shocking, isn't it?"

Jason looked around at the crowd. "Looks like the whole town has come out in remembrance of Nina," he said.

Hazel nodded. "Yes, everyone is here except for Jolene and that McGee girl."

"Nope, looks like you spoke too soon," he said, pointing to the shop entrance.

McGee stood in the doorway, looking around uncertainly. She carried a lime green cloud with her, tinged with purple.

Hazel approached her. "Hello there, McGee."

"Mrs. Dean," she said. "I...I thought it's the least I could do to come and support this cause. I just, I understand now that I made things worse for Nina's kids by publishing things too early, and I am sorry. I honestly thought I was helping."

"I know. And I'm glad to hear that," Hazel said. "Why don't you come over here and buy some brownies?"

As she motioned for McGee to head out the door, a book caught Hazel's eye. One emitting just the same lime green and purple that McGee carried with her. She pulled it off the cart. *Atonement* by Ian McEwan.

"McGee," Hazel said, holding the book out to her with a smile. "I want you to have this book."

FROM HAZEL'S KITCHEN

Brown Butter Blondies

2 sticks salted butter
1 ½ c. brown sugar
1 c. granulated sugar
4 eggs
2 ½ tsp. vanilla extract
1 tsp. butter flavoring
1 ¾ c. flour
1/3 c. malted milk powder
1 tsp. salt
2 tsp. baking powder

1.   Preheat the oven to 350 degrees and line a 9x13 pan with parchment paper
2.   Brown the butter in a saucepan until it becomes dark golden brown. Pour it into the bowl of a stand mixer and let it cool for a couple minutes
3.   Add the sugars and beat

4.   Add the eggs one at a time, then the vanilla and butter flavoring

5.   Add the flour, malted milk powder, salt and baking powder. Mix until just incorporated.

6.   Bake for 45-55 minutes until a toothpick comes out clean from the center.

* * *

Grandmama's Lasagna

1 sweet onion

1-2 lb. ground beef (or Hazel will use turkey to make it healthier)

2 cloves garlic, minced

1 16 oz. can crushed tomatoes

1 giant jar of spaghetti sauce

Dried oregano

Fresh basil (if you have it in your garden)

Lasagna noodles

16 oz. cottage cheese

8 oz. sour cream

Garlic salt and pepper

8 oz. or more Monterey Jack cheese, shredded

1.   Preheat the oven to 350 degrees

2.   Make the red sauce: sautée the onions in a small amount of olive oil. Add ground meat and cook until brown and crumbly. Add the garlic and stir once or twice. Add the crushed tomatoes, spaghetti sauce and herbs. Let it simmer while you make the white sauce.

3.   Make the white sauce: Combine the cottage cheese and sour cream together in a bowl. Add garlic salt and pepper. Stir to combine.

4.   Assemble the lasagna: Add a small amount of red sauce to the bottom of a 9x13 pan (to keep the noodles from sticking to the bottom). Add a layer of noodles, then half red sauce, then all of the white sauce. Sprinkle with half the shredded Monterey Jack cheese. Then add another layer of noodles, then the rest of the red sauce. Sprinkle with the remaining Monterey Jack cheese.

5.   Bake for 45ish minutes.

REVIEW

We hope you've enjoyed Longing is Violet Dusk, the second installment in The Hazel Dean Mysteries.

If you did, please consider leaving a review on Amazon or Goodreads. Reviews can do so much for up and coming authors, and your words would be greatly appreciated.

ABOUT THE AUTHOR

Josalyn McAllister is a cozy fiction author whose most recent works include *Love Over Easy* and *Guilt is Midnight Blue*. Josalyn started writing character descriptions at the tender age of seven, inspired by the works of LM Montgomery. In her teenaged years she moved on to Newsies fan fiction. Inspired by National Novel Writing Month, she wrote her first novel about a child she mentored in college. She has never stopped writing. Josalyn taught middle school history before deciding she would rather spend time with her own children rather than other peoples. A restless soul, she has moved all over the country and collected an eclectic array of hobbies. Her writing has a relatable quality that will charm and entertain you.